DREAM
SPARKS

THE VISION OF LIGHT SERIES

CLAIRE J. HALL

Dream Sparks

This book was printed in the United States of America.

Book Cover Design and Interior Formatting by 100Covers.

ISBN (Paperback): 979-8-9997245-0-2
ISBN (Hardback): 979-8-9997245-2-6
ISBN (eBook): 979-8-9997245-1-9

DEDICATION

To my parents, brother, grandmother, family, and friends for all of their love and support.

CHAPTER 1

THE WIND BLOWS my short black hair across my face, bringing the refreshing scent of pine with it. The branches of the trees blow in the breeze, sounding like gentle ocean waves coming to the shore. Pausing I watch as a few snowflakes are gently floating to the ground, despite the patches of sunlight that glow on the mountainside before me. My finger moves back to the trigger as I refocus on the scope of my rifle. The reindeer stops grazing, perking its ears. I freeze, holding my breath. I take aim, but before I can fire it runs off into the forest.

As I walk after it I notice how the sun is warmly shining on the land. I sigh as my communicator starts buzzing. Tapping my earpiece I pick up the call. "Hey Anna, what's up?" I ask casually.

"What's up? Franca, didn't you see the recall message?" she asks in an alarmed tone.

"No, didn't see it. What'd it say?" I ask, watching the snowflakes that are falling around me.

"There's a huge storm coming. Can't you see it? All the other hunters have returned but you."

I pause and look around. It doesn't look that bad to me, but then again the weather on Hayventh can be unpredictable. "It looks alright to me, but I'll make my way back to the settlement," I say, turning away from the mountains to go back to my hovercraft.

"Please hurry and don't get sidetracked. The settlement thinks it's going to be like that terrible blizzard from a couple years ago," Anna says, her tone becoming anxious.

I watch as a few snowflakes start blowing around me. It doesn't look like a serious storm is going to develop. Still, I know it's better to humor them and return. "I'll be there soon. I'm not too far away," I say as I put my rifle in the back of my hovercraft.

"Alright, I'll be sending out a search party if you're not back within the hour."

"You don't have to do that, I'll be fine," I say with a laugh. I wait in silence for her to respond. "Anna?" I ask, the smile fading from my face. Nothing.

We must've been cut off. Snowflakes swirl around me as I get in the hovercraft. With the press of a button it starts to hum. I turn onto a dirt path that heads deeper into the dark green forest and start following it back to Wayford. Clouds are now beginning to cover the sky, looking darker than they had before. The wind tugs at the hovercraft, causing my knuckles to turn white as I hold the wheel with more care.

I'm having some doubts. That blizzard Anna mentioned before had us trapped in the settlement for months. While we haven't had another storm come to that, it's not out of the question. Hope we have enough food stored up. The settlement's bigger than it used to be. I press onward, speeding up. I can outrun this storm easy.

My vision gradually becomes more limited as the snow thickens. The wind that was sounding like calm ocean waves now sounds like a roaring sea cascading around me. Soon I can only see five feet ahead. I wish I had gone to my usual hunting spot, instead of an area I'm not as familiar with. Thankfully Wayford has watchtowers that emit a blue light that shines through storms. The wheel is jerked out of my hands as a violent gust of wind bursts against the hovercraft, causing it to smash into a nearby boulder.

I quickly straighten the wheel, and with some struggle against the current I return to where I think the path should be. Soon after a shuddering noise can be heard coming from the engine. The hovercraft must've taken a harder hit than I thought. I look ahead, as far into the snow as I can. No blue light can be seen. The hovercraft shudders one more time before coming to a complete stop. I rev the engine, hoping for a response, but get nothing.

I get out, grabbing my tools from the back. All that can be heard is the wind. I move my hair away from my face and open the hood. Flurries of snow block my vision. Squinting through the snow I can see that the left side of the engine has smashed parts that I don't have spares for. I put the hood back down.

I can't stay here any longer. If my hovercraft was still running I'd have enough heat to stay in it. Exchanging my tools for my rifle is easier said than done. It's hard to leave something behind that you've worked on for years. Taking my rifle, I turn from the hovercraft and try my best to not look back. I glance over my shoulder after a few steps and find it has faded out of sight behind a veil of snow.

A force of wind almost knocks me off my feet, shifting my focus back to the storm. From what I remember there are some nearby caves in the area that I can take shelter in. I put my arm to my forehead as the wind and snow relentlessly move around me. Everything ahead is white, and even with my fur lined armor I can feel the cruel bite of the tearing wind. This storm is way worse than I thought it would be.

For a brief moment the wind is on my side, blowing the snow out of my vision enough to let a blue light pierce through. Maybe I made it farther than I thought I had? My pace quickens as the wind resumes picking at me. A warm light ahead lifts my spirits. Standing by the fire, listening to tales of old would be nice... I battle my way through the snow, and as I come closer I realize it's not the settlement I've reached, but a cave that some people are staying in. A warm campfire is lit, and the blue light is coming from a carrier ship. Through the wind I can just make out the low humming sound of machinery.

Normally I would wait and observe these people before approaching them, but I'm at risk of getting frostbite if I continue to hang out in the storm. I shuffle my way towards the camp. As I get closer a woman approaches me. Her steps are lighthearted, as if the storm means nothing to her. The factory manufactured clothes she's wearing are designed for cold weather, but not for something like this. I glance at my own armor that's barely doing the job.

"What're you doing out here?" she asks cheerfully with curiosity in her blue eyes. Her light blond hair blows in her face, but she doesn't seem to mind.

"I got stranded, was hoping to find shelter till the storm blows over," I say.

She laughs. "Well come on then; what're you waiting for?" And with that she starts walking towards the camp.

I reluctantly follow her, and soon find myself by the warm crackling glow of the campfire. I notice the humming sound that I heard earlier is coming from some mining equipment. To my surprise I also hear hammering and look to see a young woman with pastel pink hair working at a forge. She doesn't look up from her work, focusing on the task at hand. Hovering lanterns glow brightly, throwing a warm light on everything.

The woman I followed to the fire sits across from me and taps the communicator on her arm. A holographic screen shows up.

"Still no connection. Do you know how long it'll be out?" she asks, looking at me intently.

"Well, usually we get it going again once the snow lightens up. Should be up in a few hours."

"Good," a man says, coming over and picking up a crate. "We need to get going as soon as we can," he says, continuing on to the mining equipment.

"Are you planning on stopping by Wayford?" I ask. Maybe I could go with them.

"No, we've got some errands we need to take care of that take us elsewhere," she says. "Maybe some other time we'll be able to see the settlement. I've never been there myself... but you," she says, gesturing at me. "You look like a hunter. Why don't you tell me your story?"

"I'm just one of the hunters there. Have been since the settlement was started," I say indifferently.

"And your name is?" she asks, her eyes studying me.

"My name is Franca. And you are?"

She smiles at me, her eyes shining brightly. "My name's Fauve." She starts to say something else when a man with dark brown wavy hair comes up to us.

He makes solid footsteps with his boots, almost stomping but not quite. He carries his gun with both hands, and while it looks like it would be heavy he carries it effortlessly. "Fauve, what are you doing? Who is this?" he asks in exasperation.

"Oh! This is Franca; she's one of the hunters here. She just stopped by for a chat," Fauve says cheerfully.

"You make friends in the strangest places." He shakes his head. "Don't you realize she's now going to have to come with us?"

"What?" Fauve and I ask at the same time.

"I just came to stay by the fire for a bit," I say. What've I gotten myself into?

"You see that mining equipment, right?" the man asks, nodding his head in its direction.

"Yeah?" I ask. I look over there, and then the realization hits me.

"Exactly."

"This is ridiculous." Why hadn't I thought of this before? Maybe it was because of the storm that I had forgotten. Mining is illegal on Hayventh.

"Lance you can't be serious!" Fauve stands.

I stand as well, picking up my rifle. I believe I've worn out my welcome.

He looks at me with sternness in his eyes. "I am. She can't leave. She's seen too much."

I straighten my shoulders. "I'm leaving, and I'm not going to say a word about this." I turn and walk away from the fire. A bullet whistles past my ear, and I freeze.

"I wouldn't do that if I were you," Lance says calmly. "I'm giving you one chance to sit back down at the fire."

I turn and meet his gaze. All I see is alertness and energy. His finger is still on the trigger. I walk back to the fire and sit down without saying anything.

"That's better," Lance says.

"Lance you can't do this. What's Alex going to say?"

"Alex isn't here. Maybe now you'll take guard duty more seriously."

Fauve sighs and rolls her eyes.

"Hey Roxanne. We've got a prisoner to guard," Lance calls out. "I don't have time for this. We have to get this operation on the move," he says, looking at us one last time before walking away.

I glance over at Fauve, wondering why I had to come to this cave, of all caves.

"Sorry," Fauve says with a grimace.

"It's my fault more than anything for not noticing. Either way I'm out of here." Standing back up I turn and walk at a fast pace. I don't get far before I find myself pinned to the ground.

"Where do you think you're going?" I hear a woman's voice ask harshly.

"I'm going my separate way, that's where," I say, struggling against her.

"That's for us to decide," she says as she pulls my arms behind my back. I hear a clicking sound. She brings me to a stand and drags me back over to the campfire.

"Don't make me watch her Fauve," the woman says, sitting me down and taking my rifle.

I clench my teeth. If only handcuffs were made of metal instead of force field material they wouldn't hurt so much. The woman walks away, heading back towards the mining equipment. I look at Fauve and see she's typing something into her communicator. Before long Lance and the woman who handcuffed me return to the fire.

"Come on we're packing up," the woman says.

Fauve looks at them in surprise. "But what about the storm? The carrier won't be able to handle the wind."

"It'll be fine. We can't stay here any longer. We've spotted a search party not far from here."

"Yeah, we've got to move on. And don't you get any ideas," Lance says pointing his gun at me.

I stand without saying anything. I can see that people are taking crates into the carrier. As soon as he thinks I'm following him I run. Fauve steps out of my way. I hear voices calling out behind me but I keep running. Soon it's only me, the roaring wind, and the falling snow. I can't see well but I keep going. Not leaving home today.

I trip and fall. Looking at my foot I find that a grappling hook is wrapped around it. As I'm trying to kick it off the woman from before comes through the veil of snow.

Her long jet black hair blows to the side, revealing a long scar going down her cheek. "You actually thought you could get away?" she asks menacingly.

"Like I said before, I won't say a word about this. Who cares anyway if you were mining? Wayford has other things to worry about." I get the hook off with my other foot and make it to a stand.

"Of course it concerns you. The hunters uphold the law here. You're coming with us."

I walk away, heading towards the forest. I'm leaving, whether she listens to me or not. She catches up, grabbing my arm. I hear a smack and feel my jaw stinging. "You're going, unless you want to get hurt."

I don't say a word back to her. Why should I? I would fight back if my wrists weren't handcuffed together. We make it back to the cave finding that everything has been packed up. Lance and Fauve are waiting on either side of the door to the small carrier ship.

When Fauve sees me she puts a hand to her mouth. "Roxanne, you didn't have to go that far!"

"I did what I had to Fauve," Roxanne says sternly, pushing me up the ramp and into the carrier. "Sit down," she says, pointing at a seat.

I sit, and she takes the seat next to mine. Once Fauve and Lance board the ship we take off. I clench my teeth as another wave of pain shoots through my wrists. My jaw hurts enough that I can't clench it for long. I feel like it's already bruised. I look over and see that Roxanne is wiping my blood off of her armored glove. I thought I felt her glove scrape my face when she punched me. I was right.

It doesn't take long for us to reach a cruiser ship that's waiting in Hayventh's orbit. There must be a way out of this. Metal panels slide open, revealing the ship's hangar. When we land Roxanne immediately stands and yanks me out of my seat. "Come on, we're going!" she says, pushing me towards the exit.

I stumble, but manage to regain my footing. We leave the carrier with Lance and Fauve walking on either side of us. The other two crew members that were with us stay behind. Our steps echo eerily as we walk through the hangar. Where is everybody? For a ship this size things are unusually quiet. I can see a layer of dust on the other two carrier ships.

Roxanne shoves me. "What're you looking at?"

"Nothing," I say, looking forward again. We stop at a door that three people could go through at a time. I can hear the gears in the walls clicking and turning as it slowly opens. We pass through the door to a main passageway. From what I know of ships like this we're heading to the main area.

Before we get there a man with short sandy hair and blue eyes comes up to us. His face has a softer expression, and his tone of voice is not nearly as harsh as Lance or Roxanne's. "You came back successfully as I expected. Who is this?" he asks with concern reflecting in his eyes.

"A prisoner sir," Roxanne says standing proudly with a smile.

"A prisoner? Why, what'd she do?" the man asks with alarm.

"She saw what we were doing," Lance says, aggravated.

The man furrows his brows. "That does change things... she's going to have to stay with us for now."

"What? I don't deserve this! I was at risk of getting frostbite!" I say, jerking my arm out of Roxanne's grip. I'm tired of her holding onto me.

Lance raises his gun at me, putting his finger on the trigger.

The man puts his hand on the gun and forces Lance to lower it. "I'm sorry, but I have to follow protocol. If anyone on Hayventh saw what we were doing we would be in worse trouble than we are now. Come on, we better get going," he says, signaling for us to come with him. We follow him through a few passageways, coming to a stop at a medbay. My stomach sinks. I'm forced into the room, and see the standard rows of beds with rounded glass lids.

Over by the computer system is an old woman who comes over to us. "Alex, who is this?" she asks.

"Someone who saw them mining," Alex says. "We need her in one of the beds tonight."

She doesn't say anything, but types something into her communicator. The lid of the bed next to us starts to open. I can feel the sweat on my forehead. Alex removes my handcuffs and I immediately swing at him as he tries to pick me up.

He steps back. "Whoa, just trying to help," he says, raising his hands.

Roxanne grabs my arm and twists it behind me so fast I can barely process what happened. Crying out in pain I lose strength in that arm.

"Roxanne, there was no need for that!" Alex exclaims, forcing her to release me.

"Yes sir," she mutters, still watching me intensely.

I grit my teeth, taking a few deep breaths. I've been in medbeds before, and they're painless. I just don't trust these people. Alex starts to lift me up again. I struggle at first, but the pain is too much for me to keep on.

"It's for your wellbeing," Fauve says looking at me sincerely. She seems to be trying to help me, but I'm not sure if I believe her.

"Alex, it doesn't look like she's been hurt badly. Bandages may be enough," the old lady says.

"She might have injuries I'm unaware of... it's better to be safe than sorry," he says as he shuts the glass lid.

Everyone leaves out of my sight except for the old woman. She enters something into her communicator, and a mist starts to fill the bed. I hold my breath and shut my eyes. I can't hold it forever, and eventually breathe in the mist, drifting off to sleep.

CHAPTER 2

I AWAKEN, TAKING in a deep breath. I watch teal mist leave my mouth as I exhale. It's slightly thicker than air, but that's only noticeable when you focus on it. Every medbay I've visited has been like this, though I prefer making repairs on the outside rather than being inside needing medical attention. I gently put my hand to my jaw and feel no pain. I wish I knew exactly what they put in the mist.

I try to get a sense of my surroundings, which isn't easy from the bed. Everything is tainted in a light teal color, but from what I can see the room is dimly lit. If it's nighttime this might be the best time for me to escape. By morning I could be back home, though many days could've already passed... I try not to think about that. I yawn, feeling relaxed. I gotta remember not to breathe in too much of this stuff or I'll go back to sleep. I yawn again, feeling a bit drowsy. I better get going.

I look to my left for the emergency release. It's a small handle you can pull that will cause the filter system to turn on and open the glass lid. I find the handle and give it a sharp pull. Nothing. Sometimes the emergency release doesn't respond right away if it hasn't been used in forever. I pull again, harder this time. Nothing. Maybe I'm not pulling hard enough because I'm feeling drowsy?

I stare at the ceiling, yawning again. It's possible they disabled the release from the computer system. Since I've worked on these before I know there's a hidden button that can override that. Being a ship mechanic has its benefits. I look around, finding the button on the other side. I press it, then pull the handle and wait, yawning.

As I begin to drift off I hear the filter kick in, replacing the mist with fresh air. I watch as I exhale the last of it, feeling more awake. The glass lid opens, and I sit, moving my legs over the edge of the bed. I stretch, noticing that my wrists and arms aren't hurting. I'm feeling much better than I did yesterday.

I take in my surroundings again, trying to piece together my situation. I've gotta make the best of it, whatever it is. I realize there aren't any lights on in the room. Gentle starlight is shining brightly through the room's transparent wall.

Most of the stars are yellow and orange, but there are some blues in there too. I'm reminded of how I would stargaze out of my window as snowflakes fell among the pine trees. I can almost hear the crackling sounds of the fire in the fireplace...

My thoughts are interrupted by the booming voice of the AI system speaking over the ship's intercom. "Repairs are ninety six percent complete. Leaving Hayventh once repairs are finished."

That means we're still in Hayventh's orbit. I feel a surge of energy come over me that leaves all sleepiness behind. All I have to do is make it to the hangar. And if I'm lucky, most people will be asleep.

I walk up to the door and check it. No alarm systems. That's one less thing to waste my time on. I slide the door open, wincing at the sound it makes. I go through it and freeze.

Across the passageway Fauve is leaning against the wall. My tension dissipates as I hear snoring. In the dark I can't see exactly what she's wearing but I can tell it's not armor. I must not be much of a threat. I silently shut the door and stand still until my eyes adjust to the dark before proceeding.

I move along the passageway as quietly as I can. In the darkness the passageway feels like it endlessly leads into the void. It's been some time since I've been on a ship this large. It's hard for me not to stop and marvel at it.

"Repairs are ninety eight percent complete. Leaving Hayventh in approximately three minutes," the AI states.

Three minutes? I let out a sigh, continuing onward. There's no way I can find the hangar in time. I'm about to give up hope when I pause at a nearby door. There's a humming sound coming from the other side. The generators are in there! I can temporarily shut off their power, interrupting the ship repair and delaying launch.

I glance over my shoulder. Fauve could still notice me if I'm not careful. I hear footsteps coming towards me. I look around trying to find somewhere to hide. There are a few crates stacked to the side a little ways down the passageway. I go over to them wishing I had a better option. This takes me closer to Fauve than I'd like to be.

The footsteps are even, but forceful. They pause, then quicken. I hold my breath, staying still... relief washes over me as the footsteps pass by. I look around the crates, keeping as hidden as I can.

"Fauve! What are you doing sleeping again? Get up!" Lance says in a frustrated tone. She startles awake, looking around.

"Whaa?" she says sleepily.

"Fauve, get up!" Lance says, shaking his head. "How can someone who has so much energy in the day struggle so much to stay awake at night?"

Fauve waves her hand dismissively. "Oh come on Lance, the prisoner's sound asleep; it's not like she's going anywhere. And besides, I'd wake up if the door opened."

"Doesn't matter, you're on duty so you have to be alert," Lance says quickly with no room for argument.

"Guard duty is so boring. Why couldn't I have been assigned something more interesting?" she asks in a tone that sounds to me like she'd rather be doing anything else in the world.

"Alex isn't going to give you something better until you can prove you can handle this. Now I'll be back in an hour or two and I expect to find you awake." With that he begins to walk away, not giving her a chance to answer. He stops and turns to look back at her. "Oh and Alex expects us to wear our armor for as long as the prisoner is on board." He turns and leaves, continuing down the hall past her.

Fauve shakes her head and sighs, bringing her arm up and tapping her communicator. Its holographic screen pops up, and she starts looking at a 3d map of a forest. I can feel sweat running down my forehead. I need to get going but I can't go yet because she'll see me. She gets a notification on her screen and taps her earpiece.

"Hey Aric," she pauses. "Yeah, I can't go yet. You know. Guard duty. From what I see we'll want to try the west side. You there yet? We gotta hurry if we want to get there first..." She turns her back to me and looks down the passageway in the direction that Lance went. I take this opportunity to go back to the generator room. I quickly go through the door.

"Repairs have been completed. Launching in ten seconds," the AI announces in its booming voice.

I rush over to the main generator and look for the emergency handle. I find it and pull it. The power shuts down and I rush back into the passageway.

"Yeah I have to go, something's up," I hear Fauve say. She won't be turned away from me much longer.

I rush in the opposite direction, hoping the hangar is this way. I continue on until I find a passageway that has large windows on one side. I look in and see the carrier ships. Once the door opens I go through it, making sure it shuts firmly behind me. I walk towards the carriers, feeling my hope rising. After briefly looking at them I choose the one I think will serve me best. I make my way towards it.

"Thought you'd be getting away, huh?" Roxanne says coldly.

I look to see her leaning against the other carrier ship. Really? I have to go through this again? "The sooner I'm gone the better off we'll all be," I say, wishing I sounded more confident. The door to the carrier ship opens easily. I expect to hear her footsteps, but she doesn't come after me.

"You can try all you want, but that one's dead," she calls out.

I continue to the pilot's seat and sit down. Soon I discover she wasn't bluffing, it actually won't start up. Thankfully I know how to fix the problem. I get out my diagnostic tool to see what's wrong. The scanner makes a beeping noise as I scan around the engine area. I hear footsteps rushing onto the ship.

"Hey what do you think you're doing?" Roxanne asks, snatching the tool out of my hands. She shakes her head. "Doesn't matter. You're not doing that again." She grabs my upper arm and pulls me away from the engine. Before I can react she puts my hands behind my back and handcuffs me.

I clench my teeth. How does she move so fast? My wrists start hurting like they did yesterday. While the medbay does heal wounds usually the wounded area is still sensitive to pain for the next few days. Roxanne starts walking.

"Where are we going?" I ask.

"None of your business," she says harshly.

I think it is my business, since I'm the one who will have to deal with whatever she does to me.

As we're coming to the medbay Fauve looks at us from her communicator's holographic screen. "Roxanne, what are you doing? How did she get out here?"

Roxanne keeps walking. "I'm taking her to the prison," she says with indifference. "That's where she should've been put from the beginning and it's where she belongs if an eye can't be kept on her."

"But Roxanne, Alex said she should be in the medbay for at least another twenty four hours!" Fauve says, walking quickly to keep up with us. We're heading to the back of the ship at a speed that's making my head spin.

"Well he's not awake right now so I'm making the decision," Roxanne says as she takes my handcuffs off and shoves me into one of the cells. She taps her wrist and types something into her communicator. Nothing happens. She narrows her eyes. "You cut the power, didn't you," she says glaring at me.

I shrug. Doesn't matter now. The entrances of the cells flicker with light as the electrically charged force field walls turn on. I'm glad the other walls are solid.

"Power on, checking for damages," states the AI instead of resuming launch like it's supposed to.

"You better hope you didn't do any damage," Roxanne says threateningly.

"If cutting the power caused damage then there's something really wrong with this ship," I snap back.

"Come on Fauve, we better tell Alex what happened and check for damages," Roxanne says, signaling for Fauve to come. She hesitates. "Come on," Roxanne says, grabbing her arm and walking away.

I don't hear from anyone after that for hours. Not even Lance comes to check on me. I had expected at least for him or Fauve to come by, since they are the guards. The small cell has a bed with a metal frame. The only thing to keep me company is my own boredom.

"Power generator: fifty percent. Weather: sunny with a chance of rain," the AI states calmly. It's been making announcements like this ever since the power came back... this doesn't bode well. Pulling the emergency handle shouldn't have caused this. I wonder if these people ever took this ship to a mechanic? This ship's probably never been to one.

I look up as I hear footsteps and see Alex coming up to my cell carrying some food. "I see you're still awake," he says, setting the food on a teleporter tray. The food appears on the floor of my cell.

"When are you going to release me?" I ask, walking to the force field wall.

"What?" he asks, looking taken aback. "You expect me to let you go?"

I nod. "Yeah, I don't deserve to be here."

"It's not that simple, surely you understand there's a process I have to go through."

"It is that simple. I go home and say nothing of this, and you go your own way."

Alex shakes his head. "Even if I wanted to let you go I'm in no position to. We're not in Hayventh's orbit anymore, and we have no power due to damaged circuitry. Thankfully the emergency thrusters are working, but I'm not sure if we can make it to the next planet for repairs."

"That's not right, a ship shouldn't be having this much trouble from an emergency shut off."

"Well it is what it is. There's nothing I can do about it."

"If we go back it can be repaired on Hayventh."

"By now we're in-between Hayventh and Faratha IV. That planet is better equipped for fixing large ships."

"While my people may be mostly hunters we have some very good mechanics there," I say, thinking of some of my friends who excel at the craft. I've learned so much from them, even after my years of experience. I see his point though; Faratha IV has more resources and a more livable climate with a higher population.

"I'm sure there are. But due to all the things I have to consider this is the best path for me to take."

"What about using one of the carrier ships?" I ask. "I could buy one from you."

Alex frowns. "There seems to be something wrong with those too. They don't act right. I don't trust us using them until I figure out more about what's going on."

"If things are so bad then why are you talking to me?"

"Someone has to assess the damages, and I prefer to do that myself. Our copilot is managing things just fine." Before I can say anything else he looks at his communicator. "I've got to go, there's a report that needs looking into." With that he leaves.

I'm surprised he wasn't angry towards me for what I did. Being stranded is a serious thing. Somehow I've got to get out of this mess. I don't know how, but I have to figure something out. My communicator still works, but all outgoing and incoming communications are blocked for it, so I can't contact anyone. I look at the blank ceiling wishing it had a skylight. While I miss the view that was in the medbay I'm glad I'm not trapped in one of those beds. After a while I doze off into a deep sleep.

"Come on, we're almost there."

I look to see that a young woman with auburn hair is standing in front of me. Her hand reaches out towards me, her eyes glinting with amusement. I find myself squinting as the warm sunlight hits my face.

"The jump's not far," the woman says with laughter in her amber colored eyes.

I look at my feet and see I'm standing on a ledge. The gap between us is small. I reach out and grab her hand.

She pulls me over the gap with ease. "There, that wasn't so hard now was it?" she asks.

"No it wasn't," I say, taking in the jungle clearing around me. A gentle breeze flows through my hair. Everything is so green.

"I have something to tell you," she says, her eyes shining brightly with excitement.

I look at her, and before I can say anything she speaks again.

"This jungle has all the answers," she says, smiling.

"The answers to what?"

She begins talking, but I can't hear what she says. Everything around me starts to fade to white.

"Wait!" I say, as the ground shakes. Everything fades away.

CHAPTER 3

I AWAKEN TO everything shaking. I feel myself rolling off the bed and quickly grab the bars of the headboard as the ship continues to tilt. An alarm is faintly sounding off in the distance as the ship goes into another fit of rocking.

I can't tell if the ship is malfunctioning or if we're being attacked. The ship starts tilting the other way, and the bed slides towards the force field wall. I get off of it before it hits the wall. It'd be good if I didn't get electrocuted today. Don't need that.

If this is from the ship malfunctioning I'm leaving at all costs. I can't stay on something like this. The ship rocks again causing me to almost lose my footing. Gunfire sounds off, and shouting can be heard. So we're under attack, but by who? Marauders? Then again, I'm not sure the people I'm with aren't marauders themselves.

I shake my head. Regardless we're being attacked, and I'm stuck in this prison cell. If I could escape now no one would miss me. I hear shouting and people running as another alarm sounds off. The sounds of pounding feet and gunfire are getting closer. I brace myself, ready to deal with whoever comes my way.

The prison door bursts open, and a man and woman come running through. They look around quickly with guns raised. The man stops when he spots me. "Hey, should we take her with us?"

he calls out to the woman, studying me. I shift my weight to my other foot as he continues to stare at me.

"It depends on if she has anything of value," states the other. She comes closer to the cell to take a look at me.

The man seems to ponder that for a moment, then shakes his head. "Nah, we can't do anything with her. Come on, we gotta go," he says turning to leave.

"Wait!" I exclaim, getting an idea. If I can convince them into taking me I can escape later and get home. Usually people like this damage a ship beyond repair, and a lot of times the people on board are left to die. This may be my only chance of survival.

The man turns back to look at me. "What?" he asks.

"I used to be a ship mechanic, and I know some information about Hayventh that may be of interest to you." I say, trying to keep the anxiety out of my tone.

The man looks at the woman, and she nods. "We could use a ship mechanic," she says eagerly.

The man nods and gets out some handcuffs.

"I don't need those, I'll go willingly," I say, wanting to avoid the pain.

"I'm not sure we can trust you. Come on." He turns off the force field wall, and I come forward, letting him put the handcuffs on me.

All I have to do is get them to trust me, then I'll be on my way. We leave the prison. Burn marks and bullet holes can be found along the walls of the passageway. My eyes water from the smoke. I wish I could cover my ears, or that the alarm system would shut off. I get chills as I notice we're the only signs of life here.

My captors keep going as if nothing's wrong. It's shameful they think nothing of the destruction they caused. That's typical of marauders. Only out for themselves. That's the one regret my people have had about moving to this star system... it's full of them. The only thing that's distinct about the ones I'm with is that they both have a tattoo of a tiger on their arms with the letters T.C. sketched underneath it. I have no idea what that stands for.

They come to an abrupt stop. I look to see a figure cast in shadow standing in the haziness ahead. The figure begins to walk slowly towards us. I can feel the man and woman shrink back as the figure comes nearer. The person's cloak brushes the ground as they walk, and their bluish grey helmet under their hood makes it impossible to see their face.

The person comes to a stop, standing tall. Power and darkness radiates off of them, and the air begins to feel more tense with every moment that passes by. Time seems to freeze as my captors hesitate to go forward to meet the person.

I cough from the smoke, breaking the stillness. The figure gestures for us to come closer. The man sits me down against the wall and goes with the woman to meet the person. Words are exchanged, but I can't make them out. The hooded figure turns and walks away, disappearing into the smoke.

I can't keep from coughing. All this smoke is getting to me. My captors come back and help me stand. It doesn't take long to realize we're going back to the prison.

"Aren't you going to take me with you?" I ask, feeling my heart rate picking up. If they put me back in the cell I'll die.

"Our master has told us not to take any prisoners. We've gotten all we can here," the woman says as they quicken their pace.

I struggle against them. The man sits me down against the wall. Then him and the woman run off.

"No! Don't leave me here! I can help you!" I call after them, feeling hopeless as they are soon out of sight.

I start coughing again, pulling against the handcuffs, wondering how I can get them off. There must be something around here I can use. Seeing nothing I lean my head against the wall. What's the use? After a moment I clench my fists. I'm not giving up yet.

I bring myself to a stand and walk in the direction of the hangar. I can voice command one of the carrier ships to take me home. I walk through the empty passageway, feeling relief as the alarm system finally stops. Still no signs of life.

I eventually make it to the hangar. The door doesn't open automatically for me like it should. I hit the button that makes it open manually with my shoulder. The door starts clicking and making a grinding sound. Sounds like some metal got shoved into the gears. The door finally opens, and I rush in as the last carrier is taking off.

"Wait!" I call out, running.

Fauve is piloting it. Before I can get her attention the carrier blasts out of the hangar. I stand in the dead silence for a moment, catching my breath. I notice there's another carrier sitting in the corner. Fauve's wasn't the last one after all. It's covered with dust and looks rusted. It's going to be near impossible to get that one up and running with my hands behind my back.

"Hey!" I hear someone call out behind me. I quickly turn to see a man walking towards me. I brace myself. Once he catches up to me he speaks again. "Are you alright? We thought the marauders had you for sure," he says looking at me with concern in his icy blue eyes.

"Who are you?" I ask defensively, ignoring his question.

He smiles. "I'm Evan, the copilot of this ship. I've been busy piloting it for Alex, so I haven't had the chance to meet you."

Meet me? Why would he be interested in meeting a prisoner? "I didn't know anyone from the crew had survived. How many are left?"

"We all survived. We're hiding in a few of the rooms in the west sector of the ship. We didn't have time to get you, and barely got away from them ourselves."

"Why were we attacked?"

"The marauders have gotten worse as of late. They seem to be banding together under a new leader and are attacking whenever they see the opportunity. I'm surprised to see you're out of your cell, what happened?" he asks, changing the subject.

"I was convincing them to take me with them so I could be on my way. It almost worked too," I say simply.

"It's dangerous to do that, especially since most who go with them are never seen again."

"I shrug, "I could've escaped, had they taken me far enough."

He looks at me with admiration in his eyes. "Maybe you could've. We need to get back to the others. I was out scouting and we're not sure if the marauders have left."

I look back at the carrier. I probably could've gotten it working. I turn away from it and follow him.

He pauses. "Oh, let's also get those handcuffs off. No need for those."

"Thanks," I say as he removes them. I rub my wrists as we continue walking. The ship's lighting has gotten noticeably dimmer now. "It's much darker than before," I say.

Evan glances around. "Yeah, it is. We're low on our power reserves, and hopefully by pretending we're done for the marauders won't return."

We walk in the low lighting for what feels like a long time, turning down passageways I don't recognize. "Why is the crew on this ship so small? It seems like there's only a few of you."

Evan hesitates. "We're looking for people to hire," he pauses. "Well, we were before all this happened. Repairs will be costly."

"Yeah," I say, looking around. "This ship needs some. If it were me I'd trade it in for scrap and start over."

He laughs. "That's a correct assessment. It is what it is though." Soon we see a warm light up ahead. As we come up to it I can see that the crew has made a room into a makeshift camp of sorts.

Alex is standing at a table, and people are taking orders from him. His face is bleeding, but he doesn't seem to notice. The man I had seen helping with the mining is standing at the desk. "Blair, I want you to check on our food supply. If it's not all there bring back what's left. Once Fauve is done scouting I'll have Lance take a turn and review her work."

"Got it," he says as he turns to leave. He nods at us as he shuffles past.

Alex starts typing something into his communicator. "Hey Raya?" he calls out.

The woman with pastel pink hair comes out of a room to the left of his desk. She has a sleeve of tattoos on her left arm and a black smudge on her face. "Yeah?"

"Any luck with getting the communicators online?"

She shakes her head. "Haven't got 'em workin' yet. I'll keep tryin' though." With that she heads back into the other room and shuts the door before I can see what's in there.

Alex turns to look at us, and pauses before speaking. "I see you survived. We couldn't get to you as we had to go to our defenses immediately."

I nod in understanding. I'm a prisoner after all, not part of the crew. Not that I want to be anyway. "Are you going to make me go back to the prison cell?" I ask.

To my surprise Alex shakes his head. "No, there's no use in that. You'll just be here under guard."

"Sir I don't think she needs a guard... where's she going to go?" Evan asks.

"I don't know about that," Alex says. He changes the subject, looking back at me. "Once Roxanne has her injuries checked it'll be your turn. You go into the room over there, and Maylea will have you checked."

"Alright," I say, waiting to see what he'll tell me to do in the meantime.

Lance comes up behind us, waiting to talk to Alex. I move out of the way, and Evan follows. "I've got some things I've got to do, but you can hang out here until it's your turn to go," Evan says motioning to one of the seats that have been set up around a small table.

I go sit there and he leaves Lance finishes talking to Alex and takes his place by the door that leads to the passageway, watching me warily. I try to ignore him. Soon Blair comes into the room carrying a large box. He sets it on the desk.

"That's all?" Alex asks. "Just the one box?"

"Yeah, that's all that's left. I'll check to see if the hidden emergency rations are still there."

Alex takes a deep breath and lets it out loudly. "We're going to have to go on strict rations."

Blair nods and heads back out. Roxanne comes out of the other room with a bandage wrapped around her forearm and hand. She sees me and glares but goes on to talk to Alex. "Is Fauve back from scouting yet?"

"No, haven't seen her. She's probably checking the east side of the ship."

"She can't do anything right, can she? Now I'll have to go find her."

"Roxanne, don't be like that," Alex says as she walks away.

She catches my gaze and narrows her eyes. "What're you looking at?" she asks. She doesn't stop walking and leaves.

I know that was Fauve I saw leaving the hangar earlier. I wonder what she's up to? I realize it's my turn to see the medic. I stand and walk over to the door. I open it and go in.

The old woman that I saw in the medbay is sitting at a table typing something into her communicator. She looks at me and puts on a smile. "I see you survived. Why don't you have a seat?" she asks, motioning over to a bench that's up against the wall.

I go over and sit, watching her closely. I'm not sure how much I can trust her.

"My name is Maylea. I'm the medic here."

"Nice to meet you," I say, feeling funny about this. I'm a prisoner not a crewmate. I hesitantly let her check me over and decide to keep the conversation going to pass the time. "So how long have you been a medic?"

"I was drafted into a war long ago at the age of seventeen. It happened immediately after I completed my medical training." She shakes her head. "Back then I had no idea of the pain and sorrows I would witness from choosing this path."

"How did you finish your training so quickly?" I ask in awe. I've never heard of anyone completing it so soon.

She gives me a sad smile. "I had a passion for it since I was a child. I began learning and training way before I was supposed to. I still love doing it, but the war mentality does wear on you over time." She sighs. "I'll never approve of fighting. It's all worthless and sorrowful."

I can tell by the look in her eyes that she's trying to figure out if I agree with her. To be honest I haven't thought about it much... It's something that's always been around during my lifetime, so I'm not sure how to respond. "Yeah, it sure is rough," I say, already knowing

I said the wrong thing. Her eyes glint with a flash of sternness, but she says nothing else about her thoughts on the matter.

"Well, you look fine, besides a few bruises here and there. You don't need any further treatment."

I nod and thank her before turning to leave. She doesn't say anything more.

Alex and Raya are talking as I exit the room. She turns to see who opened the door and smiles. "Why not her? She could help me out I'm sure."

Alex frowns. "I don't know about that."

Raya rolls her eyes. "Oh come on Alex, what's the harm? I can't get all this work done on my own."

"Fine. Just make sure she doesn't get away."

"Knew I could count on ya Alex."

She walks back towards the room she was working in and looks over her shoulder. "Ya don't mind helpin', right?" she asks.

"Guess not," I shrug. I've got nothing better to do.

She smiles and goes into the room.

I go after her, noticing that Alex is watching me. "Stay out of trouble," he says when we make eye contact.

"Will do," I say, continuing on. I pause at the doorway. What a contrast. The other rooms were spotless, but this room is a mess. In the center is a forge and anvil, with clutter strewn all about. In the dim lighting I can't make out what all of it is, but I can see piles of various metals, tools, and scrap lying all around.

"I know it's a little messy, but it gets the job done," Raya says smiling at me.

"A little?"

She laughs. "Okay, maybe a lot. Either way I do get things done. I'm a little overwhelmed with tasks at the moment though."

"And what do you think I can do for you?" I ask. I don't have any experience with forging.

"Ya can help me with these metal plates." She points at some metal panels sitting on a metal table next to the forge. "I want ya to look 'em over and see if they'll do for coverin' some of the bullet holes in the ship's walls."

I carefully walk over the table and examine the panels. "You do realize this isn't the way you repair bullet holes," I say.

Raya starts hammering on another panel, sending sparks flying everywhere. I step to the side to avoid some of them. "Yeah I know that. The crew expects me to repair the ship, and I don't have the proper tools or experience."

"Why isn't there a mechanic on board?"

Her hammering pauses and she looks straight ahead. "Well we did have a mechanic, but he left a month ago. Just ran away one night, takin' all his tools with 'im. Haven't seen 'im since," she says, resuming her hammering.

"Well, I do know a thing or two about repair work," I say, trailing off as I notice a familiar bluish grey helmet glinting in the light in a nearby pile of clutter.

CHAPTER 4

I GET CHILLS looking at it. What's that doing here? The person I saw earlier... are they linked with the crew somehow?

"That's great! A ship mechanic is desperately needed here," Raya says. Is it me, or is she hammering more excitedly now? "How many years of experience do ya have?"

"Oh, about ten. I do it on the side now, but before the war I had my own business," I say, not taking my eyes off of the helmet. I need to find out who that belongs to before it's too late.

"Why didn't ya start one after settlin'?" Raya asks while examining her work.

"Hayventh was in need of food and other survival supplies. It made more sense for everyone to be focused on hunting at the time." The thing I'm wondering about is why Raya has the helmet. I look over at her. She doesn't seem like she is tall enough to have been the mysterious figure I saw earlier. Her shoulders aren't broad enough.

Raya nods. "Makes sense. Glad you're here though, havin' a ship mechanic on board will bring us a lot of relief ya know."

I take my attention off of the helmet and try to focus more on the conversation. "I'm only a prisoner here... and I need to get back home. I have my own life to tend to."

"I was afraid of that. It's just..." She pauses and looks straight ahead again before resuming pounding out a dent in the metal she's working on. "We're not in good shape, and if we don't get help we won't survive for much longer." She turns and looks at me. "If ya prove yer worth ya won't be a prisoner for long. The crew doesn't have much of a say anymore."

Her words cause me to sigh. This ship would need so much work. And how do I know if these guys are good people? I don't want to help them if they aren't, but I don't have much choice since my own survival is at stake.

"Well? What do ya say?" Raya asks, not letting me off the hook.

"I'll do it. That's better than rotting in a prison cell," I finally say. I'll do this for now but I'm still going to find a way home.

Raya smiles, "I knew I could count on ya. Just had a feelin'."

Before I can say anything else Evan comes into the room. "Alex wants us all to discuss some things now that he knows more about our situation."

Raya nods. "We'll be there in a bit!"

"Good," Evan says, smiling. He turns and leaves.

Raya looks hesitantly at her work before finally putting down her hammer. "I'll have to work on this more afterwards." She starts walking along the path through the clutter.

I follow her, taking one last look at the helmet. We enter the main room, and I'm surprised to see that the only crew members that are here are ones I've already met. Fauve is the only one missing. Seven is not nearly enough for a ship of this size.

"Alex, where's Fauve?" Maylea asks.

"No idea. Roxanne has yet to find her. If we don't see her soon I'm going to have to organize a search party," Alex says.

As Lance is beginning to speak Fauve bursts into the room. "Looks like I made it in time for the meeting," she says, out of breath.

"Fauve, where have you been?" Maylea says, rushing over to her. "You're not hurt are you?"

"No I'm fine. Just running a bit late is all."

"Why did it take you so long to get back?" Lance questions in a demanding tone.

Fauve shrugs. "Just been scouting the ship like you asked. Nothing much going on in the east sector."

Lance looks sternly at her, then sighs. "Guess it's time for the main report. Alex, what's the current situation?"

Everyone turns to look at Alex. Fauve takes a seat at the table looking less tense than she did a moment ago.

He hesitates, quickly glancing at each of us before speaking. "If we don't turn things around we won't see the light of day. Our power is decreasing, and after today I'll be shutting off the lights. Our oxygen levels are going to drop if we don't figure out something soon."

"What about the emergency power reserves?" Lance asks.

"Those have been drained. It seems that the marauders took everything they could. Even the emergency food storage is empty."

"But that was hidden in a place where not many would look?"

"It was, but they found it anyway."

"Alex, Franca used to be a ship mechanic! She can help us!" Raya says excitedly.

"Things are too chaotic right now. It'd be too easy for us to lose track of her."

"Yeah but where's she going to go? All we have to do is lock up the hangar," Evan says.

"If Alex doesn't think it's a good idea then it isn't," Lance says, glaring at Evan.

"If we had better guards we wouldn't have to worry about her at all," Evan says.

Lance stands angrily, looking like he's about to yell.

"Both of you stop. We don't have time for this," Alex says, motioning for him to sit back down. Lance sits, keeping an eye on Evan.

"Raya, I'll let Franca help with ship repairs as long as you are with her. If there's always someone watching her then I won't have to worry about that," Alex says, continuing on as if nothing happened.

"What repairs should I go with first?" I ask. If I'm honest I feel a little overwhelmed by the work that will need to be done. I may have bitten off more than I can chew with this. The ship needed a lot of repairs before the attack... who knows how much damage was done to it since then.

"Checking the oxygen generators is the first thing, then working on the ship's circuitry is next. If we can get power we can get to the next planet faster," Alex says.

"Where are we exactly?" Blair asks.

"Somewhere between Faratha IV and Rythor."

Maylea gasps. "How did we get that far from Hayventh?"

I notice the only one who doesn't act surprised is Fauve... did she already know this?

"The marauders hauled us away, so we wouldn't be able to tell anyone before they made their escape," Alex says.

"Can we land on Faratha IV?" Roxanne asks. "It'd be better to land there instead of Rythor, considering the battle and all."

There's a battle happening on Rythor? While I don't usually hear of much news from the other planets I should've at least heard of this.

Alex shakes his head. "We're not close enough. We only have enough resources to make it to Rythor, and that's if we stop using power now."

The meeting goes on for a little longer with everyone receiving assignments. Alex decides to cut the lights... while he seemed confident that we can make it to Rythor I have a feeling we're barely going to survive. I go along with Raya and Alex to the control room.

Once we get there he goes over to the control panel. "Here go the lights," he says, touching the main command screen.

I get chills as everything goes dark. I can't imagine that the helmet will remain where it was. That will have to be thought upon later. I walk over to the control panel and enter a special code in on the second screen, which brings up the statistics of the ship. Nothing looks good, but the information on the oxygen generators is alarming.

"What do you see Franca?" Raya asks.

"Well," I say, trying my best to keep the alarm out of my tone. "The oxygen generators aren't getting enough power to keep generating. We have five days' worth of oxygen left."

"Great," Alex says, as he pulls up our star system on the other screen.

"How far away from Rythor are we?" Raya asks.

"We're only able to use the ship's emergency thrusters, and they take power," Alex says. "I'd say that if we put all of our power towards the thrusters we might get there in four days. That's if things go well."

"And if things don't?" I ask.

"If things don't it's going to take us seven."

"Unless we can get the power generators going?"

"The marauders took the power cables, and we have no spares," Alex says, the frustration in his tone mixing with exasperation.

"Surely there's another way, right Franca?" Raya asks.

"I'll try and think of something," I respond, wishing my eyes would adjust quicker to the darkness.

"In the meantime I'm going to set the rest of the crew to work on power saving and using the thrusters. The sooner we get to Rythor the better." With that Alex leaves; his footsteps fading into the void of darkness.

Raya stays silent for a while, letting me think. The connectors at the end of those cables are custom made for models like this. If Raya could forge some, I'm sure I could find wires to connect them to. I'm not sure that would work, as the wires in the cable were special made too. But it's the only thing I know to do. I turn to Raya, hoping she'll listen to me. We don't have much time. "Raya, if you could forge the connectors of the cables I think I can come up with the wires, and we might get power again."

"I just gotta remember what they look like," she says with a hint of enthusiasm in her voice.

"You could go to the generators and look at how the plug in is shaped," I say. "In the meantime I could take a look at what kind of wires I'll need."

She pats me on the shoulder. "I'm on it." With that I hear her leave the room. All that's left is a void of silent darkness. I'm surprised she forgot Alex's orders about not leaving me alone so soon. I'll gladly take it for what it is. Stars are shining brightly through the windows of the control room, giving me the realization that we may be left to free float among them forever.

I was hoping to go home, and that's still all I want. Hopefully with time I'll make it through all of this. I turn my attention back to the statistics on the screen and browse till I find the power generator section. From the looks of it I can take a cable from one of the carrier ships and use that once Raya makes the other part.

I make my way to the hangar and find that the door is now stuck. It's cracked open like it didn't finish shutting. I can almost fit through the opening. I put my hands on the door and pull. It doesn't budge, and I hear a grinding sound coming from the mechanism. Whatever metal was in the gears seems to have fallen, freezing them in place. As I'm about to look for the maintenance panel I hear the echoing of footsteps quickly coming my way. I move away from the hangar to the entrance of one of the passageways.

"Oh come on Roxanne, you don't actually think she'll get away?" I hear Evan say.

"Of course she will if she gets the chance. Don't let her fool you." I hear the hangar door slam shut, and then a clicking sound.

"Really. You're going to lock the hangar?"

"Yes I am. And if you have a problem with that you can talk to Alex," she says back harshly.

I hear them both walking off as Evan continues to protest against it. Great. It's not going to be easy getting into the hangar. I move on, deciding to try to find a different cable. I make my way through the passageways to the supply room. I can't help but look behind me, feeling like the figure could appear out of the darkness at any moment. Relief washes over me as I make it safely to the supply room. To my surprise I find that Lance and Alex are there. Keeping out of sight I begin to realize what they're talking about.

"I'm sorry Lance, I should've listened to you," Alex says.

"It's fine, Evan can sound convincing at times. Where do you think she is now?"

"I don't know, but she's probably trying to escape. If we find her we'll have to keep her under tighter guard."

"And mostly in the prison cell."

"If we can find her. We've got so many other problems. There are only enough food rations for three days."

I back off deeper into the darkness. The last thing I want is to be stuck in that prison cell again. As soon as this ship is stable I plan on leaving. If I left sooner their rations would go further... but

I might be leaving them to their deaths. I'll just have to make the best of this. I decide to make my way to the east wing. I overheard Fauve say there was nothing there, and the others seem to mostly operate from the west wing.

Time seems as endless as the stars. I occasionally stop and shine the light from my communicator along other passageways to see what's down them. The end of the ship is the only convincing sign that my destination has been reached.

Pausing, I recall that according to the computer system there should be a supply room on the north side of this wing. Whether this crew ever used it is another story. Finding the right room is another journey altogether. Eventually I find myself standing in front of the doors to the supply room. The sound of the gears inside echo loudly, causing me to jump as the doors automatically open. A dusty room is revealed, filled with boxes.

I walk in and rummage through the first box. My hand touches something wet, making me quickly pull away. The smell of spoiled food causes the box to be immediately shut. Wiping my hand off on my armor I hesitantly move on to the next box.

This one's filled with old gun parts. Might become useful later. I open a third box, and to my relief I find an old carrier ship battery with its cable still attached. Of course the connector is different, but that can be cut off and changed. I carry it under my arm and continue on.

As I'm about to leave the room I notice a box in the corner that's set apart from the others. Setting the battery down I open the box and use the light of my communicator to see what's inside. To my surprise I find it's full of rare gemstones and gold. To which one of them does this belong to? I decide to leave it, trying to make it look like the box wasn't disturbed. To the best of my ability the other boxes are moved back to where they originally were.

I take the battery and leave the room, once again feeling the heaviness of the darkness around me as I let the light from my communicator fade. Alerting anyone of my presence wouldn't be ideal, and my communicator only has so much power. Hopefully the others will be understanding when I return.

Coming to a stop I realize I've forgotten which passageway I came from. Taking my best guess I walk along, hoping it's the right way. I freeze as I hear the echoing of footsteps in the distance but relax as I realize they are going further away. I continue on, noticing that there are black spots on the wall. I shrug it off and keep going. It seems like this side of the ship needs some cleaning. Either that or I'm seeing things. I shiver, noticing the temperature drop for the first time. The others weren't dressed as well as me... I wonder how they're faring?

Stopping, I find I'm going down a dead end. There's a large dark spot on the wall next to me. I shine my light on it, and immediately wish I hadn't. The hole is filled with little spider-like mechanical bugs. As the light shines on them I hear a whirring sound as they begin to dimly glow. Soon they are moving, along with the other spots on the wall. I rush out of the passageway, not wanting one to get on me. Someone at some point planted those to spy on the crew. That hole looked like it had been there for a long time. Usually a power supply is set in the wall for the bugs to recharge. I wonder if the power outage caused them to be dormant?

No matter, I'm going to have to watch out for those and notify Alex about them. I wander on but my exhaustion is taking a toll. It's been a day, and I need rest. Once I'm a good distance away I turn to one of the doors of the passageway that I'm currently in. It opens, and I find that the room is empty. I can't say I'm far away enough from the mechanical bugs, but I'm too tired to go on. Sitting against one of the cold walls I soon drift off to sleep.

"Wouldn't this be a cool place to live?" the woman with the auburn hair says, smiling and looking around.

We're surrounded by blooming cherry blossom trees. Some are a light pink, and others are dark pink, their leaves reminding me of rose petals. Other trees have white, gold, or yellow blossoms. Up ahead is a valley tucked away in the forest with a cozy cabin there.

"So this is where he lived?" a man that's with us asks. He smiles. "Not bad."

"I find it cool that he chose here, out of all the places he could live," the woman says.

"So, you're going to move to this area when this is all done and over?" I ask.

She smiles. "I think I will, and you should too. I know you like Hayventh and everything, so maybe this could be a second home?"

"Sure, I could probably live here."

The man laughs. "We've got work to do Jalyn, we're not there yet."

She laughs too. "I guess not. Come on, let's see what we can find." We walk to the house. As we get closer I realize it's much older than I thought it was.

"How long do you think it's been since anyone lived here?" the man asks.

"I don't know. I heard his son used to live here after him, but that may be a rumor," Jalyn says after some hesitation. We get up to the house and Jalyn opens the door, going inside.

"Do we have authorization to do this?" the man asks.

Jalyn doesn't answer him and continues on.

"I guess not," he mutters to himself.

I don't recognize him from anywhere, but he seems familiar. He has short brown hair and green eyes. A tall guy, with a few scars that make him look like he's been in a fight or two. We go in and find dust and cobwebs everywhere.

Jalyn doesn't waste much time, heading directly upstairs to a room that looks like some kind of office. She heads over to an old desk in the corner of the room. The walls by the desk have maps plastered all over them. I walk over to take a look. Some are labeled, but many are not, causing them to drift off in time.

Jalyn gently picks up a journal that's been left on the desk. Blowing off the dust she carefully turns the pages and stops when a map falls out. She picks up the map and starts reading the journal. The man and I wait silently, not wanting to disturb her.

After a few moments she looks at us. "In this journal he talks about his journey in the wilderness but doesn't give much detail in fear that this information could fall into the wrong hands. He did draw a map of its location though."

"So, we have a lead?" I ask.

"A small one... if we work at it enough I think we'll figure it out," she says. We stay in the house for a little longer before heading out.

"I kinda hate to leave this all behind," the man says.

"Yeah, I understand that. We'll come back sometime Greyson," Jalyn says.

We continue making our way into the forest of cherry blossom trees. There's a silence here that can only be found when you leave civilization behind. A light yellow blossom lands on my shoulder as I look around the forest. Jalyn starts talking, but her words sound muffled. Soon everything fades to white.

CHAPTER 5

I AWAKEN TO my stomach growling. I stiffly come to a stand, trying to shake off the grogginess I'm feeling. I wonder what time it is? I check my communicator and realize it's dead. It shouldn't have died yet. how long have I been asleep? Time's not on my side, I better get going. In the corner of my eye I see movement, but when I look there is nothing there. I have to admit that being in the dark for this long can be unsettling.

I continue on, and as I go the passages seem more familiar. I quicken my pace, knowing that the makeshift camp the crew made is up ahead. As I come closer I hear someone rushing towards me. I keep a calm pace, not wanting anyone to think I'm intimidated. It's best to stand my ground from the start.

"What do you think you're doing?" Roxanne asks, grabbing my arm.

"Let go of me and I'll tell you," I say.

She scoffs and drags me over to the desk. I had a feeling I'd have to talk to Alex right away. "Where have you been?" he asks. It's clear by his tone he's not as glad to see me this time.

"I went looking for a cable for the power generators," I say, wishing there was light so I could show him the battery I found.

"You were supposed to be with Raya," he says sternly.

"Well I thought things would move faster if we split up," I say back. These people don't seem very grateful.

Alex is silent, choosing to say nothing more about that. "I guess you better take the cable to Raya," he says tiredly.

I jerk my arm out of Roxanne's grasp. She doesn't say anything and lets me go. I open the door to Raya's forge and can already hear her hammering.

As I come in she stops and looks up. "Franca? Where've ya been? Ya almost got me inta a lot a trouble."

"I'm sorry about that," I say wishing these people would be a little more lax in emergency situations. "I brought this though," I say, holding up the battery before carefully making my way towards her through the clutter. It's nice that the forge emits a little light. I wonder how long we'll be able to power it.

"I'm afraid I haven't made as much progress as ya have... the connector has a lot of small details that need finishing." I come and stand by her, finding that she has done excellent work so far. She picks up the connector with tongs, and sets it in some coals next to her, before bringing it back to the anvil to hit it with a hammer.

I shiver, feeling the icy cold that has set in. Temperatures will continue to drop. After a few hours she finishes the connector, and we get the cable attached to it. My stomach growls much louder this time, reminding me that I still haven't eaten. "How is the food being rationed out?" I ask, wondering if they'll spare me any.

"It's been fine, we're down to gettin' one meal a day," she says. "Maylea will be givin' it out soon."

Right as she says this Maylea opens the door. "Everyone's eating in the main room. You two are welcome to join when you can." Before we can say anything she goes on her way.

We leave our work at the table and go to the main room. I can hear Blair and Lance talking, and Alex is still seated at his desk.

There are some other chairs against the wall, and I choose to sit there. Raya follows me.

"Man, I can't wait till we can have light again, I think I'm starting to see things," Blair says to Lance.

"At least you're not hearing things," Lance replies in a downcast tone.

Evan comes into the room and sets a box on Alex's desk. "These are the last of the supplies."

Alex looks into the box. "Well it's better than nothing. Did you see Fauve by any chance?"

"Don't tell me she hasn't come back yet," Lance says with little care in his tone.

"We'll have to send Roxanne out to find her again," Alex says.

"I just hope she's alright," Blair says, yawning.

"I wish she had more sense and would stay put," Roxanne comments.

Maylea opens the door of her makeshift medbay and walks to the desk. "I just checked my communicator. Do you all realize we haven't slept for the last forty eight hours?"

"Has it been that long?" Lance asks.

Blair laughs. "Like it matters."

"Maylea's right, we need to rest," Alex says, showing us the date and time on his communicator. "We've been in the dark for so long that we're beginning to lose our sense of time."

"But what about finding Fauve?" Maylea asks, concerned.

"She can't go anywhere," Alex says.

Maylea nods and goes back into the room. Alex sends us to the sleeping quarters, which consists of bunks. I get handcuffed to the bottom of Roxanne's bunk since the prison cell's force field wall can't be powered anymore. I'm not tired... I'd rather be working on the ship than laying here. I pull at the handcuffs and feel a wave of pain go through my wrist. As time goes on I drift into a light sleep to pass the time.

Once everyone wakes up I'm released from the handcuffs. Roxanne doesn't say a word to me, immediately heading out to look for Fauve. Raya and I go with Alex to the forge to show him our work.

Raya goes to the table and frowns. "That's odd, what'd I do with it?" she asks, rummaging through clutter.

I briskly walk over to the table. I know we set the cable on it. I can't believe it's gone. Who would've done this? I glance over at the blue helmet... or at least to where it used to be. That too, has vanished.

"Well, are we ready to try the cable?" Evan asks as he walks into the room.

"Not quite... it seems that Raya misplaced it," Alex says.

"Surely it's here somewhere," Evan says, rummaging through some of the clutter near him. We spend what feels like hours looking, but don't find it. I guess I'll have to find another cable...

"Well, if I'm allowed to go to the hangar I can get another connector off of one of the carrier ships..." I say, trying to see how the others feel about that.

To my dismay Alex shakes his head. "We can't risk having another person missing. It's bad enough that we can't find Fauve, and everyone is too busy to keep track of you."

Looks like I might have to start a disappearing act too. I wonder if Fauve does this all the time?

Lance bursts into the room. "There's a light flashing red on one of the oxygen generators," he says, trying to catch his breath.

Before Alex can say anything I rush past him into the darkness. That means one of the generators isn't producing any air. I enter the maintenance room and go to the generator. A flash of something catches my eye, but when I turn to see what it was I find that there was nothing there. Turning back to the generator, it seems that it's just not getting enough power. I wonder how close we are to Rythor? Cause we can't survive off of this for long. Examining the other oxygen generator I can see that it's running off of the last of its emergency power reserves.

I run out the door, passing Alex. He must've been trying to catch up. I shake my head. Don't have time for that. In the control room I'm greeted with alerts from the computer system saying that the last of the power has been sent to the oxygen generators. The thrusters are running off of the last of their power reserve. The power shouldn't have drained this fast, especially with so many things being shut off. Might as well report this to Alex. As I'm about to leave the door bursts open.

"You're not supposed to be here," Roxanne says in a surprised tone. "Where's Alex? Who's with you?" she demands.

"No one," I respond, waiting for my eyes to adjust to the dark again after looking at the screen.

"Great. You're always left unsupervised. I can't be everywhere at once..." As she's complaining I notice that one of those mechanical bugs is sitting on her shoulder. I rush up to her and knock it off.

"Hey!" Roxanne yells, punching me.

"There was a mechanical bug on your shoulder," I say, taking a step back. I don't feel like fighting her right now.

Roxanne is silent for a moment, then she sighs tiredly. "You know what? I'm too tired to care anymore. You go about your business. As for the bug, you're probably seeing things." She turns, and fades into the darkness.

The bug starts crawling away. I step on it. Sparks fly from it as it dies. These bugs are spying for someone, I just don't know who. Our problems leave me no room to investigate. I turn back to the screen to get an estimate on the oxygen. It says it should last twenty four hours on the ship, if nothing else goes wrong. I look at the date and stare at it in shock. The last time I went to sleep was twenty six hours ago. No wonder I feel tired. Checking our route I can see we're closer to Rythor, but it looks doubtful that we'll get there in one day.

"Checking oxygen levels?" Evan asks, causing me to jump.

"Yeah, and it's not good. We've got about thirty four hours left," I say, regaining composure.

"That's not too bad," Evan says.

"Sorry, I meant twenty four. I'm getting tired enough that I'm starting to make mistakes," I say, putting my hand to my forehead.

"It's alright, everyone is at this point. What do you think is the next step with the generators?" he asks, not leaving like I expected him to.

"Well, my primary concern now is getting more power to them. The computer says there's another spare carrier battery in the east wing that I'm going to go salvage," I say, walking out the door. I don't have time for small talk.

Evan walks beside me, matching my pace. "I'm surprised the marauders left that there. They took everything else."

"With how little the east wing is used they probably thought that there was nothing there," I say. From a distance I hear Alex call for Evan.

"I've got to go, catch up with you later?"

"Yeah, sure," I say, going on my own path. I shiver again as I head down the dark passageways once more. They seem like an endless void where death will eventually catch us. I push that thought away as I begin to feel claustrophobic. I hear a tapping sound and look to see that one of those mechanical bugs is walking beside me.

I shrug and continue on. I could destroy it but there are hundreds of them... it'll get replaced anyway. If I'm seeing it at all. It's not like it can get anything out of me. I turn the corner and run into Fauve.

"Whoops, sorry," I say, backing up.

"No worries," she says in a carefree tone with laughter. Does none of what's happening matter to her?

"Where have you been? Everyone's been looking for you," I ask, curious myself.

"Oh, I've been patrolling the ship. I'm not sure we're safe yet... it feels like we're being watched."

I glance at the mechanical bug. "Yeah, it does feel that way, doesn't it? I'd like to know why..." I say sarcastically.

"Yeah, so would I. What are you doing on this side of the ship?"

"Oh, I'm going to go get a carrier ship battery that the computer system mentioned earlier to power the oxygen generators."

She pauses for a moment. "If it's the one that was in the southern storage room... it's gone."

"Gone? What happened to it?"

"I don't know. I heard about what you and Raya were trying to do, and thought I'd bring it. But when I got to the storage room it was gone. I'd assumed you had gotten it."

"Were there any other batteries in that storage room?"

"No, there wasn't anything else like that."

"Let's get back to the others. We've got to figure something else out." We silently walk through the passageways, and the bug keeps up with me until we get to the others, then it scurries away into the shadows.

I walk over to the desk to talk with Alex. "No luck?" he asks.

"Nope."

"Have you seen Fauve?"

"Yeah, she's right here..." I turn to see that she's gone. Now where'd she go off to? "Well, she was with me..."

"She does that. Can't stay still for long."

Lance comes up to us, once again out of breath. "The thrusters aren't running anymore. We've come to a dead stop."

Alex drops what he's doing and starts walking out of the room at a fast pace.

"Shouldn't we tell the others?" Lance asks.

"We've got no time to talk. If we don't get those running we will die," he says, running into the darkness.

I keep up, and glancing at my feet I find that the mechanical bug is also coming.

"Wait up!" Raya calls. I can hear her running to catch up. I wait for her and then we continue on together.

Alex bursts into the control room and starts pressing buttons on the computer system. "Why won't they start up?" he asks in frustration. Looking out the windows I can see we're almost in Rythor's orbit. To die here after coming so far... I walk over to the computer system and start going through the administrative orders.

"What are you doing?" Lance asks defensively through his chattering teeth.

"I'm directing all of the energy from the oxygen generators to the thrusters. We have no choice now. It's the only way we'll make it."

"Lance tell everyone to get ready in case we succeed," Alex says.

I hear the sound of Lance's heavy boots pounding on the ground as he runs off.

I finish changing the settings and we wait. Sometimes it takes the ship time to process administrative changes like that. After a few minutes the thrusters start again, and Alex lets out a breath he had been holding. I go on to try to figure out what to do about the oxygen generators while everyone else gets ready. To my dismay there's nothing I can do to power them, so I return to the control room to watch our progress instead. I hope I did the right thing. I can't believe this is happening to me. Last I checked I was only on a hunting trip.

Hours pass as we slowly make it towards Rythor. I keep an eye on the oxygen level, feeling the sweat running down my face as I watch it getting closer to zero. Once it hits that we will only have what's left on the ship. I try to stop my teeth from chattering but fail. It's getting colder by the minute.

I'm about to accept that I will die here in the dark when I look up from the computer system and see we've made it to the planet's orbit. I pinch myself to make sure I'm awake and find it's true. We'll just make it. Barely. Another hour passes, and the whole crew joins me as the ship lands in Rythor's hangar.

"Alright, let's go," Alex says, leading us to the exit door on the ship. We pass through the airlocked doors, and I soon find myself squinting as bright daylight surrounds us.

CHAPTER 6

EVERYONE GOES AHEAD of me except for Lance. He walks beside me to make sure I don't wander off. The mechanical bug turns and heads back inside the ship. Despite it being a cloudy day everything feels bright. I try to look around anyway. The hangar is huge, filled with all kinds of ships. Daylight shines brightly through the hangar's skylights and windows. Many vendors are selling their wares to anyone who comes near. Some people look over at our ship, but most ignore us.

"Finally we're out of that ship," Raya says, looking around at the people.

"Hopefully we won't have to go back to it," Blair says.

Fauve looks over her shoulder at a man who is watching us. He moves on quickly and soon disappears into the crowd. A woman starts to walk up to Roxanne, seeming interested in talking to her. Roxanne glares at her, and she goes on. I take in the scenery, so glad to be alive.

Alex calls us to his attention. "Alright. Roxanne, Blair, Maylea and Raya will go and stock up on supplies. Lance, you and Fauve will guard the ship. Evan will look into getting the ship repaired, and I will be busy getting back into contact with our commander."

Commander? These people are working under someone?

"What about Franca?" Lance asks.

"You should be able to handle her," Alex says.

"Great."

"Why don't I take her with me? I won't have any trouble watching her," Evan says casually.

Alex nods. "Alright then, I'll let you take her. You're all dismissed." He goes off, leaving everyone else to their errands.

"Let's go see what we can do about the ship," Evan says.

Lance glares at him. Evan doesn't seem to notice. He lets me walk freely without grabbing my arm, which is refreshing. I'd rather be with him than with Roxanne. I wouldn't mind Lance so much if he wasn't so suspicious of me. At least now I'll feel like I have more freedom.

"Oh no you don't," Roxanne says, taking hold of me. Maybe I spoke too soon. "I'm keeping her with me."

"Roxanne I need Franca's help with buying some ship parts we need. Surely you're not attached to her so much that you can't let go of her," Evan says jeeringly.

She glares at him and tightens her grip on my arm. "The parts we need are on the list. There is no reason to involve the prisoner in this," she replies icily.

"And who put that list together? You and Lance? Franca will know what's best to get for the cost," he argues. "And by the way, holding onto her like that is a waste of energy. She's not going anywhere," he adds.

"You obviously haven't been paying much attention," she says, not letting go of me. "And Alex made the list," she states coldly.

The more they're arguing the more tense she's getting. I think my arm's starting to lose circulation. I feel so tired. why can't they just agree?

"Which is another reason why someone else should check it over. He may be the captain, but he's not a ship mechanic. I can of course, call him over and see what he thinks," he says calmly, checking his holographic screen.

"Fine, just don't let her out of your sight," she says, finally letting go of my arm. I can't help but rub it from how tight she was holding onto me.

Once we get out of earshot he stops walking. "I've got that list here of all the ship parts we need…" Evan says, pulling it up on his holographic screen. "Does this look right to you?"

I check the list over carefully. I don't see anything missing. "Looks fine to me," I say, though I still think it would be better to start over with a new ship.

He thanks me and we continue on. We stop at a vendor where a young man is standing. The mechanic smiles at us and nods. "How may I help you two today?" he asks in a friendly tone.

"I'm looking at getting the ship repaired in slot nine," Evan says.

"We'll get on that right away sir. Come back in a few hours and we should have everything ready to go."

"Thanks."

We leave and go look at some of the other ships to pass the time. I feel a bit concerned. Mechanics always discuss what repair work needs to be done. Evan brings up his communicator's screen. He types a response about me being with him, and sends it before I can see who it was sent to. He looks at me and notices I'm watching his screen. "Just letting Alex know you're with me," he says, smiling.

I let it go at that. It makes sense that Alex would be checking on me. As we're looking at all the different ships one catches my eye. It's a big silver ship with white and gold accents. I've seen this model before on rare occasions. It has everything you could possibly want on it and can house a large crew. It's a luxurious ship for travel but costs a fortune. This one looks like it's also custom made. Whoever owns it must be extremely wealthy.

"That's a pretty cool ship, isn't it?" Evan asks, looking up at it.

"Yeah, it is," I say. "I haven't seen one of these in years."

"Did you ever work on one?"

"One time I did. Those are easy to work on. The layout makes it convenient to repair." I say, still studying it.

"Well, maybe sometime you can look around inside and see what you think of it."

I look over at him surprised. "You own this ship?"

Evan laughs. "No, but a friend of mine does. I usually land my ship next to his."

"Is your friend going to stop by and see us?"

"No, he's got a lot of business to take care of this week, so he can't stop by. He doesn't get to use his ship much because of his business."

"Evan! Franca!" Alex calls out as he comes up to us. "Did you see the repairs that the mechanics are doing?" he asks with excitement in his eyes.

Evan smiles. "I've had them work for me before, they do a good job."

"I'll say they do. Did you see what they're doing to the engine? It's a huge upgrade! And it's barely costing us anything!" Alex says, beaming.

"I have a friend here who always brings his ship to this shop, and he has it arranged so that the mechanics will charge him for any repairs I need. He doesn't mind paying for upgrades for us."

"Tell him I said thanks then." Alex glances at his holographic screen. The time flashes on it. "Well, everyone's about to meet up, so if either of you need to get anything now is your last chance," he says, walking back over to one of the vendors.

"Need anything?" Evan asks, looking over at me.

"No, I'm fine," I say. There's nothing I need, and I can't buy any hunting gear anyway.

"Alright then," he says casually, getting himself a drink.

We make our way back to the meeting spot to find that Roxanne and Lance are standing there waiting with Alex. They both look at Evan with distrust and resentment in their eyes.

"Hey, what do you think of those ship upgrades so far?" he asks Alex, walking past Roxanne and Lance, ignoring them. As they talk I check my communicator. It's nice that the sun can charge these. It's still low on power, but I can see it's already seven o'clock. I don't see the others anywhere.

After some time passes Maylea comes up to us with a box full of medical supplies. She starts showing Roxanne what she got. The others all return with boxes of supplies. Even Fauve returns on her own. I look over at the ship. Its lights are glowing warmly. It looks like the mechanics got everything back in shape. The repairs on that thing must've been costly. The others start to walk towards the ship, but Evan heads in the opposite direction.

Where could he be going? I look around. Everyone else is laughing and chatting with each other. Before I can talk myself out of it I turn and walk in the shadows, silently following him. He keeps to the shadows until he is well away from the ship hangar. I follow as silently as I can. We're well into the city now. Rythor has always seemed more alive at night.

Hovercrafts traverse both the ground and the sky, and the sidewalks are filled with people. Shops glow warmly with neon lights, and lighthearted music flows out of them. Bugs can be seen flying around the streetlamps. The city never comes to a stop. Both holographic and real plants can be found throughout the settlement. Skyscrapers appear to be as high as the stars, and ships land on platforms at the edges of them. Some of the shops can be found in the outer rooms of the buildings.

There are also many towers that have a glass dome at the top of them. I remember seeing pictures of these. They're for observing the sky, which is important as a lot of scientific research is done here. I'd also like to see how the botanical research is going at some point. The night sky has patches of dark stormy clouds. Rythor used to be known for having the clearest skies out of all the planets. Over time it has gained the reputation of having unusual storms and strange weather all the time. No one seems to know why.

I feel like stopping to take in the scenery, but Evan keeps going. I'm beginning to feel nervous. He's already made quite a few turns on different streets, and I've lost my bearings. If I lose him it'll be hard for me to find my way back. I guess I'm free to go, now that the crew is okay. Once my communicator charges a bit more I could contact Anna. It'd be so nice to get back home. We reach a district that looks fancier, with mansions dotting the city. There seem to be less people frequenting this area. Maybe he's going to visit his friend? I thought his friend was too busy for us to visit him.

Evan stops in front of a large mansion. I stop quickly, hoping he didn't hear my footsteps. He looks around a little, but not behind him. He types something on his communicator, and the door opens. He quickly goes in and the door shuts with a click. I lightly pull on the handle, and it doesn't budge. Now what am I going to do? I don't know my way back, and I'd rather not wait for him.

"People like you shouldn't be wandering the streets at night."

I spin around to see a band of marauders standing behind me. The man leading them has his arms crossed with a grin on his face.

"Mind your own business and I'll mind mine," I say in a harsh tone.

The man laughs. They all have a familiar tattoo on their arms... the tiger with T.C. sketched underneath it. "Don't think you'll be getting away. You're coming with us."

I have a bad feeling about this, like I wouldn't escape if they captured me. I run as hard as I can. I can hear their feet pounding on the ground in pursuit. If I can head back the way I came I can get to the crowds of people and lose them. As I'm running I start breathing harder. I glance over my shoulder. The marauders seem to be keeping pace with me effortlessly. I'm almost to the crowded streets when I skid to a stop.

Another group of marauders are blocking the way ahead of me. To the side are buildings. I turn to the left and start running.

"Hey!" I hear their leader shout as they all start chasing after me.

I run up to one of the buildings and jump, just grabbing onto the bottom of the railing of a balcony. I pull myself up and stand on the railing before jumping and grabbing onto the one above me. I hear the marauders talking to each other below. The buildings in this city are tall, with many windows. When I reach the third balcony I climb over the railing and try the door, hoping to get inside. The door is locked, so I return to climbing. I continue working my way up as quickly as I can.

I grab onto the railing of the fifth balcony and feel my arms start to tire. The further up I go the higher the chance I'll lose them. I make my way to the sixth balcony, already knowing I won't be able to do much more.

An alarm goes off, and the marauders below run around the corner. I don't think they're giving up yet. There's a balcony to my right that has a door that's cracked open. Can I reach it? With my strength fading I know I can't go much farther. I jump, holding my breath as I sail through the air. I barely grab hold of the balcony railing. I pull myself up and go over to the door, out of breath.

It opens, and I find myself in an empty office. I stay in the room for a little bit so I can catch my breath before moving on. I leave it, entering a hallway.

"Do you think she went this way?" a marauder asks.

"She might have. The others are guarding the doors to the building," another one says.

They round the corner. I run, heading up the stairs to the next level. They chase after me, determined to catch me this time. Soon I find myself on top of the flat roof of the building. Walking over to the edge, I look at the busy city below. I hear footsteps coming up from behind. I look over my shoulder and see a few of the marauders have made it here. They're grinning at each other, knowing that I have nowhere else to go.

Or at least that's what they think. I look over the edge of the flat roof and see some ships flying by. I can't see the ground below, but maybe that's because the moon is covered by clouds. The ships are going pretty slow... if I could jump and get a hold of one I could ride it until I made it farther into the city, then be on my way. I get ready as a ship comes closer.

The men rush towards me, realizing what I'm about to do. I jump, stretching my arms out towards it. I grasp the edge of the wing with one hand, barely reaching it. I can tell right away that I didn't get a good grip on it. My hand slips before I can grab the wing with my other hand, and I feel the soft air turn to icy wind as I fall into the city below.

CHAPTER 7

I WAKE UP to the sound of rain pattering on the ground. I groan and open my eyes, surprised to see tiny blue rectangle shaped ones staring back at me. The metallic mouse watches me with its teeth bared. It takes me a moment to realize where I am... if I'm remembering correctly I've ended up somewhere in the abandoned part of Rythor's settlement. The metallic mouse looks at me with a challenging gleam in its eyes. I grab a nearby rock and try to lift myself out of the puddle of water I'm lying in.

The pain in my left leg and arm causes me to groan again. My muscles move stiffly. I gather a few more nearby rocks, not getting up from the puddle. I take one and throw it at the mouse, holding myself up with my other arm despite the pain. My shivering keeps me from holding the stones as steady as I'd like to. The mouse growls at me but backs off.

I put the rest of the rocks in my pocket and try to stand. I feel a sharp pain in my leg, but manage to get up, putting my weight mostly on my other one. I look around to get a better sense of my surroundings. Moonlight can be seen reflecting brightly on shattered glass and nearby puddles. I see that the moon and a few stars are peeking around the shadowy dark clouds. The light from them shines all around me as a light rain hits my face.

The sound of the rain is almost comforting and would be if not for the sound of metal being dented and torn. I look to see that the mouse has moved on to chewing on a metal can. I stare at the creature, trying to remember what happened… everything feels kinda hazy. I remember starting to fall, but nothing after that. Now I'm at the bottom of a ravine. If it weren't for the armor I still had from Hayventh I would have died.

I try to take a step forward but stumble. I put out my hand and lean on the dirt wall beside me. Taking another step hurts but leaning on the wall helps a little. More metallic mice come scurrying up to me, with their teeth bared.

While they have no interest in humans, metal is what they live on, and they are always seeking it. I'm not in the best position to run away, so my only other choices are to either give them pieces of my armor or defend myself. I move my foot a little and hear the sound of my boot clinking against metal. I look and see it's another can.

With some pain I grab it and throw it past the mice. They scurry away after it as if it's their last meal. I begin to limp my way down the abandoned street I've found myself in. One lonely streetlight remains lit, as if it's trying to make a last stand. I continue towards it, going at the best pace I can, leaning on the wall beside me when I need to. My hand brushes over the old door of a house. The metal is rusted in some places, and mostly covered in dirt.

I place my hand more firmly on the door and try to push it open. To my surprise it opens easily, almost causing me to stumble. I step inside, and the lights turn on automatically. They're dim and some are flickering, close to giving out forever. The one room apartment has a few furniture pieces, but there's not much to it other than that.

A bookshelf along the wall stands empty, and a cabinet door has been left open. From what I remember of when Rythor was first being built, the people felt more paranoid about being found than the rest of us did, so they started to build their settlement underground. Over time they began to feel safer and moved to the surface.

I'm about to turn and leave when I notice a piece of paper laying on the floor. I pick it up and turn it over to find a picture with strange writing sketched underneath it. The picture is of a young man standing on a hill, surrounded by shadows. A beam of light is shining from his fist, piercing through the darkness. The writing below the picture is in symbols I don't recognize. I fold the piece of paper and put it in my pocket, looking around the apartment one last time before moving on.

The going is slow, but I make it down the abandoned street until I come to a dead end of sorts. I stop and rest a bit, keeping an eye out for more of those mice. The street does continue on, but it's on ground that has been raised up by about six feet, creating a ledge. Maybe an earthquake caused this? I decide to sit with my back against the ledge, taking a break.

I almost cry out in pain as I sit, but I bite my tongue. I don't want the mice, or anything else that's down here to think I'm weak. I roll up my sleeve as much as I can to see why my arm is hurting so much. It's scraped up pretty badly, and my communicator has been smashed and broken. A small piece of the metal is lodged in my arm. If I take it out it'll start bleeding, so I let it be.

After checking my arm I try to get my boot off, but the pain is too great. I give up and try to stand. I need to get over this ledge if I want to find my way to the surface. The ledge is taller than me, but there are a couple of places where I could put my hands. I briefly put weight into my injured leg as I put my other foot on a rock that's sticking out of the ledge. I manage to pull myself up, but the effort leaves me in more pain than I was in before. I stop and rest for a time before moving on.

The street continues onward, lined with abandoned houses. More mice are scurrying around, and some are gnawing on the corners of the metal doors of the houses. While Rythor has always been focused on science and nature, they used to also be interested in creating synthetic nature to fill the city with when real animals wouldn't stay in it.

Robotic animals were made to help the city feel like it had more nature, but that didn't go well. We've never been good with AI, and we've found it's best to stay away from it. The scientists regretted creating these things and disposed of them not long after they were made. Some escaped and live here... Mostly the mice from what I've seen so far. I continue on, occasionally looking up at the sky as I go. Sometimes I can hear the faint sounds of music... I feel so close and yet so far away from the settlement. I pull my coat closer to me and continue to limp on.

I go five feet before I have to stop and rest again. The pain has been catching up to me. At this point I also can't stop shivering. I look to the sky to see what time it is. It's going to be awhile before dawn, and even then sunlight won't shine on these streets until midday. I can't see the moon anymore because of the dark clouds.

Thunder starts to boom, and waves of rain start to fall. I need to stay out of the rain if I can. I come to a stop at an old intersection. I wish I knew my way around here. It's hard to tell which way to go... each street leads off into an eerie silent darkness, going further away from the opening of the ravine. I was hoping to stay away from darkness like this for a while.

Chills go down my spine as I hear coyote howls in the distance. Probably synthetic, but you never know. Looking at the abandoned houses it appears that some of the doors have rusted shut. I may not be as lucky this time. The howling continues, being echoed left and right. I slowly make my way to one of the houses, wincing as I go up the step to the door. Unlike the one I found earlier, this one's locked. I lean against the railing, taking a moment to catch my breath. I don't feel like going over to another house.

The howling sounds closer this time. As much as I want to stay here and rest I know I have to find a safer place. I try another house door without success and decide to look for a street that leads up out of the ravine. I can't help but glance behind me every few moments to make sure I'm not being chased down. I wish I could signal the ships that are flying over the ravine. I come to another intersection and have to decide which way to go. My boots sink into mud with every step as the rain continues to pour down.

This area of the city is different, having apartment complexes instead of houses. If I can get to the top of one I'll be able to see things better once the rain dissipates. I carefully walk up to one of the buildings and try the door. To my surprise it opens, but it takes a lot of effort to get the door to open enough for me to get through. I gladly take a break and rest until it quits raining. Once my shivering stops and I've recovered enough to walk again I make my way up to the top floor of the building and open one of the windows.

Now that the rain has stopped everything lies in complete silence. I had no idea how huge this underground city actually was. From here the view of houses and apartment buildings go on forever. Some roads go downward to another level of the city. I spot three roads going up to the surface, with only one that is close enough for me to get to. Even so, it looks like it may take me a few days at this pace to get there. I better get going.

I look through the building on my way down to see if I can find anything useful, but it's been emptied out. I'm starting to feel the effects of not eating for a day. Normally I would hunt for food, but I don't know if I could find any real animals down here. Leaving the building and heading west seems like my best option. If only the clouds would clear up and sunlight would come through to give me some warmth. The pain in my leg is getting sharper as time goes on.

I jump as I hear howling that sounds like it's close by. I turn and see that a metallic coyote is standing behind me. Its blue rectangular eyes glow with a fierce look. Faint glimpses of light reflect off of its shiny metal coat. It growls, baring its teeth at me. I stand taller, despite noticing that there's nothing around me I can use as a weapon. Showing no signs of fear, the coyote starts making its way closer to me.

I try to step out of the way as it makes a powerful jump. A bullet hits its head. The coyote's claws miss me by a few inches as it lands back on the ground. The bullet made a dent, but didn't go through. I turn to see Evan standing there with a gun in one hand. He's using his communicator as a light. The coyote growls, then runs off into the distance.

"Evan? How did you find me?" I ask, surprised. How would you find anyone in these ruins? How would he have known to look for me here?

"Everyone's been looking for you, and I've lost friends down here before." He says, coming up to me. "Hey, are you alright? You look like you're injured," he continues with concern in his eyes.

"Yeah, I hurt my leg in a fall... I'll be fine in no time," I say, not wanting to tell him I jumped off of a building. I also don't want him to know that I was following him.

"Right, that blood on your arm isn't anything at all," he says sarcastically.

"Oh, that," I say, looking at it and shrugging. "It's just a scrape."

"What about your communicator?" Evan asks, motioning to it.

"Oh, it got smashed in that little fall I had. I'll fix it up in no time," I say, trying to shift the attention to the communicator instead, but I don't think that helped.

"Must've been quite the fall," Evan says, still looking concerned. I try to stop my shivering and stand up a bit straighter.

"It wasn't that bad," I say casually. "Which way is the way out of here?" I ask, once again trying to change the subject.

Evan gives me a look that tells me he doesn't believe me. "I landed a ship down here. It's not far off," he says, starting to walk.

I begin walking beside him, but it doesn't take me long to start limping again.

He slows down. "Why don't you just admit you're hurt?"

"I'm fine, really." I say, doing my best to quicken my pace again. On one hand it's nice to get out of here, but on the other I know Evan will try to take me back to the others. "Look," I start to speak up. "I need to get back home, and I wasn't planning on going back to the crew. If you let me go I'll pay you for your troubles," I say, hoping he'll take me up on the offer.

He waves his hand dismissively. "Ah it's fine, I was planning on taking you back home anyway."

"Really? Why would you let me go?" I ask, unable to help feeling skeptical.

"Why should we keep you with us anymore? We're going to make repairs and head back to headquarters."

"Well I'd appreciate that," I say, feeling hope rise in my chest. If I can get home everything will be okay. Even my pain feels a bit more manageable. I don't let on how I'm feeling though and continue to act casual.

"I could use some help with a mission later on though... You think you'd be able to help out every now and then?" he asks, sounding like he wants me to agree. For some reason I get this bad feeling in my gut...

"Well, to be honest I don't feel like working with this crew, so..."

"It's not with the crew," he interrupts. "Me and my friends are doing some research on a mining project and could use some help keeping the machines running smooth."

That sounds like something I would do well with, and if it was every now and then I might not mind. "Well alright, I can't promise how much I'll be able to help out though," I say, hoping that didn't come out as harsh as I thought it had. I just miss home so much that I'm reluctant to leave it for a bit until things settle back down.

"Fair enough," he says sounding disappointed.

I feel a little guilty that I didn't offer to help more, but I want to spend some time at home when I get back. I've missed it so much and honestly I've thought I might not see it again a few times already. I stop, having to rest. Evan waits patiently for me as if he's not in any hurry. Howling sounds pierce the darkness once again.

"There are more coyotes down here?" I ask in disbelief.

"We're not out of danger yet. If we can make it up to my friend's ship we'll be out of here soon though."

That's enough to motivate me to start walking again. We hear the clanking sound of paws hitting the pavement. I can tell there's more than one, but I'm not sure how many.

Evan glances over his shoulder. "If you can move any quicker we need to. They're coming fast."

I nod and try to move faster despite the pain. I can't keep this up for too long...

A small carrier ship lands in the street to the right of us. We turn as the door opens.

"You guys going on an adventure without us?" Fauve asks, stepping out of the door.

"We've got to get out of here, we can chat later!" I say. As I start to get in the carrier Fauve notices my leg. "Hey what happened to you?" she asks, sounding worried.

I shrug. "Oh I fell and hurt my leg. It's nothing."

"Oh, we'll have to get Maylea to look at it."

I was hoping she wouldn't say that. We all get in the carrier ship. Blair is also there, and seems glad that we've been found. Fauve powers up the carrier's engine, and we begin our ascent, leaving the coyotes behind. Evan doesn't look happy about this but goes along with it. I find it odd that he doesn't mention his ship... he leaves it behind.

"How'd you find us?" I ask, both surprised and relieved, though I don't know why.

"Oh, I know my way around. I used to live here!" she says excitedly. "We need to get going because the ship has finished being repaired, and who wants to stay down here under the city anyway? There's not much to do here," she says.

CHAPTER 8

I LOOK OUT the window at the city as we emerge from the ravine. The city is just as busy when it's stormy. We travel along the sky path, making our way back to the hangar. Fauve struggles to stay on course with the wind that's blowing. Thunder is once again rolling across the sky, and lightning can be seen off in the distance. Evan doesn't say a word and watches the scenery. Fauve keeps glancing behind her. I look behind as well, but don't see anything.

Soon we land in the hangar, and getting out I can see Alex pacing in front of our ship. He looks up and rushes over to us. "Finally you're here! I thought we'd lost her for good this time."

"She was with me the whole time," Evan lies. I start to speak up but he looks at me to stop.

"We've got to get going, and fast," Alex says.

"What's wrong?" Evan asks.

"I can't tell you in front of her, but we have something serious that needs addressing."

"Hey, what about me going home?" I ask. There's no way I'm spending any more time in those cells. Maybe I'll call it quits now and run away.

Alex shakes his head. "I can't do that until I get this current situation cleared up."

"And what is that exactly?" I ask in a demanding tone.

"I can't tell you that."

"If it concerns me then I deserve to know."

"Maybe later on I'll be able to explain it to you. For now you're expected back in your cell."

I shake my head. "Oh no, I'm not going back in there. In fact, I'm not going with you at all unless I can move about freely on the ship. I've done nothing wrong, and you have no right to be treating me this way."

"Alex, it'd be alright to let her go freely about. One of us would always be around her," Evan says.

Alex shakes his head, wiping sweat off his brow. "You know what? I don't have time for this. I just need her on board. Disable all of the carrier ships and lock the hangar, and I'll allow it." He walks away, boarding the ship.

"Let's go, shall we?" Evan asks.

I nod, not saying anything. Fauve looks behind her one last time before getting on the ship. Evan and I get on next, with Blair following close behind. The doors of the ship shut, and a part of me wonders if I could've escaped at the last minute. I can't help but feel a little trapped. Evan looks at his communicator. "Gotta go," he says, rushing off to the control room.

I'm left to admire the work that was done on the ship. There are no bullet holes or burn marks, and the power is working again. Feels like a new ship. The repairs easily cost more than what the ship was worth. I guess that didn't matter to Evan or his friend.

"Hey, ya do realize that yer arm's bleedin', right?" I turn to see Raya looking at me with concern in her eyes.

"Oh it's nothing," I say, not wanting to let on how bad it is. I'd rather not burden these people with my problems. They've got other things to worry about, and I don't want to end up in the medbay.

"I think ya should have it checked. Come on, I'll go with ya."

"Really, I'm fine," I say, standing still. If she sees me limp she'll probably force me to go to the medbay.

"That doesn't look fine... let that go and it'll get infected."

"Okay," I say with some hesitance, knowing she's right.

"Alright, this way," she says, looking relieved.

We make it to the medbay, and I try to relax my shoulders.

"Welp, here we are. Let's head on in," Raya says.

I turn to the door, dreading to go in. I hate being in those medbeds, and Maylea will probably put me in one.

I open it, and Maylea looks up from the computer system. "Need something?"

"Raya thinks I need to have my arm checked," I say, starting to limp as I come in the room. I'd hidden it pretty well from Raya so far, but I can't do that forever.

"I knew it was worse than ya were sayin'!" Raya says, sounding a little hurt.

"Looks like your leg's not doing good either," Maylea states, ignoring Raya's comment.

"It's fine," I say.

"I'll check your arm first," she says, motioning for me to sit on one of the beds.

I limp over and sit down.

She carefully checks my arm. "Nothing's infected. You're lucky that metal didn't go further into your arm." She moves on to try to check my leg. I cry out in pain as she takes my boot off. Her brow furrows. "Looks like you've got a micro fracture in your leg. You'll need to spend at least a few days in the medbay."

"Can't I do something else instead?" I ask, feeling a bit annoyed.

She narrows her eyes. "Look, if you want to get better this is the best way."

"Alright." It looks like I can't avoid it.

She works on my arm next, and then instructs me to lay down in one of the beds. Once I lay down she types something into her communicator. The glass lid shuts and she leaves from my view. As the mist starts to fill the bed I drift off to sleep.

"Hey Franca, a little help?" I hear Jalyn say.

"Yeah, no problem," I respond, looking around. We're in some sort of underground location.

Jalyn is trying to open a door that's partially buried. I get my shovel and scrape dirt away until we can open it. "Thanks Franca. Where'd Greyson go off to now?" she asks, sounding like she's tired of him wandering off.

"He'll be back I'm sure," I hear myself say.

"I don't mind it usually, but since we're being chased I think it's best to stick together." We go through the door, and I recognize where we are. This is a part of Rythor's underground settlement! But why are we here? "You feelin' okay?" Jalyn asks in a worried tone.

"Yeah, I'm fine," I say, trying to hide how disoriented I feel. The look on her face tells me she doesn't believe me, but she continues on. We look through the abandoned house but find nothing of note.

Jalyn looks around quickly before turning to leave. A picture falls out of her pocket. "Just leave it, I don't need that one anymore," Jalyn says as I was starting to bend down to pick it up. I leave it, and we step out of the house and look up the street.

Greyson comes towards us, running. "We've got to get out of here. He's caught on to us!"

I look and see a man who's wearing a hooded tan cloak running after us. Everything fades away before I can do anything.

The ship shudders, waking me from my sleep. That can't be good. I pull the emergency handle like before. The filter kicks in, and after a few moments the glass lid opens. I sit up, feeling a bit stiff. I look at my arm and am glad to see it has healed. It feels strange to see my arm without my communicator there. I'll have to look into getting a new one. Now to see how my leg is doing. My first step is more painful than I expected it to be. I sigh, knowing I needed to spend even longer in the medbed. I would ponder the dream I had, but I don't have time.

I wait for the pain to pass, before limping on. The ship shudders again, causing me to put my hand alongside the wall to catch myself. If I want to find out what's going on I'll have to head to the control room.

As I go I keep catching myself expecting to see bullet holes in the walls. The mechanics even did a new paint job. You can't tell anything was wrong with this ship… besides what it's doing now. I've also noticed that the mechanical bugs are gone. Those were probably cleaned out as well.

As I get closer to the control room I can hear Alex talking. "I just don't understand it. Yesterday the ship was running smoothly," he says with frustration in his voice.

"Relax, it's working out a few things. These do that sometimes," Evan says calmly.

"We'll have to keep a close eye on it. We've already passed Durath, but we may need to go back and land there," Lance says.

"Oh I hope we don't have to stop there. I'm not a fan of deserts," Fauve says. "They're so boring… what's there to see?"

Evan laughs. "They're not all that bad Fauve. If you observe them closely you will discover many things. Durath's semi-arid climate has a lot of greenery when it rains."

Alex clears his throat, and everyone goes silent. The ship shudders yet again, dipping a little then going back on course. "Seriously, this can't be good. We need to take a look at what's wrong."

"Yeah, a ship shouldn't be doing this after two days of running," Lance says.

Two days? I must've been asleep for a lot longer than I thought. I head into the control room so that I can join the conversation.

Everyone looks at me, but before I can speak the AI does. The words are garbled and staticky at first, then they get clearer. "Extreme heating of the engine...Evacuation recommended..." then the rest of what it says goes back to being impossible to understand. The power starts to flicker on and off.

"I'm going to try to turn us back to Durath, but I'm not sure if I can. Franca, I need you to check on the generators and engine. Everyone else check on the other rooms and see if there are any damages," Alex says, rushing to the pilot's seat.

Everyone springs into action, and I head to the generator room as quickly as I can. I open the door and go into the room, shutting it behind me. Usually the humming I hear is ongoing, but now it's stuttering. Judging by the heat the generators are producing I can tell they're being overworked, but I don't know why yet. This ship is nothing but a headache. I continue to look at things and discover the fourth generator has been shut off. That could be causing the engine to stress out. I don't remember doing that, and the mechanics should have known better.

I go over to it and find that the cable that connects it to the other generators is also missing. I'll have to get another one. I go over to a box of spares the mechanics left. It takes me some time to find the right one. Everyone's counting on me to fix this. I get the cable and realize I'm going to have to turn the generators off again.

"Hope this works right this time," I say to myself as I pull the emergency lever. I make my way over to the generator and connect it to the others. I go back over to the lever and flip it back on.

Everything seems to power up fine, but the AI makes no comment. It might not when powering on, but usually that's not a good sign. It might have been better if I had left it alone this time around. Hopefully what I did fixes things.

I leave the generator room and find that everything is eerily quiet. There's no sign of anyone around. I get a chill down my spine as I feel the ship shudder again. Then I notice it. There's no mistaking the smell of smoke. I try to open the medbay door since it's the closest room to me but it's locked. I check another door and find that it too, is locked.

"Franca?" I hear Evan calling up ahead.

"I'm over here!" I call back, going in his direction as fast as I can.

"Come on, this way," he calls, entering the hangar.

Maybe everyone's evacuating? I follow him and find him standing next to one of the carrier ships with the door open. I wonder why they haven't started it up yet? I guess Alex decided we were in too much danger to stay here... I get on board and see that no one is there. I start to have a bad feeling in my gut. The door begins to close. "Wait!" I exclaim, pushing the door open and getting off.

"Franca, we don't have time for this, we've got to go," he says. "The others have left already."

I look and take a quick count of the carrier ships. "All the carrier ships are still here though," I say.

"You're miscounting them. One has left already," he says, his tone barely masking his aggravation. "Don't you want to go home anyway?"

"No, the others are still here. I know how many carrier ships we have. We have to get them to safety."

"The ship's already catching on fire. We don't have time for this."

The smell of smoke is getting stronger. A sense of danger grips me, and I decide to walk away. "Fine go ahead of me then. I'll catch up," I say.

I glance quickly behind me. Evan is pulling out his gun. I dart behind another carrier ship next to me.

"I'm trying to save you Franca, don't be like this," he says.

I move to a different one as I hear his footsteps. I remain silent as he looks for me.

"Fine Franca, be that way. You'll die with the others!" Evan yells as he runs to get into the carrier ship. He takes off, heading into space.

I leave the hangar, returning to the main ship. I hear Roxanne yelling. It sounds like she's in the crew's bunk room. I can't help but feel my anxiety rise at the hint of panic in her voice. I quicken my pace at the cost of my leg hurting more.

I grit my teeth. She needs me to hurry, I'll deal with the pain later. I go to the door of the bunk room and see that it's locked. I get out some tools I have on me and get to work on deactivating the lock. It's hard to work under this kind of pressure, but I try my best to focus. I can't believe what Evan did... it looks like Roxanne was intentionally trapped here. I successfully deactivate the lock and press the button for the door to open. It opens half way and I rush in.

The room is full of smoke, and I can't see anything. "Roxanne?" I call out before holding my breath as I try to find her. I hear her coughing and rush over to the bunks. I find her crouched next to one struggling to breathe. I try to pull her up to a stand but quickly realize she's been handcuffed to one of the wooden bars.

Through the coughing Roxanne tries to speak. "Save the others, leave me behind." I notice a blade laying under the bunk across from us and grab it, starting to saw through the wooden bar. It takes me longer than I wanted it to, but eventually I get her free.

I drag her out of the room as some of the ceiling lights catch on fire. Roxanne is wheezing at this point, struggling to breathe. My eyes are stinging from the smoke. It takes all my willpower to ignore my leg. "We need—" Roxanne starts coughing again. "We need to get to Alex," she starts to make her way over to the control room.

I limp after her and see that she's entering a code into the key-screen. It displays that the password is incorrect. Alex is pounding on the door and yelling. Roxanne starts hacking the system and gets it to unlock. She glances over at me. "Don't tell a soul about this."

"No worries," I respond. Her knowing how to hack into a system is the least of my concerns right now.

Alex bursts out of the door, looking disheveled. "The extinguishing system isn't working right," he says, with a cough.

Roxanne rushes past him going straight for the computer system. Alex heads to the other rooms, and I painfully follow him. We pass the hangar. I get chills down my spine again. "Alex, there's something I need to tell you…" I begin to say.

He shakes his head. "There's no time for that. The cameras in the control room are showing that people are locked in the medbay and in Raya's workshop."

I can tell he won't listen to me right now, so I let it go for the moment. As we go down the passageway we see ceiling lights catching on fire. That seems kind of odd to me, why would those be catching on fire? We get to the medbay and find that Blair is trying to kick the door down. Alex goes up to the key-screen but it has melted. I rush to the door and open the emergency panel. A wave of heat hits my face.

I search my pockets, hoping that I still have my old gloves. Thankfully I still have them. I used to work on things that were extremely hot, but it's been a while. I need to manually open the door if I can. I press the override button and the door opens a couple inches. I take off the maintenance plate and see that the wires have melted. Before me or Alex can do anything Blair pries open the door with his bare hands. He groans but continues on, running into the room. Flaming wires are hanging down, blocking the way. He runs through them, dodging the fire and ignoring Alex's calls.

He comes out of the room carrying Fauve. Alex runs in to get someone else. I start to feel relieved as the ship's air vents shut off. They were blowing air onto the fires. Maybe Roxanne will get the rest of the extinguishing system working soon. Alex comes out of the room with Maylea in his arms. He gently sets her down on the floor. She lays there unconscious. The air vents keep slowly flickering on and off, along with the lights.

"Maylea..." Alex says, crouching beside her. He takes hold of her hand and checks her pulse. She's still breathing but shows no sign of waking up. My eyes are stinging and watering, making it difficult to see.

Blair takes off in Roxanne's direction, wanting to check on her. I hear some sounds coming from Raya's workshop. I limp stiffly over to the door. I look over my shoulder to see that Fauve is following me. Besides a burnt piece of hair she seems uninjured. Concern is written on her face, and I can see an intense focus in her eyes.

She moves to the door, ignoring the wires that are exposed and sparking next to it. "Raya are you alright?" she asks.

All we hear is coughing in response. I get to the door and check the key-screen. I had hoped this one would be in better condition, but it's melted and cracked like the others. I kneel by the door's maintenance panel and get to work.

CHAPTER 9

As I STRUGGLE to get the maintenance panel open Fauve continues to talk to Raya. I get it open and see that the gears seem to be jammed in an area that can only be worked on from the other side. At this point Fauve has gotten Raya to talk, so I start calling to her through the door.

"It's gettin' harder to breathe in here," Raya says with worry.

"I'll have you out soon," I say.

"Hurry, everythin's burnin' up."

"The gears in the door are jammed. I need you to unscrew the maintenance panel on your side of the door. That way we can figure out what's going on."

"Give me a moment, I'm sure I have a bar turner with me somewhere." I hear coughing and the sound of junk falling.

The ship rocks, and Lance can be heard yelling in the distance. It sounds like he's in the prison. I try to focus on what I'm doing, but it's hard with all the chaos around me.

"Got it! Now what?" Raya asks.

"Do you see anything stuck in the gears?"

"Yeah, there's a piece of metal stuck in them."

That's odd. That shouldn't be there. "Try to get that out," I say. I hear Lance yelling again, and this time it sounds more urgent. I turn to Fauve. "Once she gets that out I need you to try the button again," I say, handing her one of my heat resistant gloves.

"You can count on me!" she says, moving into my spot as I start to limp towards the prison.

The air vents keep turning on and off, and the extinguisher system hasn't been activated yet. The ship shakes, throwing me off balance. As I fall to the ground I hear a loud crashing sound behind me. I look and see that the passageway has caved in. The ship's main frame is probably still intact, but a part of the ceiling has fallen.

I can hear Alex trying to wake Maylea up, but to no avail. I slowly get back up, barely able to ignore the pain now. I can't turn back. I can only go onward. I make my way to the prison. When I finally make it there I find that Lance is locked in my cell. Burning wires are falling from the ceiling. "Franca," Lance says coughing. "The cell's about to cave in," he says, looking at me desperately.

I rush up to the key-screen and find that this one is intact. I look at it for a moment, then enter in the password I remember Roxanne using earlier. This one doesn't have a maintenance panel. The key-screen is the only way to control the force field wall without one of the crew's communicators. The smoke is getting a lot worse, and we're both starting to have trouble breathing. Lance moves over as more burning wires fall. "Don't you have your communicator?" I ask.

"Evan took it from me," he says angrily.

I squint at the key-screen. It says the force field wall should be shutting off, but it's not. It's hard to tell what's wrong with all this smoke in my eyes.

"Hurry up, what's taking so long?"

"I'm trying," I reply, pressing the button for the force field wall to switch off again. It starts to flicker on and off.

"Can you get it to turn off for longer?" Lance asks, watching the wall.

I press the button again, but there's no response. "No, it's not doing anything."

"Aren't you the mechanic who's supposed to know how to override things like this?"

"I'm trying!" I say, pressing more buttons. There's gotta be a way to get this thing to work.

He watches the force field wall, and when it shuts off he runs past it, barely making it. More wires begin to fall from the ceiling, with flames running along them.

"We better go," he says, running towards the passageway. I follow him as quickly as I can, which isn't fast. "Great, now we gotta get through this," he says, looking at the cave in.

As I'm walking up to it to get a closer look the ship shakes causing me to lose my balance. I cry out from the fall. Now my leg is hurting a lot worse. Lance turns to me and tries to help me up. "Are you okay?" he asks, focusing on me for a moment.

I try to stand but can't. "My leg's gotten worse," I say.

"Don't worry, I'll carry you out once I get through the cave in," he says, picking up some debris and ramming it into a spot that looks weak. I flinch from the loud sound of metal hitting metal. He hits it again and again, trying to at least make a dent. Despite Lance putting all his strength into it the wall of debris doesn't move.

"Lance! Are you and Franca okay? We've been trying to get this wall down but we haven't made much progress yet," Alex yells through the cave in at Lance.

"Well we're surviving. Could be doing better," Lance yells back, ramming at the weak spot of the wall again. This time it shakes a little.

"Keep hitting it, I think we'll make a break through," Alex calls out over the noise of a metal cutter. "Careful Raya."

"No worries, I got this," she replies.

"I think Maylea is starting to wake up," Fauve says.

"I have to help Lance with this, would you mind looking after her for me?" Alex asks Fauve in a worried tone. He seems to care about Maylea a lot. I wonder why I have so much trouble with her?

"No problem!"

I stop listening to the conversations that are going on and turn my attention to a cracking sound I've been hearing. I look at the floor and see that there are cracks in it with smoke coming out of them. The cracks are steadily moving closer to me. Lance and Alex are still talking. Their focus is on the wall. I try to call out to Lance but he's busy shouting through the debris to Alex. I yell again, this time as loud as I can.

He looks over at me. "What?"

I point at the floor, having another coughing fit.

"Alex we need to get through now. The floor is splitting and smoke is coming up out of the cracks," Lance yells urgently through the wall.

I hear commotion on the other side. I watch the cracks to make sure they don't spread closer to me or Lance. There's not much else I can do anyway. After what feels like forever Alex, Raya, and Lance finally break a small hole through the debris. Lance rams into the wall one last time, and it comes crashing down. We both raise our arms over our eyes as pieces of metal and debris go flying.

As this is happening a hole breaks in the floor where my foot is and it gets caught. Lance turns to pick me up, but I'm stuck. I can't help but groan in pain at his efforts. The heat of the fire getting more intense. It must be getting closer to me. If we stay here for too long it'll be too late for all of us. The heat from the floor is hot against my boot. "Leave without me, I'm just a prisoner," I say. I feel scared, and I didn't want my life to end yet, but at least they will make it.

"We're not leaving without you," he says as he works to get my foot unstuck. He picks me up and moves just in time as the hole in the floor gets bigger. He puts me down when we get to the others. The air vents have been running nonstop for a while, and for some reason the ship's heating system has been activated. It's already hot and smoky enough in here as it is.

"We need to shut the airlock. The ship looks like it's going to break off there," Alex says walking over to the keyscreen. He's right, that hole my foot was in looked deep. With great effort the gears in the airlock turn. It shuts, and the airlock loses power.

"The ship's power is getting weaker," Lance says.

"Where's Blair?" Fauve asks.

"I don't know. He left to try to find something to get me out."

I try to stand but can't. I need to see what's going on with the power generators. I start to crawl. "I'm heading to the power generators. They need to be checked," I say, coughing.

"Let me help ya," Raya says, helping me to a stand and keeping her arm around me. I feel funny accepting her help, but I know I need to. We make it to the generator room. It's as bad as I thought, if not worse. The wiring to some of the generators has melted. One generator is sparking.

"How do we deal with that?" Raya asks. "It's too hot to go near them."

"Well, all I can do is shut them off," I say. With her help I get over to the emergency handle. I pull it and the sparking slows to a stop. Once again we're in the dark. Hope no one needed the lights. "That should keep things safe for now," I say, coughing.

We turn and leave the room. The burning wires hanging from the ceiling dimly light the passageway.

"Come on we better go," Raya says. I hope we can make it... I can barely stand, even with her helping me. We finally make it back to everyone and I sit, leaning against the wall. I happened to sit next to Maylea, who is wheezing and coughing. The ship keeps shaking.

"We need to shut the next airlock and move. The floor is cracking here too," Alex says.

Lance and Blair help Maylea and I further up the passageway while the others work on the airlock. Roxanne calls for help. They set us down and everyone else runs off in her direction. I hear an earsplitting cracking sound as the ship shakes violently. I have a feeling I know what that was…

"Welp, there goes the prison," I hear Fauve say in the distance.

I try to get up, but the pain is too much. As I lay there I can't help but think that this might actually be the end for me.

Maylea stands and grabs my arm. With great struggle she brings me to a stand, wrapping her arm around me. I wave dismissively. "It's okay, leave me behind. They need you more than they need me."

"It'd be wrong for me to leave you behind as long as I'm able to save you." At least she has more morals than Evan does. She tries to help me walk, but I can tell that she's still weak from earlier. We manage to get to the front of the ship near the control room and find that everyone is there, trying to put out a fire. Blair comes out of the room holding his arm. Maylea goes up to him immediately, and I lean against the wall for support.

I hear Blair groan. I slowly make my way over to him and Maylea.

He looks at us and winces. "Don't mind me. The others need help putting out the fire."

"It looks like it's broken," I hear Maylea say as I limp over to the control room. I don't know if there's much that I can do. Burning wires continue to fall from the ceiling, and one of the walls is black. Alex and Lance are working to keep the fire from the control panel. Fauve and Roxanne are trying to keep the fire away from the doors.

It takes us the next few hours to put out the fires and repair what we can. Once the fires are out I get sent back to the medbay. I feel bad that I can't help much right now. At least I'm not alone, Blair and Maylea are with me. While there's no power there Maylea can still treat us with medicine. Alex checked the hangar as soon as he could and found that I was right. Evan is gone, and hopefully he won't return.

CHAPTER 10

IT TAKES US all of the next day to get the ship in a stable state. We managed to put out all the fires, but it took us keeping everything shut down. We repaired the generators that were salvageable, but as long as the ship was running new fires were starting. I've been trying to help best I can despite my condition. "See anything?" Blair asks.

"Not yet," I respond, removing another part. We both stay silent for a while as I'm looking. I shine a light further into the engine and keep removing parts, but nothing seems wrong. In fact, things look pristine. I'm about to put everything back together when something catches my eye. "Can you hand me that bar turner?" I ask, putting out my hand.

"Sure," he says, using his good arm when he hands it to me.

I loosen some small bars to get to the part I noticed. It's a part that's designed to rotate, but it doesn't look right. Sure enough, upon closer inspection it's not hard to see that the part is meant for a larger ship. "Found the problem!" I say, turning to look at him.

"What is it?" he asks, sounding apprehensive.

"See that rotator? It's designed for a bigger ship. It's getting stuck, causing too much stress on the engine—"

"Which is what's starting the fires," Blair says, finishing my thoughts.

"Exactly. We won't be able to run the ship with it like this unless we want more fires. I'm surprised the ship made it as far as it did. It's a shame that we don't have any spare parts."

Blair is sitting near me in a chair that we brought into the room. We're using his communicator as a light. The others are all busy working on other things with the ship. Blair was the only one left who could help me. His right arm is in a sling. He'll need to spend time in the medbeds once the medbay has power. "I guess we're in a similar boat to what we were in before huh?" He asks.

"Yeah but worse in a way. As long as we need power for the oxygen generators there will be fires. I don't have a way to replace the part for this, and the rotator has to be there."

"I guess we'll have to tell Alex then. We need a plan of how we should proceed."

"Where is Alex?" I ask, realizing that I haven't seen him for hours. Last I saw he had shut himself in the control room, seeming upset about something.

"He's still in the control room. He's upset about how things are going."

"I can understand that. Things haven't been going very smoothly."

Blair hesitates. "Well… things are going worse than you think."

"What? How?" I ask a little louder than I needed to.

Blair shakes his head. "No, I'm not supposed to tell you… Alex wouldn't want that."

"Well I'm stuck in this situation anyway, so I might as well know," I say, feeling a little frustrated. Why do I keep getting stuck in messes?

"Alright. Might as well. We're part of the military Franca. We were supposed to fight in a battle that was taking place on Rythor, but we missed it. We were mining on Hayventh because we needed to make emergency repairs from a previous marauder attack. Maybe we would've made it to the battle had we not had that second attack. The army believes Alex has made off with the ship and are warranting for his arrest. And ours."

"What? There was a battle on Rythor? Everything seemed fine when I was there. Also if Wayford had known of your situation you would've been given permission to mine," I say unable to keep the frustration out of my tone.

"There was a battle, but it took place away from the settlement. The people don't know about it. Being as late as we already were we didn't feel we had time to contact Wayford."

"And now what are we going to do? We're stranded and outlawed?"

"I don't know. Alex believes the only option is to visit the commanders over on Pike III. Then he can explain everything."

"And why do I have to be here for this?" Can't I go home yet?

"Alex has rules he has to follow. If things aren't taken care of properly we could accidentally start a war with Hayventh, as we're pretty sure Wayford wouldn't be too happy knowing we took you with us."

"No they wouldn't, but I've already explained that I wouldn't say anything about what's happened. Why can't that work?" I ask, wondering why they won't trust me on this.

He shakes his head. "Alex doesn't want to take the risk. He wants to make sure that things will go smoothly down the road."

As we're talking we hear the door open. We turn to see that it's Alex. "Thought I'd come and see what's wrong with the engine," he says in a somber tone. I tell him what was wrong, and he frowns. "That couldn't have been an accident."

We don't say anything. We all know it was Evan, and that Alex has been having a hard time with that. He thought Evan was his friend and could be trusted. "Regardless we've got to figure out what our next step is. The next planet we can make it to is Yenath, but it's to far away for us to drift over to it. We would have to run the ship and deal with the fires." Alex says.

With the condition the ship is in I highly doubt we can make it to Yenath. "Is there a way to establish connections and get someone to tow us to Yenath?" I ask.

"Well, with our network down we can't contact anyone long range. If there's anyone nearby it's possible they would get our S.O.S," Alex says, deep in thought. "We might as well try," he finally decides.

"You think Evan might get it?"

"Evan... is long gone. He knows we could start tracking him if we were to see him. He can't do that much to us anyway." We stay with Alex as he sends out an S.O.S. I have no idea if there's anyone out there. It's a bit risky too, we could get plundered. We have no choice... drifting off into space will do us in eventually. An hour later Alex calls us over to show us the response he got.

"What's it say?" Roxanne asks.

Alex brings it up on his communicator. "It says, 'We're a merchant ship. Here's the deal: If you take a ship off of our hands that we've been unable to sell we'll tow you to Yenath for free.' What do you think Roxanne?"

"Does it run? If not then no," she says with her arms crossed.

"Why would they expect us to take a ship that's not running?"

"I've seen it before," she says, shrugging.

"Alright, I'll ask," Alex says, sending his reply back. In a few moments he gets a response.

"It says, 'Yes of course the ship runs. What do you take me for? I can't sell it because it's an old model that's considered worthless, and I don't want to put up with it anymore. Take the deal or leave it.'"

Roxanne doesn't say anything at first, thinking. "It sounds okay. It's not like we have any other options."

Alex nods in agreement and types a response. After a while he gets a reply back. He looks at us and smiles. "Okay, we'll be picked up in a half hour. If you three wouldn't mind telling the others so that everyone can get all their stuff together I'd appreciate it."

Blair, Roxanne, and I set out. I'd rather not talk to Maylea if I can help it. She still treats me coldly, and I feel tired from the whole ship burning event. I know Roxanne will be harsh on Raya, so it would make more sense to me if I talked to her instead.

After a bit of silence I decide to speak up. "So," I start to say, feeling funny for breaking the silence. "If you talk to Maylea, I can talk with Raya, which will probably make things more convenient for us." I say, looking over at Roxanne.

She doesn't bother to look over at me and keeps looking ahead. "I don't care who I have to talk to, but if that's what you can handle better fine, we can do that." She says, still sounding cold, but not as cold towards me as she used to be.

Maybe the whole thing that happened changed her mind about me a little. I nod and waste no time heading over to the workshop. I stand at the doorway, looking in. We decided to remove the doors to the rooms for now until we can get them fixed. Now that we'll be moving on to a new ship it doesn't matter anyway. Raya is working on something, but I can't tell what it is from here. She seems absorbed in what she's doing. She turns and picks up some metal and starts hammering on it. After a bit I knock on the doorway.

She looks at me and smiles, stopping her hammering for a moment. "Hey Franca, come on in," she says cheerfully, resuming her work.

I walk over to her and stand by the worktable. "What're you working on?" I ask. It looks like she is adding some embellishments to a shoulder piece of armor. I didn't know she could work with gemstones.

"Oh, I'm workin' on a set of shoulder pieces a friend ordered. He wants his armor to look fancier now that he's won some battles," she says cheerfully.

"Have you made everyone's armor here?"

"Yeah, all the armor and weapons here are managed by me. It's my way of avoidin' fightin' in battles while still doin' my hobby," she says as she carefully looks over her work.

"So I take it you don't know how to fight?"

"Never learned, have always been afraid of fightin'. Was a blacksmith by trade, figured out how to use that to my advantage when I was drafted."

"That must've been hard, how long have you all been in the military?"

Raya covers her mouth. "I wasn't supposed to say that... Ya won't tell Alex, will ya?"

"No, why should it matter to me? I'm focused with getting back home. This does explain some things," I say as she continues adding embellishments to the armor. After a few moments of silence I decide to speak up again. "So... I'm guessing Alex won't release me because he needs me to help explain things?" I ask, getting right to the point. Why hide how much I know?

Raya bites her lip. "I shouldn't say anythin..."

"No, you shouldn't," Roxanne says. I turn to see her leaning against the door frame with her arms crossed. "In fact," she says, starting to walk towards us. "You've said too much already. We've got to get ready to go, as Alex has found us a ride. If you say anymore to Franca I'll report it to him."

"Roxanne, I—" Raya says.

"Just be glad I'm going easy on you this time," Roxanne says, walking away.

Raya looks relieved once she leaves. "I guess I'll have to finish workin' on this later." She looks around the room with a discouraged expression. "I have a lot of work ahead of me... and a lot of equipment to move."

"I don't know if I can do much because of my leg, but I can try."

"Naw, it's fine. I wouldn't mind ya stayin' to chat though."

I end up helping her some, but I can't put much weight on my leg.

"All members of the crew report to the hangar, we're about to get aboard the merchant's ship!" Alex says over the intercom.

Raya and I begin to make our way to the hangar. As we go I look out one of the windows and see a massive ship coming close to ours. It's twice as big and looks expensive. It's a shiny silver color with some dark red metal panels, making it stand out. It would be easy to spot. Maybe I could help out with hooking our ship to it to be towed.

A voice I don't recognize becomes clearer as we make it to the hangar. The man speaking to Alex has shoulder length cherry red hair, and his armor looks like a mismatch of whatever he's found. I go up to them curious of what they're talking about.

"Then it's a deal. We'll tow this thing to Pike III and you and your crew will take that old ship off our hands," the man says with an air of confidence.

"Yes, agreed. You'll get us to Yenath to pick it up?" Alex asks.

The young man pays no attention to me as I come up to them. "How else did you expect to get there?" he asks sarcastically. "Yenath is on the way, so we'll drop you off there." He digs through his pockets and pulls out a keybar.

Keybars often have passwords stored on them for vehicles or homes. They're used the first time you get something like that, and then the info is stored in your communicator, so you'll be recognized as the owner from then on.

"Here's the keybar to the ship. Towing's usually a rough ride, so you're welcome to hang out with my crew on my ship. Cause trouble though, and we'll leave you behind," he says in a serious tone. He seems to me like someone who doesn't take well to any nonsense.

Alex notices I'm standing next to him. "Oh, this is Franca," he says, looking over at me. "Franca, this is Bayu, captain of the merchant ship."

Bayu scoffs. "I'm captain of The Burning Rift," he says proudly, giving off a sense that he thinks less of Alex for not mentioning the name of his ship.

Alex ignores this and continues speaking. "Franca has worked on ships before and can probably help with the towing."

Bayu looks my way with his shocking blue eyes and turns his focus to me for the first time. Right away I feel like I'm being analyzed. "If you feel like working my crew will be setting up the towing cables once your crew is done loading supplies on The Burning Rift. Don't expect pay, we're feeding all of you and it'll take extra time dropping your crew off on Yenath."

Not that I'd expect pay from such a small job anyway. I nod in response. He turns his focus back to Alex. "Let me know when your crew is done so that mine can get going," he says, walking back to The Burning Rift.

His ship is next to ours, and the entryways of both ships are temporarily connected. Lance calls over to Alex needing him for something. He immediately goes over to him, so I have no chance to say anything else. I end up helping Roxanne with moving some more things over to the other ship. We're setting our things at the entryway of their ship since we'll be leaving as soon as we get to Yenath, which isn't all that far. The Burning Rift is a much larger ship than ours and should be a lot faster. I can tell it's custom built, so I don't know much about it compared to pre-built models.

I hope I don't get lost on it at some point. Many people are going around doing different things; this ship has a crew of at least one hundred and fifty people, maybe two hundred. I don't want to be left behind with them since I need to make it with the others to get things sorted out so I can go home... I might as well keep everyone up to date with where I am. I decide to say something to Roxanne. "So, I'll be working with their crew to get our ship set up to be towed..." I say.

Roxanne doesn't look over at me, just keeps looking straight ahead as we work. "You're getting paid for that, right?" I'm a bit surprised she'd ask that.

"No Bayu, the captain said that since he's feeding us and dropping us off at Yenath I shouldn't get paid. It's a small job anyway."

"That's sky merchants for you. They never pay for anything unless they absolutely have to," she says, sounding jaded.

I can't tell if she's aggravated that they aren't paying me or if it's because they don't do things the way she thinks they should. She doesn't seem to care much for them regardless. We have no choice though; our ship is ruined and won't go much further. Once all our stuff is aboard The Burning Rift Alex notifies Bayu that we're done. I put on my helmet and take an attachment cable for when I get to the outside of the ship.

He sets his crew to work right away, and I join them. They have me get on top of our ship. I attach the cable to my armor, and connect the other end to the outside of the ship. The cable follows a track so that I can go wherever I need to. I get up there with the others. I notice they don't use the cables for their armor and just hold onto the ship with one hand. They don't seem afraid of falling off into space. The Burning Rift is ahead of our ship. Bayu's crew has already been working on the tow cables on that side. I change the communication channel in my helmet to theirs, and immediately hear that they're singing a tune as they work. I'm not familiar with it, but the melody is catchy. I watch as The Burning Rift moves into position ahead of us.

The crew on The Burning Rift throw thick cables over to us. The cables have tiny thrusters on them so that they can be sent over to other ships. I catch one and attach it to the cable socket nearby. Other members of the crew do the same. I've done this before with other mechanics, but never with a group of people this large. The work gets done much faster since there's so many people. We attach twenty five cables to our ship.

When the work is done the people on my side grab onto the cables and pull themselves across to get back to their ship. I had expected them to use a carrier ship to cross back, but I guess they don't work that way. Soon I find that I'm the last person standing on our ship. It feels funny to leave it behind. It's been a big part of my life for quite some time. I shake my head. Life's a journey and it's time for me to begin a new chapter.

CHAPTER 11

WATCHING THE LAST of the crew cross over to the other ship, I turn my attention to the void below me. I grab tightly onto one of the cables I helped connect, and with a deep breath release the cable that's attached to my armor. I watch it slowly float away and look at my feet as I move to the edge of the ship. Below me is a vast endlessness filled with stars. I grab tighter to the cable with both hands and carefully shift my feet in position to step off the ship. Far below me a ship passes by. I step off, letting myself float above the nothingness.

I slowly move one hand and then the other as carefully as I can. It'd be easy to float away. The crew moved much faster than me, as if they do this all the time, which they probably do. I wouldn't have believed anyone if they'd told me I'd be doing this a few months ago. It feels surreal to be floating in space holding onto a cable halfway between ships. I forgot to change my helmet's communication channel, so I can still hear the crew singing. In a way it helps distract my mind from what's below.

They must've gone to work on something else. There's always a lot to do on a large ship like this. It doesn't seem like they've noticed that I've fallen behind. That means if I get lost here I'll have to rely on myself. I continue to move along the cable at a slow pace. It's better to go slow and careful in my opinion. It's probably good to give my feet a rest as well. Maylea had given me some painkillers, and while I don't feel like I can always trust her I decided to take them anyway. According to her it was either that or more time in the medbay. I have a lot to do and can't be held back because of my leg.

When I get three quarters of the way I look and see Bayu standing on The Burning Rift next to the cables that his crew set up. His helmet and armor are red and gold, instead of the silver and gold that everyone else wears. I speed up as much as I can while still being careful. My hands ache from holding onto the cable so tightly. Both ships have a flat top to them, with a ramp that goes down to a door that the mechanics go through for ship maintenance. I set my feet on the ship, and follow Bayu down the ramp to the airlocked door. He doesn't say anything or look back to see if I'm following him. Once we get inside we take off our helmets.

"What took you so long? The crew's already moved on to other things," he asks, looking at me like he's studying me. "You don't look like much of a mechanic. It seems like your captain is getting everything wrong."

I feel a little aggravated with the way he's talking to me. I'm not part of his crew and was only helping out. I stand up straighter and look him directly in the eyes. "When I've done this in the past we always used a carrier ship to get back to the ship. I'm not part of Alex's crew either, I'm just making my way home." I say, feeling defensive.

Bayu scoffs. "What a waste of resources. So that's how they teach people to work on them now huh?" he shakes his head. "I'm glad I didn't learn to repair ships from wherever you learned. You musta run into bad luck being stuck with that lot. You'd do better working with my crew than with them. I bet I pay mine better than he does. Not sure if they even get paid."

"Oh, and you learned from somewhere better?" I ask in a challenging tone. I know where I stand and I'm not backing down. "You're misjudging Alex. Circumstances have been rough for him and his crew. Why'd you check on me anyway?" I ask, ignoring what he said about me joining his crew. That's not happening.

Bayu laughs. It's the first time I've seen him smile. "I learned from my father, and he learned from his father. My skills have been passed down from generations. I've no idea how mechanics are taught now, but I know better than that. Wouldn't be captain here if I didn't. I only checked on you because I don't care to be held liable for anyone outside of my crew." With that Bayu walks away, not even bothering to hear my response.

I shrug it off. Whatever. Then I start to follow him, remembering that I don't know my way around the ship. I should at least ask him where Alex and the others are. I'm too far away to call out to him without making a scene, so I try to hurry and catch up. As he walks crew members part ways to make room for him. He strides on by, nodding at some of the crew as he goes.

I follow after, but I have to say "excuse me" a lot to get through the crowd. I couldn't keep up with his pace because of my leg. I slow to a stop, looking around me. I'm surrounded by all kinds of people, both young and old. Some people are standing around talking to each other, while others are passing through, probably on their way to work on something.

I notice a girl standing near me looking at her communicator. She has platinum blond hair that comes past her shoulders. "Um, excuse me?" I ask, trying to get her attention. Maybe she can give me directions.

She looks up from her holographic screen. "Need somethin' fellow crewmate?" she asks with a grin.

"I'm looking for my friends. We recently got on this ship, and I was helping out with attaching cables to our old one," I say, hoping that'll help. There are so many people here.

"Oh, you're a new crewmate then?" she asks with a spark of curiosity in her eyes.

"No, we're on our way to Yenath."

"Sorry kid, no idea who your friends are or where they would be. The midday meal is almost ready, so you might see them in the mess hall."

"Thanks, would you mind telling me where that is?" I ask, not wanting to ask her to take me there since she might be busy.

"Sure, no problem. I'll show you how to get there. The name's Wynter by the way," she says, starting to walk.

"Thanks. My name's Franca," I say, following her best I can. I struggle a little to keep up, but I manage. The passageway we go through is twice as wide as the ones on our ship and is full of people. We get to the mess hall, and it's a lot bigger than I expected. It looks as if it could hold at least seven hundred people!

"Might as well sit with my friends and get a bite or two," Wynter says.

I follow her to a table and sit next to her. Her friends are already talking to each other and pay no attention to us. I look around for Alex and the others, but I don't see them anywhere. I do see Bayu seated at a table not far away from mine talking and laughing with some of the crew. He doesn't notice me; not that I'd expect him to. Looking at the table I find that there's already food at my spot. I ask Wynter who it belongs to.

"Why it's your food silly, haven't you ever been on a merchant ship?" she asks in a curious tone.

"Only to do some mechanic work when no one was on them."

"Oh, well then I guess this isn't usual for you. The merchant ship is full of workers. The crewmates are all divided into different crews that handle different things. The kitchen crew cooks and serves the food before we come to the mess hall, so all we have to do is picka seat and eat."

Some of the crewmates at Bayu's table start singing, and he joins in. I can't hear them too well over the noise of all the people talking, but it almost sounds like one of the songs I heard earlier when I was working with the cables. Wynter notices where I'm looking. "I assume you've met Bayu by now?"

"You could say that. I don't know anything about him though," I say with indifference.

She smiles. "He's one of the best captains I've worked for. The crew's like family to him. He knows most of us by name."

"Have you worked on a lot of other ships?" I ask, changing the subject.

"Eh, I've worked on a few here and there. This one's the best. Bayu's motto is that he belongs and answers to no one. Besides answering to him, he tells us it can be our motto too," she says, brushing off my question. I can tell she really wants to tell me about Bayu. I keep looking for Alex and the others, but I still don't see them.

"He used to run this ship with his father, but his father died in a duel against another captain. All his ancestors either sailed the seas or flew the skies. Some people say Bayu flies the ship as if he's sailing the skies," she continues on, not letting me say anything. "He's a loner though; doesn't stay around to get to know anyone well."

"That must be a lonely life," I say, still watching him and his crew. Their song is ending. He looks in my direction and his blue eyes focus on me. I look away feeling embarrassed. I didn't want him to see that I was watching them. I wasn't meaning to; I was caught up in listening to Wynter talking about him.

"Yeah, maybe it is," Wynter says, not noticing what happened. "He has all of us though, and there's currently five hundred and fifty strong. It's hard to be lonely on a ship this size."

I quickly glance over and see that he's still watching me. He gets up from his seat and is making his way over to us. I look back at Wynter, trying to act casual. "Yeah I guess there's a lot of people to keep you company. Do you know where you guys are headed after you drop our ship off?"

"I have no idea. We go where we feel called to I guess." She stops talking as Bayu makes his way over to our table. He seems to have a commanding air about him that the crew reacts to.

I look over at him and find that he's still looking at me. "What're you doing here? Your crew is on the other side of the ship eating."

Wynter tries to stifle a laugh.

"Oh," I say feeling embarrassed. "I uh, lost my way and Wynter brought me here. We thought that I might find them in the area," I say, feeling like I shouldn't be here at all.

"You mean to tell me you and your crew don't stay in contact with each other at all?" he asks in exasperation. I still haven't taken the time to get a new communicator. I should've gotten around to that.

"Like I said before," I say, trying to ignore that Wynter is still struggling not to laugh. "I don't belong with that crew, I'm just staying with them until I get home," I say a little harshly. I immediately feel guilty. I don't have hard feelings towards them anymore. What happened with me was all a big mistake.

"I don't think I would trust them to take you anywhere. Your ship is so close to falling apart it's not even funny. It may not even make the trip. I wouldn't stay with them if I were you."

What choice did I have? My circumstances have made it hard to get away from them. Wayford has probably reported me as missing by now. "I still have some things I have to take care of with them."

By the expression on his face I can tell he doesn't think that's enough of an excuse. "If it weren't for the deal I'd keep you all here until I could straighten Alex out on how to manage a ship. Cause he's gonna ruin things if he keeps going on the way he does. I don't have time for that with all I've got to do," he says, sounding more irritable now. I think he knows I'm not going to listen. "Whatever. Once you're finished let me know and I'll get you over to them," he says, walking back over to his table, not waiting for me to respond. We watch him sit down. He says something to the others, and they burst out laughing.

"I know you might not agree, but I think Bayu's right. You'd be better off with us; you'd get fair pay and meals," Wynter says, smiling at me. What is it with people wanting me to work on this ship? I already know that if I joined this crew I'd be expected to stay for a long time. Most of these people look like they live here and never stay on planets. I don't want to work for Bayu. He's too critical for my liking.

"What planet did you choose as your home planet here?" I ask, wanting to change the subject. After our people escaped and decided to colonize here everyone got to choose a planet to call their home planet. Most people are interested in which one you chose and why.

"I don't belong to any of them, I spend my life living on ships like this one. And," she adds, "I plan to stay on this one for as long as I can." Wynter has to be the first person other than Bayu that I've met who doesn't care to have a home planet. It feels strange to me since I've never even thought of not having one. I finish eating, and then say bye to Wynter.

"Yeah, see you around. You'll say goodbye to me before you leave, right?"

"I will if I get the chance." I can't guarantee that I will. Things seem so busy on this ship that it's likely I won't see her again. Wynter nods and then turns to talk to her friends. I turn to look at where Bayu is. He's still talking with his friends. I'm about to start making my way over when he looks at me. He stands and comes to our table. I'm kinda glad he saw me; I didn't want to go over there and draw attention to myself. "Come on, this way," he says, walking past me.

I turn and start walking behind him. I can barely keep up with his stride as he moves forward through the crowd. They move out of his way, and because I'm closer to him this time I get to move past them as well without trouble. It's when we get into the passageway that I start having to slow down.

I feel the pain killers wearing off and I can tell that my leg is going to be hurting a lot soon. Sensing that I'm not right beside him, Bayu turns to look for me. He sees me and waits for me to catch up. I try not to limp much but it's easy to tell that something's wrong with my leg. "So, your ship didn't have a medbay either?" he asks.

"It did, I just haven't had much time to use it. Our ship was on fire the other day."

We start walking again, this time he goes slower and decides to walk with me. "And no proper extinguishing system I assume. That ship we're giving your crew may be a real upgrade then."

"No, we did have an extinguishing system, but it wasn't working right, and there was also a fight going on..." I say, remembering Evan for the first time today. I get chills thinking of how he betrayed us.

"I'm surprised your crew made it this far. Your captain needs to take some more classes, for his own good. I know you may think I'm just being judgmental of him, but I've been traversing the skies on my own for at least twelve years," he says, stopping us at a huge medbay.

"Why are we here?" I ask, already knowing the answer to that. If he thinks I'm going to stay here he's wrong. Looking through the doorway I try to see if I can spot Maylea. I don't see her anywhere.

"It's going to take us a day to make it to Yenath. We have some trades to make, and something is off with space up ahead, so it may take a bit to navigate around some things."

"What things? And if you think I'm going to spend all my time here in the medbay you're wrong."

"There's been some patches of distortion forming in space, causing it to be unstable in spots. I'm not sure why it's happening, but it's not good. And yes, you are going to the medbay. I refuse to be held liable for you or your crew in any way, and if you're staying with that crew you need to be as well off as you can be before you leave," he says in a no room for argument tone.

I don't care what he says, he can't keep me in the medbeds.

We walk in there, and a young woman comes up to us. "Got us another patient Bayu?"

"This one's got something wrong with her leg," he says. His communicator starts buzzing, and he taps his earpiece. He is silent for a few moments then responds. "I'll be right there." He ends the call. "There's something wrong up ahead; I'm needed for some navigating. You better follow orders and at least use the medbay for the rest of today and tonight," Bayu says walking off, once again not waiting for my response.

"He's always so busy," the woman remarks. She then turns her focus towards me. "So, what exactly is wrong with your leg?"

"I have a small micro fracture," I say, standing with most of my weight on my good leg. I might have to stay the night here, but I will not stay longer than that.

"Hmm I see. Well, let's try the medbed for a while and see if there are any improvements. These medbeds were built by the captain's father and work better than any others," she says confidently.

"Like I have a choice," I say, getting into one. She closes the lid, and a light purple mist fills the bed. I drift off, once more in a deep sleep.

We emerge from the ruins, and Jalyn frowns. "This doesn't feel right," she says, looking around. I look too but don't see anything out of place. Just the jungle like always. As we walk away from the ruins we hear a thud. Turning around we see that a man is there. I notice that there was a small platform above the entryway.

"So, you thought you could escape from me?" he asks with no expression on his face.

"We've got our own business to attend to, it has nothing to do with you," Greyson says, stepping in front of me and Jalyn.

"It is my business, and you'll hand over that map," the man says through his teeth. He glares at us, his brown eyes filled with trouble. Two scars run over his left eye, reaching to his jawline. Walking up to Greyson he grabs his shoulder and effortlessly pushes him to the side. Greyson falls to the ground. Jalyn gets out a blade and so does the man, striking at her immediately. She blocks strike after strike, backing up as she does so. I feel helpless, looking to see that I have no weapon. He knocks the blade out of her hand and raises the handle of his to hit her.

"No!" I shout, jumping in front of her. Everything goes black.

"You think she's going to make it?" Jalyn asks, biting her lip.

"I don't know, she took quite a hit," Greyson says.

The ship rattles and shakes. I instinctively touch my hand to my head and feel something wet.

"Hold on Franca, it's going to be okay," Jalyn says, trying harder to pilot the ship. The distortion in this area has gotten much worse in the past few months.

Greyson puts a damp cloth on my head. I groan... my head hurts. "Easy there, it's going to be okay," he says with concern on his face.

My vision becomes blurred as everything starts to fade away.

"No! Greyson, we can't lose her!" Jalyn says.

He starts shaking my shoulders, trying to keep me awake. Everything fades, then becomes clear again. I'm back at Wayford, in the midst of a snow storm.

"Go back home Franca," Jalyn says in frustration.

"But why? He needs to be stopped."

She shakes her head. "No, I'm not risking losing you again. I can't let you come with me. It's best that you forget about me and go back to the way you lived before." She turns and starts to walk away.

"I don't know how to do that anymore!" I call after her as she begins to fade in the blizzard. I can't be left behind like this.

She stops, then turns to face me. "You belong on Hayventh with the hunters. It'll be easier to go back than you think."

"No, I belong with you, working on the mission. I don't want to be anywhere else." Jalyn runs towards the forest, tears in her eyes. I run after her but lose track of her. The pain in my head keeps me from continuing on. I watch the snowfall wondering if there's a way I can catch up to her.

CHAPTER 12

I WAKE UP to what I thought was the ship shaking. I lay there in the medbed waiting to see if it happens again, or if I was imagining things. It does, but it's slight. I've come to a place where I'm apprehensive when I feel a ship doing that. I wipe a tear off of my cheek. It's time for me to get up. I was serious yesterday about not staying in one of these things. I can't shake that dream I had last night… I wonder what it means and why I keep having them. It's kinda weird to me if I'm honest.

No matter, I've got a long day ahead of me. I press on the glass lid, and it unlatches, beginning to drain the light purple mist and opening. I thought I was going to have to use the emergency release again. I wish Alex had set theirs up this way. I sit up and take in my surroundings. The medbay here is huge.

Most of the medbeds are empty with their lids open. A couple of them are shut here and there, but it seems like the people are doing well. The young woman I saw before comes over but stops halfway to take a call from her communicator. I would get up and go, but I can tell that she wants to talk to me. So I wait. After a few minutes she comes over and starts to check on me.

"How are you this morning? Last night you were tossing and turning, muttering something about someone named Jalyn?" she asks while she begins to check my leg.

I shrug. "I guess I was having a crazy dream."

Her communicator buzzes, and she stops to reply to someone. "Sorry about that, my daughter was asking me a question," she says.

"I didn't know that kids are on this ship too," I say, surprised. Most ship captains make you leave children at home with other family members while you work.

"Oh yes, the captain supports us bringing family along to live here too. He seems to understand people better than most captains do," she says, still looking at my leg.

"This ship's bigger than I thought."

"That it is. Currently we have five hundred and fifty crewmates and that doesn't include family on board. Some people still went the traditional way and came alone. Well, your leg's condition has improved. It needs more healing, but I can tell you're not going to stay in bed much longer."

"Yeah, I should get going and find my friends," I say, feeling the ship shake again. "By the way, why is the ship shaking like that?" It's not happening much, but from my past experiences I've yet to find it to be a good thing.

"Oh that. The captain is busy navigating through some rough patches of space. A lot of distortion in this area, but he has no idea why. If anyone can get us through it he can."

I wonder what it looks like out the windows. I get up and feel some pain in my leg. It's not as bad as yesterday, but still hurts enough that I want to use the painkillers. I get them out and take the last ones. I'll have to find Maylea before the day is over.

"Where'd you get those? I don't remember giving you any," the young woman asks.

"The ship I was on had a medic that gave them to me."

"Oh I see. Mind if I take a look at the bottle?"

At first I hesitate, but then I give it to her. She looks at it carefully, and then nods. "Yes, these are correct. Let me refill this for you," she says, walking off.

I'm glad I got that taken care of. I'm also relieved that they are the correct ones, not that I'd think Maylea would try to hurt me... it's just that I don't feel as trusting of her since I can feel that she doesn't like me. My thoughts are interrupted as the medic comes back. That didn't take her long. "Here you are. Try to take it easy today if you can. We did make some progress on your leg, and it would be good if you came back tonight."

"I'll try to do that," I reply, taking the pain killers from her and leaving the medbay. We shouldn't be here another night, but if we are I'll come back. Once again I'm not too sure where Alex and the others are. Bayu's busy and I don't care that much to bother him. I decide to continue on in the direction that we did yesterday. As I continue down the passageway I pass many people that must be on their way to the mess hall. Breakfast is probably ready. I don't feel like going back that way, but I'll miss breakfast if I don't. My friends won't be saving a meal for me because they don't know where I am.

I turn back. I might as well eat first and then search for the others. I look for a place to sit and end up sitting in a random place. I eat my food, and no one talks to me. That's fine with me. I can focus more on looking for the others that way. I don't see Bayu anywhere; he must still be piloting the ship. Alex never ate with us. He always ate in the control room. In fact, now that I think of it, this is the first ship I've been on where it's normal for the captain to eat with his crew.

I guess merchant ships do things differently. As I'm about to get up I spot Fauve leaving the mess hall. I rush over as fast as I can, which isn't easy since people don't move out of my way without me saying something. She makes her way to a different passageway than the one I've been in. I go down the passageway, but I can't catch up with her.

When I finally do, I call out to her. "Fauve!" she stops and turns to face me. It's not Fauve, but someone else.

"Oh, I'm sorry, I thought you were someone else."

"No worries, hope you find who you're looking for," she says, continuing on her way.

"Thanks," I say, turning to go back the way I came when I hear the pounding of hammers. They must have an armory! Raya is sure to be there. I follow the sounds, turning down another passageway. Once I get there I'm amazed at what I see. The armory is huge, and there's at least sixty people working at smithing stations. Everything is neatly organized and clean. The walls are lined with armor and weapons I've never seen before.

Bayu must have people who invent new technology here as well. I start to walk through the place. Most of the people keep working and ignore me. Some look at me as I pass. I continue on and sure enough I find Raya working at one of the tables. I go up to her, but she doesn't notice me because she is so absorbed in her work. I look at what she's making. It looks like she's making an armored glove prototype.

"Looks good so far," I say. Raya looks up at me, startling a little.

"Oh hey Franca! Didn't see ya there. Where've ya been? We've been lookin' all over for ya."

"I was helping with getting our ship set up to be towed, but I got lost, and then I ended up in the medbay because of my leg..." I say, surprised they had been looking for me.

"Oh did ya see Roxanne there?" Raya asks excitedly.

"No I didn't, is she alright?"

"Yeah she's fine, she got into a fight! Ya should've seen it she was fightin' with this other crewmate who was rude to her. She won of course. The captain got wind of it, and she was sent to the medbay because he doesn't want to be held liable for us."

This doesn't surprise me at all. It's just like Roxanne to spend her free time fighting. "Yeah, that sounds like something the captain would say. Glad Roxanne's fine. What about the crewmate?"

"Oh yeah, the captain's not too happy 'bout that. The crewmate's fine, but he's holdin' Alex accountable for what happened."

"Alex already has enough on his plate... where is everybody?"

"Well, I've been here in the armory most of the time, but from what I know Maylea's been at the medbay seein' if she can learn anythin'. Blair has been buyin' us extra supplies. Alex has been tryin' to keep an eye on all of us while avoidin' the captain as much as he can. The captain doesn't seem to like 'im all that much. Oh and Lance has been checkin' on us along with askin' some of the guards here for any tips he doesn't know. No idea where Fauve is, but that's normal for her."

That's funny, I didn't see Maylea in the medbay earlier. Maybe she was in a different section of it? As I'm about to respond the ship shakes again, this time harder. "Do ya know why it keeps doin' that?" Raya asks.

"From what I know the captain told me there are some patches of distortion that are causing areas of space here to be unstable."

"Huh, never heard of that before, did he say why that's been happenin'?"

"He doesn't know why, but he says he thinks it's not good."

Raya looks at me curiously. "Ya seem like ya've talked to the captain a lot already, are ya friends with 'im?"

I can't help but laugh. "No, I don't think he likes me that much. He was pretty frustrated with me getting lost yesterday, and he keeps telling me how bad off we are," I say, leaving out that I've told him that I'm not part of the crew. I feel kinda bad about that now...

"He sounds like he has a lot of pride," Raya says as the ship shakes again. "Hey, I wonder if we can see the distortion out of the transparent wall?" Raya asks, picking up the armored glove she was working on. We start walking towards the wall. I look behind me to see that someone's already taken her place, working on their own project.

"I was supposed to make a pair of these and send 'em off to my client, but with the ship on fire and everythin' I wasn't able to focus on 'em much," she says when she notices me looking at it. We make it to the wall. Stars can be seen shining gently as the ship moves by them. Like I expected, we didn't see anything unusual. Yenath is much closer than I thought it would be.

"Hey, it looks like we might be leaving today," I say.

"Yeah it does. I wonder what our new ship'll be like?"

"It depends on what shape it's in. If it's anything like ours I won't like it. You think you'll like it?"

"Yeah, as long as it has a workshop, or at least a place where I can set one up," Raya says, looking out at the stars. "I've got a lot of work to do, so it'd make things stressful if I can't get it done." Before I can say anything we hear footsteps coming up to us. I turn and see that it's Alex.

"There you two are. Franca I've been looking for you. The captain says we're going to be landing on Yenath today. I'll need everyone to help get our stuff onto the carrier ship."

"Right," Raya says, already on the move. I follow her since I'm not sure where our stuff ended up. It should still be at the ship's entry way, but the crew might have moved it. Alex goes off to find

Fauve. It takes time to get there since the ship is so large. We see lots of people on our way. It doesn't seem to matter what time of day it is, there are always people about. We get our stuff and start moving it to the carrier ship in the hangar. The hangar is huge and has lots of fighter ships in it. These people must get in a lot of battles.

"These fighter ships are the newest model! Man I miss flying those!" Alex says.

"You used to fly fighters?" I ask. I'm surprised he knows that they're the newest models as well.

"Yeah, all the time. Of course, merchant ships like this need them to defend against marauders. If they defeat them out of self-defense they're allowed to sell the ships and whatever's on them," he says before entering the carrier ship with a box.

We get all of our stuff set up as The Burning Rift reaches Yenath's orbit. The hangar door opens, and Bayu walks through. "You all look about ready to move on," he says, turning to Alex. "Here's a keybar code to the ship and a map code for your communicator. It's stationed off in the forest, out of sight. We do that with our ships because they're less likely to be stolen that way. Your old ship will be stationed at Pike III. It won't be hard to spot, none of the others will be as beat up as that."

"Thanks," Alex says, taking the codes and entering them into his communicator.

Bayu turns to me. "And good luck to you, you'll need it," he says before walking away. I didn't expect him to say anything to me. I get this feeling I'll need all the luck I can get. everyone gets in the carrier ship, along with some of Bayu's crew. They bring another carrier that has our supplies. I can't help but remember when I was on that carrier ship with Roxanne... I try to shake off the memories of me being captured. I'm not there anymore, and things are different now. By the time I get in I find that there are two open spots left.

One is by Blair and the other next to Roxanne. Not wanting to relive memories of the past I decide to sit next to Blair.

Bayu's crew is piloting it for us, so we don't have to worry about flying. Roxanne is leaning back in her seat, looking straight ahead with her arms crossed. Raya is looking out the window listening to music. Blair is writing something on his communicator's screen.

I watch out the window as we pass Yenath's settlement. Starlight is gently shining on the land. I can see people around campfires laughing and playing music. The settlement is made up of cabins, instead of the sprawling neon city that Rythor had.

The branches of the pine trees are moving as the wind weaves through them. I wish I could smell the scent of pine. I miss things like that when I've been on a ship for a long time. While ships can simulate fresh air, it's just not the same. We start to go into the forest, and I'm reminded of all my hunting trips. I've never visited Yenath before; I'll have to come here again sometime and plan a trip.

Several minutes turn into a half hour, and I start to wonder how far out this ship is. Forest is all that can be seen for miles. We descend and land in a meadow next to a cluster of trees. Bayu's crew gets to work, unpacking our supplies and taking them over to the group of trees. Alex gets out, and we go with him. We follow the crew, apprehensive of what we'll find.

"Let's see what we've gotten ourselves into," Lance says as we get closer to the trees. I hope that I won't have to spend the rest of the night getting the ship into flying condition. Roxanne points out some yellow eyes that are in the forest to the left of us. They watch us, but don't come near. She thinks that they are wolves, but can't tell for sure. The creatures move on, heading deeper into the forest.

One guy from the crew tells us that they are leaving now that they've unpacked our things. They go, leaving us to check out the ship on our own.

"Oh you've got to be kidding!" Lance says as he shines light from his communicator on it.

"Well, it's better than nothing," Blair comments.

"What do you think of it Franca?" Raya asks.

"Oh it's something alright," I say as I look at it. To say it's not what I expected would be an understatement, though it's no surprise Bayu had trouble selling it. It's a custom built model that's a cross between a fighter and a cruiser. I've seen models like this before. Most of them have issues and are more difficult to repair since they have a lot of custom made parts. They're faster than a cruiser, but slower than a fighter.

"Might as well get a look inside," Maylea says, making her way to the ship.

Alex goes with her. Roxanne and the others begin to bring supplies in except for Fauve, who's looking over at the trees. I look to see what she's looking at and see the silhouettes of some people just within the edge of the tree line. They turn and disappear, almost as if vanishing into thin air. Fauve turns and quickly boards the ship saying nothing about it. I follow her, not wanting to be left behind.

CHAPTER 13

I STEP ONTO the ship, looking around. It's smaller than our old ship but I think we'll adjust. It's an older model for sure. I'd say at least forty years old… hopefully it still runs. Entering the ship I'm greeted immediately by the main area. There's no hangar in this one, so no carrier ships if we need to escape. I try to ignore that I'm beginning to feel trapped.

Right now everyone's looking through the rooms, so I go at my own pace. I already know this model, though it's been a while since I've been on one. I make my way to the front of the ship to see the control room. As I get up to the room I notice that like all the other rooms this one is also missing a door. Alex and Lance are already looking things over.

"Hmm, I hope that being so close to the main area without a door won't be too distracting to me," Alex says.

"I think that's going to be the least of your problems. Look at this control panel! The thing is ancient," Lance complains.

Alex moves over to take a look at it. "Oh, that's not that bad. I used to fly something similar all the time when I was younger."

"Well, I guess it won't be as much of a problem for you as I thought then."

I take a look at the control panel. This ship has an almost nonexistent AI system, which will take a bit of getting used to. The screens that it has are grainy compared to what I'm used to seeing. I wonder if I could replace those... it's probably not worth the time. The ship has an old navigating system on it, so it doesn't fly as smoothly either. I can't wait to get to Pike III so that I can get this over with and return home. I'll get to go back to working on my hovercraft and living as a hunter again.

I head back to the main area. It's a rectangular room, with two small rooms off of one side of it. Then there's one room at the back. This room is the bunk room, which has two med beds in it. It looks like there aren't enough beds, but we'll figure that out later. The next room is a storage area that will only fit one or two people in it at a time.

I head to the back room and find that it already has armor and metal laying around. I think I know who moved into this one. Raya couldn't bring her workshop along, and instead has a small workbench set up. I stop there and rest my leg for a bit. It's almost better. I think I need one more night in the medbay and I'll be all good. Raya comes and stands next to me, looking at the room.

"It's a bit cramped, but I think I got it lookin' nice!" she says.

Her idea of nice is different from mine, but each to their own I guess. "I'm glad you were able to get everything settled in. It seems like it's smaller than what you guys would usually want."

"Yeah, it's a bit small, but we'll adjust to it fine. Oh, we do have to figure out where everyone's goin' to sleep though."

"I could always sleep on the floor if I need to."

"Nah, we couldn't do that to ya. We'll figure somethin' out," she says.

"I'm used to sleeping on the ground from all the camping I've done, so it wouldn't be all that bad," I say, truly feeling that way. I'm not staying with them for much longer, so why should I be taking up one of the bunks?

"Ya know," Raya says deep in thought. "Maybe I can build a bed in here and that would open up a bunk," she says wistfully. I can't help but laugh a little. In this clutter it would be hard to see her. She laughs with me. "Anyway, I've got some things I gotta do. Maybe ya can help me with 'em."

Before I can respond we hear the ship make a whining sound as it tries to start up, and then it stops.

"Hey Franca! Would you mind taking a look at this?" Alex calls from the control room.

"Gotta go," I say, making my way past some clutter.

"No problem," Raya says casually, going back to her business.

I make it to the control room and see that Alex is reading an error notice on the computer system's screen. "I'm not sure what it's saying here. It's all a bunch of numbers," he says, stepping aside so I can look at it.

I start to read the notice. These older models are known for using the old number code system when reporting errors. It's been so long since I've seen it that it takes me time to read it. Alex stands there patiently waiting, not saying a word so I can focus. "Oh, it's saying that the power generator needs to be reset before starting the ship," I say, glad to be finished reading.

"Will we have to do that every time we start it up?" Alex asks.

"We shouldn't," I say. I hope we don't. Something's wrong with it if we do. "I'll go reset the generator."

"Sounds good."

I go to the generator, which is in a small room to the side of the control room. It's a compact design, making it hard to work on. Some of the metal has rusted and will need cleaning. I find a power lever and pull it, then head back over to Alex.

"Okay try it now," I say. He nods and tries to start up the ship. This time it starts successfully, though the engine sounds rough. I've heard this sound so many times. "The engine hasn't been run in a while and needs warming up."

"Okay, I'll let it run a bit before taking off."

After a few moments I head back to the main area. Lance is there with Blair organizing our stuff.

"You know, something's a bit odd with this ship," Blair says.

"And what's that?" Lance asks.

"There's barely any storage space on it. I've never seen one with an area so small."

"Yes, that is unusual. I guess we'll just have to leave some of our stuff here in the main area."

"Hey, Franca! Could you help me with something?" Fauve calls from the other side of the room.

"Sure," I say, going over to her. "What is it?"

"I don't want anyone to hear this yet, but I've been thinking of getting away from being a guard," Fauve says. "Lance and Roxanne won't agree with it, but I think I'd rather be the copilot. I was wondering if you could ask Alex for me? I don't think he'll listen to me."

"You've been a copilot before?"

She laughs. "I've flown more ships than I can count. Used to fly all the time back at home. Me being on guard duty was Alex's idea. He also wanted to be friends with Evan and chose him because he seemed to know more than I do."

"Well, it sounds like you have enough experience."

"Thanks Franca, so you'll ask?"

"Sure, all I can do is try."

"Thanks, I'd appreciate it!"

I go back to the control room, and take a seat next to Alex. I observe the control panel carefully as the ship begins to rise. It launches fine, but still sounds rough. Sometimes I wonder if we'll ever get to Pike III. We might not make it in this thing. Yenath is the last planet before Pike III, so at least we won't have to make any stops. Alex turns to look at me. "At least it's running, right?"

"Yeah, hopefully it'll do alright. Pike III isn't far off," I say, trying to give him some hope. "Hey Alex, Fauve wanted me to ask you if she could be the copilot? She's bored with guard duty and says that she grew up flying ships."

"After what happened with Evan I honestly don't feel like having a copilot at all," Alex says.

"It's important to have one though. Especially with a ship like this," I say.

I can tell by Alex's expression that he knows I'm right. "To tell you the truth I'd rather have Lance be my copilot. Fauve is... not a very focused person. I'm not sure if she'd do well with flying if she needed to."

"Maybe she doesn't focus because she doesn't like what she's doing right now?"

"Well, I'll give it a try," Alex says after some hesitation. "Tell her she can start whenever she's ready."

"I'll go get her," I say, heading back to the main area again. I also know how to fly these, but I don't want to be in that position. I like working on ships more than flying them. I go and tell Fauve the news, and she excitedly heads to the control room. I look out one of the windows and see that we've already left Yenath's orbit. The ship is flying well considering that it's probably been sitting on the ground for at least ten years.

"You'll be on your way home soon," Lance says.

I jump a little. I didn't hear him come up to me. "Yeah, I'll finally be out of everyone's way."

"We don't mind having you here. You weren't the one we needed to watch out for after all," he says, looking at his feet. Yeah, Evan was much worse than me. "I was going to see if you know anything about Evan? You did spend some time with him."

"I don't know much; he said a lot to me but didn't actually say much about himself. I'm not even sure if what he did tell me was true…" I say. That guy was creepy.

"Alright, thanks anyway. I'm going to hunt him down and make him pay for what he did," Lance says, with anger in his tone. "I hate these marauders that are all over our star system. They're always hurting and killing people."

"Well we do need to fight them off. They've caused us a lot of trouble. Do you think Evan was a marauder?"

"I can't be sure. He didn't act like one. I think we moved to the wrong star system. While it was important that we got away from The Sarthrian Empire we needed to have more care in where we went."

Our ship starts shaking. I can hear Alex and Fauve talking, but I can't hear what they're saying. I excuse myself to go see what's wrong. Alex is trying to navigate the ship, and Fauve is looking at the radar system. "That's strange, I don't see anything," she says.

"Well something's causing the ship to be thrown off of its path," Alex says, desperately trying to keep the ship straight. It keeps rocking and heading off course.

I look out the windows to see if I can see anything. I notice that some areas ahead of us look a bit blurry. Maybe this was the distortion Bayu was speaking of? I look out the front window and see that there are many blurry patches ahead. Some of them are hard to spot, while others are large. "Alex, don't some areas up ahead look a bit blurry?" I ask.

He looks up from the computer screen and squints his eyes. "No, I don't see anything."

"I don't either," Fauve says. "Though, maybe the area to your right looks slightly darker than the rest," she says pointing at it. Alex turns the steering to maneuver around it. When he does that he accidentally hits another spot to the left, and it sends the ship rocking again.

Roxanne comes into the room. "Hey, my communicator isn't working, are yours? Mine isn't receiving any comm. links." Alex and Fauve check theirs. I'm reminded that I still need to get a new one.

"Hey, mine's not working either. How am I going to get in touch with my brother now?" Fauve asks.

"Something's not right here," Alex says.

"Maybe it's the distortion Bayu was talking about?" I ask.

"That captain doesn't know what he's talking about," Alex mutters.

"Merchant ships aren't to be trusted Franca. They just want to sell you something. They sure did get a fine deal out of us. This ship's not worth a thing," Roxanne says.

I don't say anything. I think he was right. I would wait a bit before ruling it out. The ship keeps rocking. Blair comes in the room next.

"What now?" Alex asks, trying his best to get control of the ship.

"I just came to say that we need to be going easier on our food supply or we're going to run out," Blair says.

"We haven't eaten anything yet," Fauve says.

"Yeah, we've still been unpacking," Roxanne says.

"Well someone's been eating some of it, because a third of it is already gone," Blair says.

Everyone but Alex looks at me. "Don't look at me, I wouldn't do that. I've been busy talking to people," I say. Everyone seems to agree and tries to think of a different reason.

"Do we have to discuss this right now?" Alex asks in exasperation.

"You think we have a creature in here with us?" Fauve asks, ignoring Alex.

"It's possible that we have ship mice," Alex says, sounding distracted. He flies over another distorted spot.

"Alex..." Fauve says.

"What kind of creature would eat a third of our food supply? I say those merchants took some of it as payment," Roxanne says.

"Why would they want our food? They had plenty of their own." Alex says.

"Alex!" Fauve says.

"Well I think someone or something got into it. Should we check to make sure no one is stowing away?" Blair asks.

"Why would we do that? No one would go on this ship unless they were forced to." Roxanne says insultingly.

"I think it's better to be preventative, especially where our supplies are concerned. You don't need to get nasty about it."

"Alexxx," Fauve says again. I look ahead and don't see anything. Blair and Roxanne start arguing. Maybe this is why Blair is always so quiet...

"What is it Fauve?" Alex asks. She says something but he can't hear her. "Quiet!" Alex yells. Everyone falls silent. "What is it Fauve?"

"Do you hear that ship?"

"What ship?"

"Listen. I think one is coming behind us."

Alex takes his focus off of the distortion and checks the radar system. What it shows isn't good. A group of marauders are after us. "We've got to speed up!" Alex says, putting the ship into full throttle.

The engine sounds like it's struggling, but nobody seems to care. The ship rocks harder, repeatedly being thrown off course. The marauders are also thrown around, but their ships are more stable so they recover from it quicker.

A shot fires past our ship, narrowly missing us. It's hard to dodge anything, and it was more of the ship rocking that saved us. Lance comes in the room to see what's going on, along with Maylea and Raya.

"Alright, I need everyone except for Fauve out of here, I can't focus. The rest of you go about your regular business until I call for you," Alex says.

Everyone leaves but me. I feel like I can help in some way, and I know I won't be able to just sit and wait. Alex is looking ahead, trying to navigate the ship. "I think something's wrong with the ship, it shouldn't be flying like this," he says.

Fauve is busy watching the radar system. "Alex... there's a bigger ship following us now," she says.

I look at the screen and see she's right. A bigger ship is coming up behind the rest. Something about the way it moves seems familiar to me. It navigates around the distortion with ease. The marauders scatter as the ship starts firing at them. It hits some of the ships, and they explode. Some of them try to retreat, but they're too late. In a few moments it's only us and the other ship. A call comes in on our ship's computer system, and Alex answers it.

"I had a feeling you might have trouble here. If you follow me I'll get you to Pike III without anymore trouble," Bayu says.

"Fine, I can't pay you for this though," Alex says.

"Well since you're not aboard my ship I can't reasonably charge you anyway." With that he passes us, and we see that our old ship is still in tow.

"Huh, it's almost like he expected us to have trouble," Fauve says. "You think he sent those marauders?"

"Why would he destroy them if he sent them?" I ask.

"Yeah, I guess he couldn't have done it then."

"Hey Fauve? I need your opinion on something," Raya calls from the main area.

"Coming! You're okay with me leaving for a bit Alex?"

"Yeah sure," he says, sounding a little disappointed.

A copilot shouldn't leave during a situation like this. Fauve runs off to see what Raya wants.

"I guess you were right, there is distortion out there," Alex says. "I haven't done anything right since I've been leading this crew."

"That doesn't mean that you can't learn from things and try again," I say. "It's through experience that we get better at what we do."

"Thanks Franca, but whenever I made a good decision it was actually Evan that had the ideas. I wasn't doing the work to learn. I recently checked my files with the army to see my standing, and it looks like there was a glitch with the test I took to prove I could be a captain. The test said I passed when I did not. All this time I thought I was able to do this when I wasn't even close to being qualified," he says, sounding down.

"All we can do is to learn from our mistakes and try our best moving forward," I say. I don't know what to tell Alex. If it wasn't for him I'd have already been back home.

"I'll try to do better if I don't go to prison from the accusations the army's made against me," he says hopelessly.

"I think we'll get it straightened out," I say. Now we're in Pike III's orbit.

"Would you mind telling the others to get ready to land?"

"Sure," I say, wishing I could help him more. I'm not used to encouraging people. I mostly look out for myself. The rest of the day is uneventful, and when night comes the crew decides that I should get one of the medbeds. I drift off into a restful sleep.

CHAPTER 14

I IMMEDIATELY GET out of the medbed when I wake up. I still don't like being in them. As I bring myself to a stand I find that there's no more pain in my leg. This ship may be old, but it seems that the healing technology did me a lot of good. I make my way to the control room, and find that we are close to our destination.

As we get closer to Pike III, I notice how much greener the planet is than the others. Filled with emerald forests and sapphire seas, the planet shines with a radiance of prosperity. Some areas of Pike III are blanketed gently in white clouds. A mix of yellow and blue stars surround the planet. I've never been on Pike III myself, but I've heard that the rainforests are huge.

It's funny to think that Hayventh is just north of here and that I'm not that far from home. The closer we get the harder it is to see because there is heavy cloud cover over the area we need to go towards to land. If our ship was newer it would have a more reliable radar system, but we'll have to make do with what we have.

"Look at all these clouds. I wonder if it's always like this?" Fauve asks.

"There's a lot of rainfall on this planet. Our ship isn't fit to land here, but it's what we ended up with," Alex says.

Looking into the distance ahead I can barely make out the back of our old ship. If it weren't for Bayu I'm not sure how we would land. The clouds are like a thick fog. Navigating through this without a radar system would be out of the question. I look over at the side windows. The clouds are flowing past us. Once we emerge from the them we are greeted by a world of deep green trees.

We follow Bayu's ship, flying over the top of the forest until we arrive at a gap in the trees that has been cleared for ships to come through. The gap is at an angle, cutting down through the dense branches, leaves, and vines. At first sunlight can be seen shining in patches through the overgrowth of the trees, but once we make it below the top layer of the forest the sunlight fades and holographic lanterns light the way in its place.

The trees of this forest are extremely tall; much taller than I could've imagined. Below us I can see the next layer of the forest, and from what I can tell that's about seven hundred feet below us. All the buildings here float in the air and have holographic lanterns near them.

Ships are flying all around, making the place feel busy to me. Bayu lands in the emergency side of the hangar. It has longer stationing areas in case a ship is being towed. We land next to him and step out to see that his crew is already working to detach their cables from our old ship. The back is broken off, leaving burnt jagged edges exposed. We hear a crashing sound as a piece of the ship falls to the ground. Someone gasps, and many people stop to look at the ship. Some stare in wonder, while others look at it in disgust. The hangar was spotless before our ship arrived.

The walls are made of a white gemstone, with vines covering parts of them. The trim on the walls is solid gold and the king's emblem, a hawk flying over a white wolf, is engraved in the golden doors leaving the hangar. Guardsmen from the royal palace are stationed about armed with the best armor known to us. Their armored uniform is green and silver, with the king's emblem on their left shoulders.

Pike III is a prosperous place, and the settlement has a lot of resources that the other planets don't have. The king lives here, and he has placed his guards all throughout the settlement and palace. Each planet has one settlement, and they are all responsible for their own security, with leaders that have to answer to the king. I've never seen him myself, but I've heard that he rules with a steady hand.

"Alright," Alex says. "It's time to go." The crew goes silent, feeling more somber. We all know if things don't go well we'll be imprisoned.

"You can do this Alex," Maylea says. "We will pull through."

Alex stands a bit taller and begins to walk steadily ahead of us. We follow, ignoring the stares of the people nearby. Some of them are still looking at the ship. I wonder how we'll get rid of that thing... Bayu certainly has washed his hands of it. We leave the hangar, getting ready for the last part of our journey. High above us nests can be seen in the top layer of the forest. Joyful birdsong can be heard along with the sound of the wind blowing through the trees. Looking down we can see the middle layer of tree branches.

"I wouldn't want to fall down there," Fauve says, looking at the branches below.

"Yeah it looks like a long fall... ya think it's farther than where ya fell in Rythor, Franca?" Raya asks.

I look and take a step away from the edge of the platform. "Yeah, that's much farther than when I fell in Rythor." I don't know if my armor would save me from a fall like that. Alex silently walks across the platform, getting ready to hail a transport service. Both Fauve and Raya hesitate in following him closer to the edge.

Lance rolls his eyes. "If you two would stop thinking about it you wouldn't have a problem here," he says, sounding a little aggravated.

"Hey, don't talk to me like that," Fauve says.

The crew all look tense and on edge. "I'm sorry Fauve, I'm just stressed out from this," Lance says.

"The transport will be coming anytime soon," Alex says more to himself than to us. "All we can do is try our best. That's all we can do." His shoulders slump. Before anyone else can say anything a long hovercraft stops and hovers next to the platform. We get in, and Alex tells the driver where we need to go.

After showing the driver his information on his communicator. He agrees and starts driving us through the settlement. "I'll take you to the airway, then you'll have to go the rest of the way on your own," the driver says.

"That's fine with me," Alex says, trying his best to sound like nothing's wrong.

Sometimes I wonder why I decided to stay here. I had my chance to get away but felt like I needed to stay and help. The hovercraft lifts away from the platform, starting to make its way through the settlement. Houses and buildings can be seen hovering between branches wherever they can fit. Some of the houses even have yards attached to them. The houses look peaceful, and a lot of the yards are decorated with flowers of all colors. Since they hover they don't harm the trees in any way.

The trees are far apart enough that you can fit a few houses between them. The forest seems to go on forever, with warmly lit lanterns floating among them. Hovercrafts go to and from the buildings, and some can be seen descending below the layer of branches, most likely to another part of the settlement. Other hovercrafts can be seen going up instead. I knew Pike III had the biggest settlement, but I didn't realize it was like this.

We make it to the gap that leads up to the top layer of the trees. The hovercraft comes to a stop at a floating platform. We get out, and Alex pays the driver from his communicator. We turn and see a building with small carrier ships stationed next to it. We go inside the building with Alex leading the way. A young man greets us, and after talking with Alex he lets us take a ride to the royal palace.

"Alex, weren't we going to headquarters?" Maylea asks as we get in the carrier ship.

"Unfortunately the generals and commanders are all out fighting battles against marauders that are attacking Durath. I got some information about it on my communicator."

"What are we going to do then?"

"We have to go higher up." His tone sounds tense. I'm not sure who we should go to since we can't speak with a commander. Having to visit the palace must mean that we'll be talking to someone of high authority. I doubt that they'll care to be bothered with something like this. The carrier takes off, and we're in the clouds once again. It feels surreal to spend a few minutes not being able to see anything. The carrier moves through the layer of clouds, finally making it above them.

We skim along the layer of golden clouds as if the carrier were a boat sailing along the sea. The sky is an amber orange, reflecting the light of the setting sun. The clouds go on as far as the eye can see. Mountain peaks poke through them in the distance behind the island. As I'm looking around my attention focuses on the palace. It has many windows and sits on a floating island that sets in the clouds, reminding me of an island in the middle of a vast ocean. As our ship gets closer to it I see that the island is covered with pine trees, and is surrounded with a beach.

The carrier makes it to the island, landing in a hangar that is separate from the palace. We are greeted by the royal guard immediately as we leave the carrier ship. The driver nods at Alex and then flies off, leaving us to face our fate. The guards approach us standing tall and fearless, as though nothing could keep them from doing their duty. Their guns look to be of a newer technology I've never seen before.

As the guards begin talking with Alex I take in the details of the hangar. The floor is made of brown crystal, with white walls that have intricate patterns woven throughout with gold. The guards walk away from Alex, talking amongst themselves. They keep looking over at Alex as they talk. After a minute or two they come over and ask for our weapons. Everyone hands them over willingly except for Roxanne. She hesitates, but in the end hands her sniper over when she's told she won't go anywhere past the hangar otherwise. One of the guards comes over to me.

"I have nothing," I say.

"I don't believe that," she says sternly.

I shrug. I know it seems odd, since everyone else had at least two weapons on them. She asks that I empty my pockets and quickly finds that I was truthful.

"I guess I'll have to make new ones if we don't get them back," Raya comments with disappointment, looking over at our weapons.

She worked hard on those, hopefully we get them back. To her they're like art pieces. The guards lead the way out of the hangar, with two on either side of our group and three in the rear. The doors of the hangar open to a walkway that leads to the palace. Lamp posts glow warmly, and at the top of each set of stairs a fountain can be seen on both sides of the pathway. The walkway is made of crystal. Fireflies are flickering throughout the pines as the last light of the sun is dissipating.

We come to a stop at the palace doors. They stand tall, and are made of solid wood. The emblem of the wolf and hawk is engraved in gold on each door. A guard stands on either side, and after some discussion with the others they open them. The palace has white walls that are embellished with gold and emeralds. Light shines through the many windows. Looking up at the tall ceiling I can see that there are windows higher up as well. The windows on the ground level have long white curtains that look to be of the finest silk. Chandeliers hang from the ceiling with intricate designs embedded in the glass. Everything in the palace looks to have been made with the best craftsmanship.

It's hard to believe that it was only a few years ago that we moved to this star system. We came from The Sarthrian Empire, where we were all slaves. Nareth, Gunner's father planned for us to escape during an all out space war with another empire. It worked, and we teleported to a far away star system that we've named Ohniran. Everyone chose a home planet to live on, and built a settlement there. Nareth ruled for a time with Gunner and his other son, Ty. He passed away only six months ago, leaving the throne to Gunner.

Our steps echo as we make our way along the main hallway. Other hallways and rooms branch off of this, with guards standing at each of them. We get to a long stairway and continue on in silence. I'm curious to see where we're going. Hopefully the people we talk to are understanding. At the top of the steps is another hallway that leads to a set of large doors that are shut. These are made of the same heavy wood that the exterior ones are. They also have the king's emblem engraved on them. The guards that are guarding the doorway step forward, and the two guards in front of us go ahead to talk to them.

"Wait a minute, this is where the throne room is," Raya whispers. "We might be talkin' to the King himself."

"Oh dear, I've heard he can be harsh in his judgments if he thinks you've done wrong," Fauve whispers back, sounding a little fearful.

"Where'd ya hear that? I've heard he's kind."

"You two shouldn't worry about that. From what I know, Nareth's son rules fairly and with wisdom," Maylea whispers. "And silence would be wise here."

Roxanne nods to that, and they both grow silent as the guards return. Light shines through the doorway as the doors are opened.

CHAPTER 15

I DON'T THINK any of us have seen so much wealth in our lives. Out of everything I've seen in the palace this room has the best lighting. The ceiling is domed with windows so that the remaining sunlight can still shine brightly through. There are many lower windows as well. The walls are decorated with different kinds of gemstones, some I've never seen before. There are even some in the golden floor. All of the lamp stands appear to be hand carved with excellent craftmanship. A large chandelier hangs above the center of the room. The king, Gunner, sits upon a throne of carved silver.

His layered aqua blue hair just touches his shoulders, and upon his head is a silver crown. At first I thought the crown looked like it had white gemstones in it, but as I look closer at them I can tell that they're something different. I can't tell what they are exactly, but they radiate with a brilliant white light. It's not blinding, but it's still bright. There's a feeling of power and might coming off of him, but there's also a feeling of light. It is said that his father Nareth had the same light about him when he ruled, along with the great peace he brought to the people.

Two smaller thrones are on either side of him. Two men sit on these, one being old and the other young. I'm guessing that they must be his advisors. I wonder if they are the same ones that served

Nareth in his time of rule. The young man has wavy black hair and light grey eyes. He has a sternness about him and watches us with caution. The king looks at us curiously. The guards bring us closer to Gunner, saying something lowly to him.

As Alex is about to speak a scout comes running into the throne room. "My king, I have a message for you," she says, sounding out of breath.

He lifts his hand. "It can wait, I want to know why these people are here," he says in a calm voice.

The scout shifts from one foot to the other but remains silent. Gunner's hazel eyes meet mine briefly as he studies the crew. I didn't get the chance to change my armor to something that would be more fitting for the climate here, so I know the fur lining looks out of place.

"Now," he says, looking at all of us. "What is your business here, that you have to speak to me personally?"

The guards step out of Alex's way as he comes forward to speak. He wipes sweat off of his brow and clears his throat. "My king, my name is Alex, and I am a captain of one of your military ships..." He starts. "I would've taken this to one of the commanders, but because they're all out on the battlefield I had to bring this to you instead..." He says, starting to stammer.

"Yes, and?" Gunner asks patiently.

"Well sir, uh my king," Alex says before starting to explain our ordeal. He talks of his problems at Hayventh, how I was captured, the attack from the marauders, our landing on Rythor, then our long journey here and how the military ship was destroyed in the process. Gunner listens quietly and patiently, not interrupting him once.

Alex then goes on to explain the glitch in the system and that he actually wasn't qualified to be the captain in the first place. "This was all my fault, and I take full responsibility. I don't want my crew or Franca to be punished for any of it since they didn't cause this. If the law says that we should be imprisoned I am willing to pay the sentence for each of them," he says sounding nervous, but sure of himself. Fauve gasps.

"Alex, you can't do that," Maylea says.

Alex shakes his head and holds his hand up, stopping her from saying anything else.

After a moment of silence the young man on his right speaks up. "Imprisonment seems like too harsh of a punishment, but something must be done."

"I agree with Faine," the man on his other side says.

Gunner looks over at both of them. "We must all remember that sometimes circumstances are not what they appear to be, and that even the best of us can be caught up in them."

"But something has to be done," Faine protests.

Gunner nods. "And something will." He turns his attention back to Alex. "Alex, I will renew your status with the army, but you will be assigned to a ship as the second in command, or the copilot as some of you call it. That way, you can learn how to be a captain."

"But sir," Faine says.

"How can he learn if he's not given a chance?" Gunner asks.

"Thank you my king," Alex says, sounding greatly relieved. "I would like to request that my crew stays with me. We've been through a lot together and know how to work as a team."

Gunner looks at us again, his eyes staying on me a few moments longer than the others. With everything that happened I know we look pretty beat up. I look at everyone's armor, then down at my own. We all have places on our armor that are dented, scratched, or covered in burn marks and soot. The fur lining of mine is matted and torn. The man on Gunner's left speaks up. "To me they look like they would do well separating."

"And why is that, Arlan? It is clear that separating them would be foolish. It would be well to let them be since they already get along," Gunner responds. He turns his attention to me. "Since your situation is different, and you were a prisoner aboard their ship, I will have you wait in another room while I finish discussing matters with the crew."

I follow one of the guards out of the room. I would have asked about going home, but I didn't want to endanger the crew's standing with Gunner. I'll have to speak with him about that later. The guard takes me to another room, and shuts the door behind me. There's nothing but a chair and table here. On the table sets a gemstone lamp that's casting the room in a gentle yellow glow. After a half hour I'm brought back into the throne room to join the others. Alex is still speaking with Gunner.

"Is there anything else you would like to say?" Gunner asks.

"I would like to say that Franca would like to be returned home, and that I'm sorry about the troubles that I caused with Hayventh's settlement," Alex says, seeming to have relaxed a little since I last saw him. The others still look nervous.

Gunner looks at me. "I will take care of any issues with the people of Hayventh concerning this. I'll also pay for the minerals that were taken to repair the ship." I didn't expect him to deal with this issue personally.

"But sir!" Faine protests.

"Faine, I will handle this," Gunner says calmly.

"Yes sir," he says, going silent again.

"Franca, I will have transportation ready to take you home tomorrow morning. As for the rest of you, you know too much for me to just let you go back to your own business. You will report tomorrow for your mission briefing."

"Sir, I don't think this is wise," Faine starts to say, knowing where this is going.

"I will take care of this," Gunner says evenly, speaking to Alex again. "Once I get control over the current situation you'll be allowed to go back into the army. For now you and your crew will work for me as we discussed earlier."

"Yes my king, it will be an honor," Alex says, sounding stronger and more confident. The rest of the crew remain in a shocked silence.

Gunner smiles. "Good. You can stay at the guest rooms on the other side of the palace. Training starts tomorrow."

With that the guards turn around, getting ready to take us to the guest rooms. We turn and follow. Soon the doors are shut behind us. It takes time to reach the other side of the palace. It seemed so much smaller to me when we were coming to the island. The others talk casually like usual, and don't say anything about what happened in the throne room. How do they know too much? After going through many hallways we make it to the guest area.

There's a living space with hallways branching off of it. The guards leave us here, and everyone chooses a room. I take mine last. One look in the room tells me it's better than anywhere I've stayed at in my life. I should be happy I'm finally going home after all of this, but try as I might I can't seem to shake the downcast feeling in my heart.

I know if I go home I'll be missing out on all the adventure here and will also be constantly wondering about how the others are doing. I do miss Anna and my family, but I recognize that I don't feel like going home. I've heard people say before that adventure changes a person, but I never believed them.

What can I do though? A ship has already been arranged for me in the morning. Raya told me that I should be excited to see what the ship that takes me back is like. She gave me her comm. link data and wants me to tell her about my trip home once I get a new communicator.

I'm sure I'd be interested in the ship, but I feel I would rather see what happens with the crew. I set a bag of supplies that I was given by the guards at the side of the bed. Gunner had given them to me for the trip. I feel tired. I think I will look at what's in it tomorrow. I go and lay down on the most comfortable bed I've ever been in, and slowly drift off into a troubled sleep.

I wake up in the morning feeling no different than I did last night. My thoughts return to yesterday. I don't feel like going home at all, which is so strange. Maybe adventure does have a strong call. I sit up and take note of my surroundings. Bright rays of sunlight shine on the floor next to the bed. Birds are chirping outside the window, though I'm not sure what kind of birds they are. The room I'm in has white walls with an intricate gold pattern weaved throughout it. The gemstones in the walls are smaller than the ones in the walls of the throne room. Even so I still feel like I'm in a wealthy place.

I decide to check the bag of supplies. Inside I find food, a generic travel kit, and a new communicator. I put it on and boot it up to see the time. It's seven fifteen. I think I'm supposed to meet the guards at nine. I get up and to my surprise the crystal floor isn't cold like I expected it to be. I wonder if all the floors in the palace are heated like this? Or is it only the bedrooms? It doesn't matter since this is the only time in my life that I'll be here anyway.

I have no choice in this, I have to go. But what if it's not too late to stay? I shake my head, that's just nonsense. I put on my boots and armor before walking over to the long mirror that's on the wall. My black hair is a mess and I still have soot on my face. My armor is scarred and covered in dents, burn marks, and soot. I've been on a long journey already... maybe it's time to call it quits?

I decide to contact Anna. Maybe that will help me to feel better. As I start to enter in her comm. link data I feel surprised, realizing that I can't remember it. Have I been gone that long? I start to hear voices talking outside my door.

I open it quietly and stop at a crack, hearing Roxanne. "It's not fair she gets to go home, and not me. After all, I've been through way more than she has and have paid my dues."

"But what would you be doing back at home that would be cooler than this? Going home sounds boring to me," Fauve says.

"Look Fauve," Roxanne says in a get this straight tone. "I've been in the military for a long time, and these secret missions are usually a lot harder than the regular ones. I've seen more battlefields than any of you, other than Maylea perhaps. And while we must fight on against evil like we always have I long for the day when all this blood and strife will end," she says, weariness evident in her tone. Before Fauve can get a word in she continues.

"Back home on Hayventh things are… somewhat distanced from the rest of Ohniran. I'm a lead hunter there, and when I return I will receive great honor for the things I have done here. But no, it's Franca who gets to go home; the one of us who has done the least."

I gently shut my door, deciding not to go out yet. Now I know that I can't go home. Not with what Roxanne reminded me of. On Hayventh it takes a lot of hunting and serving the people to become a lead hunter. You have to earn a good reputation over years by doing honorable things like providing meals to the poor and hunting down creatures that are a great danger to the settlement. In Wayford the lead hunters are the ones who help govern and guard it.

They are looked upon as some of the strongest people. There is a council above the lead hunters, but it's the votes from the hunters that decide things. It took me a long time to get the position myself… That giant bear I had to hunt almost killed me. I don't know if I could do something like that again. For some reason I had thought that the crew didn't need me anymore, but I know I'm wrong. The right thing to do would be to stay and help.

Most lead hunters were assigned to a sector of Wayford, and rarely met with each other. That must be why Roxanne and I never knew of each other. If I go home now, and she comes back later and talks about how I abandoned them and came home early I'll be looked at as dishonorable and will lose my position. Depending on how the crew fares I might even be exiled if staying with them would've made a difference.

Living the rest of my life shunned to Hayventh's wilderness would not be an easy life. To me that would be worse than being imprisoned here. I can't let any of that happen, not after how hard I worked to build my life there on Hayventh. I pace in my room for a bit, trying to think of how I can stay. Time goes by quicker than I thought it would, and before I know it my pacing has gotten me nowhere, and now it's eight thirty, giving me only a half hour before I'm supposed to leave.

I open my door and make my way down the hallway, not sure of who I should talk to about this. I could talk to Gunner, but he's the king and has bigger concerns. Who am I to be talking to him anyway? The people who are getting a ship ready for me will have to report to him if I choose to stay so he'll find out about it eventually… I might as well go talk to him.

My pace quickens as I remember how far away my room is from the throne room, turning down another hallway. Last night I didn't mind the stroll there as I was taking in all the sights of the palace, but now I may not make it there in time.

"Franca? Aren't you going the wrong way?" Fauve asks, stopping in front of me.

"Actually I'm thinking of staying," I begin to say.

Fauve's eyes light up. "You better hurry or you'll miss the mission briefing! It's this way," she grabs my hand and starts walking in the opposite direction.

"Hey wait a minute! I have to talk to Gunner first. The ship is going to be ready for me to go soon." I say, trying to stop. My communicator reads eight forty five now. Fauve doesn't listen and keeps going.

I manage to get my hand out of her grip and she turns to look at me. "Come on Franca, Gunner's supposed to give us instructions at the briefing and should be there," she says, looking down the hallway and fidgeting.

"If I can I'd like to talk to him before it starts. My ship is supposed to leave at the same time as that briefing, and I need to at least talk to the people who are preparing the ship," I say, heading back in the direction of the throne room after she nods in response. I'm not sure who to talk to, but I should be able to find out from the advisors if I can't speak with Gunner.

I make it there, and one of the guards gives me a stern look. "What's your business here? You're supposed to be boarding the ship."

"I need to speak with someone about that. I wanted to discuss it with the king if I can."

The guard says something lowly to the other one, and after a few moments they move to open the door.

"You'll have to speak with one of his advisors," one of the guards says. I move past them, preparing myself to speak with Faine. The windows of the throne room are letting in so much sunlight that I have to resist putting my hand above my eyes. As they adjust to the lighting I see that the advisors are sitting at their thrones, but Gunner's is empty.

"What brings you here?" Faine asks, looking at me sharply. The old man sitting on the left throne remains silent.

"I need to speak with the king about the ship that's supposed to take me home."

"Why, is there something wrong with it?" he asks with sternness and suspicion in his light grey eyes. He doesn't let go of eye contact, and I shift my weight to my other foot.

"Well no, actually it has to do with the scheduling of it," I blurt out before I get a chance to think of a better way to word what I'm trying to say.

"Meaning that you don't want to leave this early in the day?" he asks.

"Yeah, you could say that," I say as confidently as I can sound, trying to think quickly of what else to say. Spies are often looked out for and are imprisoned if suspected.

After a moment of Faine silently studying me he finally speaks. "Since the king made a specific order regarding this he's the only one who can change it, especially since it's one of his personal ships that's being used."

I start to feel bad. The king was even going to the inconvenience of sending me home on one of his ships.

"You'll find him at the shore," Faine continues. "He was wanting to reflect on some things before the mission briefing."

"Thank you," I say, feeling relief wash over me. "Where do I go to get there?"

"One of the guards will take you there." With that a guard steps out from among the others and guides me out of the throne room. I hope this goes well.

CHAPTER 16

I LOOK AT my communicator. I'm late to the ship. Not much I can do about that now. "This is as far as I'll take you," the guard says, stopping at a door facing out towards the back of the island.

I hadn't been paying close attention to where we were going since I was busy thinking about things. "You're not going to be there when I talk to the king?"

He laughs. "The king is well armed. Only a fool would attack him, and they would not live long if they did." The guard leaves, not caring to continue the conversation.

I go out the door and am immediately greeted with bright sunshine and hot weather. I'm reminded by the heat of the sun that my armor is bad for this climate. If I could I think I would change my armor out for a set that doesn't have fur. I start to make my way down the pathway, taking in the scent of pine. I can't help but be reminded of Hayventh, and for a moment I think about how much I would love to be home. Then that feeling of not wanting to go returns. This is it, if I go beyond this point I'm leaving the crossroads and will be choosing a new path. I take in a deep breath and step forward.

In the distance I can see the tips of a mountain range poking through the clouds from the planet below. The pathway I'm on winds down to the edge of the island. As I get closer I'm amazed by what I see.

The land gradually tapers off instead of looking like a rigid cliff. Sand, sea shells, and stones make up the beach surrounding the island. Large clouds roll like waves up to the shore, dissipating into nothing once they crash into it. The wind almost sounds like the ocean, bringing wave after wave to the shore.

Gunner is standing at the edge, looking off into the distance. I make my way carefully to the shore and come to stand by him. I step up to the edge like he is but feel uncomfortable being so close to it.

"So you have decided to stay," he says without even looking at me.

"How did you know that?" I ask, unable to hide the surprise in my voice.

"You don't seem to me like the kind of person who gives up easily," he responds, still looking ahead. A light breeze blows through his aqua hair. He doesn't seem to mind how close he is to the cliff edge. "The crew needs you, whether they know it or not," he adds.

"They do?" I ask. That's hard for me to believe… they got along fine before I came into their lives.

"People need each other more than they realize. There's so much that can be learned from others if time is taken to observe things."

I don't know if I agree. I've always done well by myself. "So it's alright if I stay?" I ask, thinking of the effort that was probably put into the ship being prepared for me to go.

"It would be welcomed by your friends if you do. I already canceled the ship's preparation, but I can order it up again if you change your mind."

I look out at the clouds, watching them rolling in. I sense I'm in for more adventure than I asked for. But what would things be like if I went home? "I'll stay then," I say, making a final decision.

"Your friends will appreciate it."

I spend the next few moments of silence trying to think of what to say next. After all, he's the king, and who am I? "It seems like things are busy here," I say, feeling silly right away. I should've asked about the briefing...

"There is much going on, and a great darkness is on the horizon. We must be prepared for whatever may come."

"How soon is this darkness going to be upon us?" I ask. I don't get the feeling that he's referring to the marauders.

"I don't know, but a storm is coming. And the people..." he pauses, "I must save them and keep them from harm at all costs," he says with weariness in his voice. It seems like he feels a great burden, but unless I know what that darkness is I can't fully understand what that burden is.

"I didn't know things were this bad," I say, now feeling like I can't ask about the briefing just yet. I'll have to wait for another opening in the conversation.

Gunner looks back out towards the waves. "I'm beginning to doubt that my father was right to move us here."

"Is there any way to stop this darkness from coming?" I ask. There must be something that we can do.

"My special force team was working on something important that would have helped. I need to find them soon," he says, looking at me again. "For now the best thing we can do is get the mission started. We'll deal with the rest as it comes." While he said that lightheartedly I can see the seriousness in his eyes. "The mission briefing is about to start. You'll need to go to it now that you're staying," he says, turning his back to the wind and waves.

I turn as well, very much aware that the edge of the shore is right behind me. He walks beside me as we make our way back to the palace. I can't help but still be amazed at how much wealth has been put into it. I heard that Pike III had lots of gold and gemstones, but I hadn't believed it till now. Gunner takes me to a different entrance than the one I came out of. The guards open the doors without hesitation and we head in.

It takes my eyes a bit to re-adjust. After walking down a hallway we make it to a large room with a high ceiling. There are racks of equipment and weapons as far as the eye can see. There are even ships at the end of the room. The crew is standing in the center, with guards positioned nearby. A man is talking to them.

"Amazing isn't it?" Gunner asks. I look and see that he's looking ahead.

"That it is."

"My father went to a lot of work designing it," Gunner says in a tone that's mixed with pride and sorrow.

"I've never seen anything like it," I say, which is the truth. In my opinion it doesn't compare to the throne room or the shore. There is more equipment here than I've ever seen in one place.

"It was one of his favorite rooms. He spent a lot of time trying to design equipment and inventions that would help protect the people. It has more to it than what you can see from here," he says, sounding as if he feels that others don't appreciate it enough.

"Did you design any of the palace rooms with him?" I ask, instantly regretting the question. Nareth passed away only six months ago, leaving everything to Gunner and his brother.

"Most of them," Gunner says with a trace of sorrow in his voice. Now that we're closer to the center of the room I can see that it is ten times larger than what I originally thought it was.

"I've got to go deal with some other things, I'll be back towards the end of the briefing," Gunner says, starting to turn back.

"Alright," I reply, not knowing what else to say. I make my way to the crew, and Fauve spots me right away.

"Franca, you made it!" she says excitedly, ignoring that the man in front of the group is still talking.

"What did I miss?" I ask in a hushed tone, trying to not cause a distraction to the others.

"Nothing yet, we just started!" Fauve says, not quieting her voice at all. Some of the others glance back at us, looking surprised that I'm here. Maylea doesn't look happy to see me, but Lance smiles at me. Maybe Gunner was right.

"Fauve, hush," Roxanne whispers harshly.

Fauve rolls her eyes. "Come on Roxanne, this'll be fun. You're so boring."

"Why didn't it start sooner?" I ask, whispering. It was supposed to start a while ago.

"Will you two shut up? This isn't the time for small talk," Roxanne says.

Fauve grins. "Don't mind her, she's always in a mood."

"Fauve," Roxanne says angrily, turning to glare at her with her hand in a fist. Fauve laughs.

Roxanne grumbles under her breath and turns her focus back to the man. I try to pay attention. If darkness is on its way like Gunner says, we've got a lot of preparation to do. What if a civil war breaks out among our people? It's bad enough that we are fighting so many battles with the marauders. The man is talking about the equipment that we'll be using and how we must be as low key as possible.

"For this mission you'll be spending your time aboard one of our best stealth ships. Since the only type of battle you'll face should be in space we'll focus on the ship's equipment more than your own," he says.

"Sir, we should at least have updated armor and weapons," Roxanne speaks up.

"She's got a point there," we all turn to see Gunner walking up to us. I thought he was going to come at the end of the briefing? "They're to be equipped with the best weaponry and armor that we have," he says in a calm but commanding tone. He has a heavier set of armor on. It has the same coloring and design as the guard's armor, except that the emblem is in silver instead of white. He doesn't have his crown on. Under his arm he holds a helmet. Two guards stand beside him, prepared for anything.

"Yes sir," the man says without question. "This way then," he continues, walking towards some of the equipment racks. We follow him to the armor section. Next to this section is a large rack of add-ons that you can choose from depending on what your skill set is. "On your communicator you will see what armor you're supposed to wear. Once you get it you can then choose whichever add-ons will best suit your needs," the man states.

Everyone starts picking out armor sets. I look at my communicator, and as I expected it's not showing anything. "My communicator's not showing anything," I say to him.

He looks at me with disdain. "Weren't you paying attention at the beginning? You were supposed to get the comm. link data."

"I was late to the briefing, so I didn't hear the first part." I could've said more, but I didn't feel like this was the appropriate time to go into a longer conversation. Fauve forgot to mention that this is what I missed by being late... it must not have been important to her.

"Try to be more punctual next time," he says. "Let's see, there is another name on the team list. Your name is Franca?"

"Yeah."

"So you're the mechanic," he says to himself while he types something into his communicator.

A notice comes up on mine showing me what armor I should pick up. I walk over to the rack, and take an armor set that's not as heavy duty as Gunner's, but not as light as what a scout would wear. I look and see that there is an add-on kit for mechanics. I pick it up and look at it. It comes with a personal force field bubble for my armor, and it also has an add-on for fall resistance. That's good to have, I might not ever get injured from falls again. My leg is still sensitive from that fall I took.

The armor is maroon and dark grey in color with a circular symbol on the back that glows green. The shoulders and other parts of it are highlighted with green lighting. A slot on one arm was made for my communicator to fit in. It's a big difference from my fur armor, but I'm glad for the change. There's a matching helmet sits on the rack.

It has an add-on that combines x-ray vision with detection software that highlights parts that need repairing. This will come in handy. I notice that night vision isn't included... hopefully I won't need that. Once everyone gets their equipment we're taken over to the gun racks. Roxanne takes a sniper rifle, Fauve takes a pistol, and Lance takes a machine gun.

I look at each gun and decide to go with a lightweight rifle since that's what I'm most familiar with. I'm glad to finally have a weapon again. I walk over to Gunner, who is waiting for us to finish picking out our equipment.

"All right everyone, it's time to get aboard the ship," the man who's been instructing us calls out. Gunner leads the way to the back of the room where the ships are. They are behind a transparent wall. The room behind it is actually a hangar. We go through the airlocked doors as he leads us to a ship that looks like a small cargo ship.

"We're going to be riding in this?" Roxanne asks with disapproval.

"Don't let looks deceive you," Gunner says. "It has some of the finest armor and weaponry. This is a stealth ship."

We go ahead and board it, looking around. Instead of areas for cargo storage there's a bunk area and a small main area. The ship was designed in a way that makes it not as convenient for everyday living as what we're used to. In the bunk area I notice that the bottom bunks are medbeds, like our other ship had. I make my way to the control room to find Alex and Gunner are already there.

"This'll be easy to fly," Alex says confidently.

Gunner nods. "We'll see how you do with it before trying a larger ship. This one suits our mission best anyway."

"Does this mean I won't be a co-pilot this time?" Fauve asks as Gunner sits in the co-pilot seat.

Gunner turns to look at her. "Not this time, but you can watch what I'm doing if you like."

"Wait, you're coming too?" I ask. I didn't expect him to come with us... shouldn't he be taking care of other things?

Gunner nods. "I am. Finding the special force team is crucial, and you may end up needing further instruction... we are in troubled times." For a moment Gunner reminds me of the stories I've heard about his father. His father was always thinking of the people and would often do things personally for them. He always believed that was the best way to rule.

Alex prepares the ship for launch. I head back to the main area, and pull Blair to the side.

"Blair, what happened in the throne room when I wasn't there?" I ask.

"Oh that's right, you weren't there for that. Now that you're a part of the special force team you are supposed to know about what we discussed. In the throne room the scout that was waiting to talk to Gunner blurted out that the storms on Rythor are getting worse, and that it's believed that Ty is responsible for it. It seems that he has decided to not work with Gunner anymore, and has been ruling Rythor on his own. Since we know too much, Gunner has decided that we're his new special force team, and that we will be helping in searching for the old one."

I'm surprised by this news. Ty was the head of our army, our best strategist. He always worked with Gunner and his father in ruling our star system. And now he's taken over Rythor? "What's Gunner going to do about his brother?" I ask.

"We don't know yet. It seems like this special force team has something to do with it."

I watch as we leave the palace behind. In some ways I wish I could've stayed and rested there for longer. The island looks so tranquil floating among the clouds. I for one would prefer to spend more time on land. I wonder if Bayu ever gets sick of being on a ship all the time?

I guess some people like spending all their time in space. Before I know it I'm looking out at the stars again. We pass Yenath by the end of the day and head onward towards Durath.

"So where exactly was the special force team last seen?" Lance asks Gunner.

"They were supposed to go to the asteroid field near Durath."

Lance furrows his brows. "Why would you want them to go there? There's nothing to see in an asteroid field unless you're there to mine metal."

"They were there on business that I'm not sure I'm ready for you to know yet."

Lance looks at him with a hint of suspicion in his eyes. It seems that Lance is slow to trust anyone. At night we all go to the bunks except for Alex and Gunner. They have a bunk in the control room. I take the bunk below Raya. I can see Roxanne on the bottom bunk across from me. Memories from before make me glad that I'm not over there.

Roxanne is staring straight up at the top bunk. A tear goes down her face. She's been through more than what she lets on, but I already know she'd attack me if I ask her questions. Soon I find myself drifting off to sleep.

I squint at the bright sunlight as the familiar sounds of the jungle greet me. I look to see that I'm surrounded by three tents and a campfire.

"This must be it!" Jalyn says excitedly. She's standing at a table that has a big map and a journal setting on it.

"I can't believe we've made it this far," I hear myself say as I walk over to her, taking a look at the map. This does look like a location that matches it.

She turns and smiles at me. "Everything's going to be so much better after this!"

Greyson laughs, shaking his head. "We haven't been in the ruins yet Jalyn. We've yet to discover if we've actually found it."

Jalyn rolls her eyes. "Whatever. All I know is that we're closer than we've ever been."

I start to say something and she looks at me, but I can't hear myself speaking. Everything around me gets blurry, and when things get clear again I find that I'm somewhere else.

"Hmm, it should be this way," Jalyn says. I look to see that she's way ahead of me, standing under some torch light with the map. Many torches are mounted to the walls of the ancient hallway, but only a couple near Jalyn have been lit.

"Franca, you coming?" Greyson calls back to me.

"Yeah, I'm coming," I say, shouldering my pack and quickening my pace. I shiver from the cold and pull my coat closer to me. It's been getting colder the further we travel into the ruins. While Jalyn leads the way Greyson stays behind to blow out the torches as we go. We don't want that man to catch on to where we are. He'd be here in an instant if he knew. The hallway opens to a large room.

"This is amazing!" Jalyn exclaims, taking the last lit torch off the wall. Four large stone columns support the ceiling, and the walls are lined with cracked stone bookshelves. She pushes in a stone on one of the rounded columns. A part of the floor moves, and a chest comes up out of the ground. She walks up and examines it carefully. Greyson and I come up beside her.

"I doubt we'll find the key to that," Greyson says.

"I know, but I don't want to break the lock," she responds.

"If you don't we'll never know if it's in there."

She hesitates, never being one for damaging historical relics. I wouldn't be either, but it feels like we're in an urgent situation. Greyson gets out a lock cutter and breaks the lock. Jalyn hands the torch to Greyson and opens the chest.

The disappointment on her face tells me we have yet to find what we're looking for. "Back to square one," she says, looking discouraged.

"We'll find it, we just need a little more time," I hear myself say.

She smiles at me and says something in response, but I can't hear what she says. Things get blurry again, and everything fades away.

CHAPTER 17

THE MORNING COMES and we get ready for another day. I discover that everyone has already left the room but me. I wonder what Jalyn was looking for? I know these dreams mean something, but I'm not sure what. Maybe I'm supposed to be looking for something? I try to shake the dream off... I've got a long day ahead of me. As I'm about to leave something catches my eye. I walk over to Fauve's bunk and look under it. I find gold bars and ancient artifacts that I had seen once on our old ship. So she's the one who has been collecting those things?

I'll have to ask her about that sometime. I push the gold further under the bed so it doesn't glint in the light like it was before leaving the room. As I'm walking through the main area I notice Fauve is looking out the window at an angle so that she can see behind the ship. She's biting her lip.

"Hey Fauve, everything okay?" I ask, walking up to her. She jumps, then smiles.

"I'm fine Franca, just making sure we're not being chased down by marauders again!" she lets out a fake laugh, "I doubt they will though. Like they'd want to mess with us again after what Bayu did."

"You sure you're alright?" I ask, pressing. I don't usually do that, but it does seem like something's wrong.

"Yes I'm fine…" she says, not sounding convincing enough for me to let her off the hook. "Okay, I guess I'm not." She looks around to make sure there's no one else around before continuing. "I'm being hunted down."

"Hunted down?"

"Shh, not so loud," she says in a hushed tone. "I'm living two lives Franca. One as a co-pilot on a military ship and the other as a treasure hunter." She looks around again before continuing. "I have an artifact that some men are looking for. They've been tracking me since Rythor, but I think I lost their trail once we got to Pike III."

"How long have you been pulling this off? Do any of the others know?"

"No one knows. I thought these men would give up, but now I'm getting worried. They're like marauders."

"Well, let's hope they lost your trail. Do you think they would attack us?"

"No. Promise you won't tell anyone?" she asks with a pleading look on her face.

"As long as they don't actually attack us I don't see any need to."

"Thank you Franca."

I don't know what to do anyway. It doesn't feel like my place to tell anyone about it. It's Fauve's responsibility unless we end up in danger. She resumes looking out the window and I decide to go on to the control room.

"Now you see that area over there?" Gunner asks, pointing to a spot that's slightly to the left.

"I don't see anything," Alex says with frustration.

"It's okay, keep looking," Gunner says, slowing our ship to a stop.

Alex is silent for a few moments before speaking. "Oh I see it now, I can barely make it out." he pauses. "Isn't that one over there as well?" he asks pointing straight ahead.

"Yes, that's also one. Now avoid those," Gunner says, getting the ship up to speed again.

"Do you know why those distorted spots are here?" I ask.

"We don't know that yet, but I've sent out scientists to investigate it," Gunner says.

"It seems like it's only out near Durath and Yenath," Lance observes.

Gunner nods. "There are some between Yenath and Pike III as well, but that's as far as it goes. Whatever's causing it is somewhere around those three planets."

"I wonder if Bayu's figured out what it is," I say.

"Who's Bayu?" Gunner asks, looking at me with curiosity in his eyes. Lance starts talking with Alex. The ship shakes a little, but not as bad as it was earlier. Gunner looks at Alex. "That one was much better," he says. He turns his attention back to me, waiting for a response.

"Bayu is a merchant we got help from when we were stranded in space," I say.

"There are many of those merchants around here, especially around Pike III. They can't all be trusted though so I'd watch out with them." He's right, though it doesn't seem like Bayu's out to cheat anyone.

"We made it to Durath!" Lance exclaims. I look and see that we're close to being in it's orbit.

"Alright we need to turn to the south," Gunner says. Alex nods and turns the ship. I watch for the asteroid field on our radar system. It's late into the night when I can finally make out the asteroids up ahead. A few are moving gently past others that stand silently in the light of the stars. Gunner directs Alex on where to go, and soon we are surrounded by them. The ship is equipped with a deflection field, so we don't have to worry about them crashing into us. I wish that would work on the distortion. From what I've seen, nothing can move those spots. It's as if they are a part of space.

"Hmm, this doesn't look right," Lance says, looking at the radar system. As we're getting farther away from the edge of the field the asteroids are all missing pieces, and some have been cut in half. "Wasn't there a law against mining this particular field?" he asks.

"There was one put into place so that we would have an emergency supply of metals we could mine. The field wasn't like this a week ago," Gunner says. He instructs Alex to continue until we get to the center of the field. Even with a ship this fast it will take some time to get there. "If anyone sees even a part of a ship tell me immediately." His shoulders tense as his gaze focuses on asteroids ahead. I don't get a good feeling about this. We spend the rest of the day searching through the asteroid field and find nothing. There's no trace of the special force team.

"So what do we do now?" Lance asks.

"We'll have to head back to the palace and decide our next move... the mining here is a concern," Gunner says.

Alex turns the ship to head back to Pike III. I keep an eye on the radar system. I want to see if all of the asteroids have been mined in this area, or if it's only some of them. Nothing shows up, and after awhile I decide to head back to the main area. Fauve is sitting at one of the windows with a concerned look on her face. I go over to see what she's looking at.

At first I don't see anything, but as I look farther off in space I notice a few black ships that are barely visible in the distance. "Do you see those Fauve?" I ask, turning to her.

"Yeah... those are the people who have been following me." The ships turn away and leave.

"We need to tell the others about this."

Fauve looks down. "Yeah, you're right. I'll tell them when the time is right." But when will the time be right? In my opinion it's now or never. I watch the asteroids go by. Most of them are missing pieces. I wonder why this is so important to Gunner?

Raya comes into the main area, sitting in a nearby seat dejectedly. "I can't do any work here. How long are we goin' to be stuck on this ship?"

"Probably the same amount of time it took us to get here. What work needs to get done so soon?" I ask.

"None of it really... it's just that I'm bored. There's nothin' to do."

"Yeah I hear you there," I say. Things have been pretty slow today. It will take us two days to get back to Pike III. The ship starts rocking again. It seems like there's distortion even in the asteroid field. Hours pass without much changing. I spend my time both in the main area and in the control room. We finally make it out of the asteroid field, and turn in the direction of Pike III.

When it gets later in the day we stop for the night. Usually a ship would be put on auto pilot, but the distortion tends to get ships off track. In the morning we resume our journey and make it to Pike III the next day. Instead of following the other ships to the hangar we continue above the clouds until we get to the island.

Once we land in the hangar Gunner immediately leaves us to take care of business. We make it to our rooms, and everyone starts doing their own thing. I make my way to the living area to see what everyone's up to. Roxanne is sitting in one of the chairs, talking to Maylea while looking out the window.

Maylea is sitting across from her, watching and listening. "When do you think it'll all end?" she asks.

Roxanne leans back in her chair, looking more tired than how I usually see her. Maybe she hides it more when I'm around. "I don't know. It feels like it'll never end," she says, making eye contact with me. Her shoulders tense, and she sits up straighter. Called it.

Maylea turns to look at me, slightly narrowing her eyes. "If you're looking for the others they've gone to the armory to do some training. An order came through on our communicators to train if we wanted."

"I saw that. Why aren't you two training?"

"Because I've been fighting for years and don't need it," Roxanne says icily.

By the way they're looking at me it's clear I've interrupted their conversation for longer than they wanted me to. I was just asking out of curiosity. "I'll be on my way then," I say, trying to defuse the situation. I turn to go, and as I get to the door I can hear them talking again.

Soon I find out I don't recall where the armory is. I head to many rooms, but almost all of the ones I come by are either other living areas or are locked. While I can't see any guards I feel as though I'm being watched. I could go back to Maylea and Roxanne, but I don't feel like it. I continue on, wondering if I got turned around at some point.

The guards are most likely watching my every move from surveillance. They're probably wondering what I'm doing. I start to feel a little frustrated but keep checking different doors. Soon I come to a stop, finding myself standing in front of the doors to the throne room. I'm about to turn away from the doors when I notice that one of them is cracked open. Beyond the door I can hear people talking.

"Sir," someone says out of breath. It sounds like the scout that was there the first time we met the king. "I have a message—"

"Go on," Gunner says.

After catching her breath she responds. "The people of Rythor are feeling oppressed. They're crying out," she pauses again to catch her breath. "Something's gone terribly wrong with the weather there... it's just storm after storm... Ty isn't doing anything about it, and it's getting worse the longer he's been there."

"This can't be good," Faine says. "Something bad is happening there, and it's your brother's doing. You're going to have to face him soon."

"If we let him be things will probably smooth out over time. Why cause more strife?" Arlan argues.

"I'm afraid your son is right Arlan," Gunner says. "We can't let the people suffer no matter how much my brother's relationship means to me."

"I know you don't want to face him, but you should start training again in case you have to fight him," Faine says.

"There must be some way we can work things out with him," Arlan says.

"Father, the only way Ty will work with us is if he takes Gunner's place as king. That was against Nareth's wishes and I think he was right. Ty is too violent and aggressive to be a good ruler," Faine says.

Another man I don't recognize speaks up. "And what of the special force team? What's your next move on that?"

"The only way to stop Ty is to get frosthur. I don't know what happened to the special force team, so I'll have to send out the new one to try to mine some," Gunner says.

"We don't have any other miners who are experienced enough to mine it. Radek was the only one who knew the best way to do it without wasting any, and now we've lost him with that team," the man complains in an agitated tone.

"Maybe someone on your new team would know? You don't know much about them," Arlan says.

Faine scoffs. "They seem like a rag-tag group to me. I doubt they are skilled enough for it."

"You'd be surprised at what people can do Faine," Gunner says. "People have a lot more potential and grit when they believe in themselves."

"Well I guess they might know something…"

"I'll be meeting with them anyway. If they know how to do it I'll be sending them out right away."

"Are you going to leave with them again? We need you here," Arlan says.

"All that's going on right now is fighting with marauders. The army can handle that. You and Faine shouldn't have trouble managing the other regular tasks. I have my communicator in case a ruling needs to be made."

"But why go with them? What if something happens to this team too? We would be doomed to Ty's rule if you died," Faine says.

"I know that Faine, but I get a sense that I will be needed. I can't shake it."

"Alright, if you think that's what's best we will support you on it."

"Thank you. I've got to get going. Time is not on our side."

Once I hear that I quickly back away from the door. I don't want to be caught listening in. I'm surprised no one noticed that I was there. Why wasn't the door guarded? I decide to head back to our living area. I quicken my pace. He'll be on his way there too, and I don't want him to see me. I make it back and find that Maylea and Roxanne are still talking. Lance and Blair are there too, talking and laughing about something.

"Franca, where were you? Maylea was telling me you were going to be at the armory, but I didn't see you there," Lance says.

"Oh, yeah I got a little lost and couldn't find it," I say, not wanting to mention that I was listening in on Gunner's meeting.

Roxanne scoffs. "Don't you pay attention to your surroundings?"

I feel my shoulders tense. "Of course I do, we've just had so much going on..."

Roxanne shakes her head and continues to talk to Maylea. Before anyone can say anything else Gunner comes through the door with guards on either side of him. He takes a quick moment to look around. "It looks like most of you are here, who's missing? It's time for another mission briefing."

"Alex and Fauve are still training. I'm not sure where Raya is, but if there's a forge here that's the first place I'd look," Blair says.

"She works with metal?"

"She spends most of her time at the forge," I say. I know she could help with that metal Gunner was talking about. I don't recognize frosthur, but maybe it's a different name for a metal I already know of.

"I will ask her about that then." Gunner says, typing something into his communicator. "I've sent orders for the three of them to come here. In the meantime we'll start to discuss your next briefing."

Blair pulls up a seat. Lance continues to stand and observes Gunner with a watchful gaze.

"As Franca already knows, we'll be on a mission to mine a metal called frosthur."

I look up in surprise. The others look surprised as well. "Franca was part of a meeting?" Roxanne asks barely hiding the envy in her tone.

"You could say that."

I feel so embarrassed. I didn't think anyone saw me, but Gunner knew I was there the whole time.

"How is frosthur different from other metals?" Blair asks.

"It's a metal that is incredibly strong against heat. It's too cold to hold without gloves, and it takes a special method to shape it.

From what we've seen it can cut through any other metal we've tried. My sword is the first weapon we've made from it," Gunner says, pulling his blade out from its sheath with his left hand. The handle is blue and a white light shines along the silver colored blade.

"Will we get weapons made from it?" Roxanne asks, sounding impressed.

Gunner looks at her warily. "I'm not sure if any of you are capable of using one yet. This blade takes skill to wield."

"I've had years of training with blades."

"Even so the weapons made from this are extremely dangerous."

"Why is the sword glowing with a white light?" Lance asks.

"I can't tell you that yet, but maybe another time." Gunner says.

Alex, Fauve, and Raya come into the room. "We tried to get here as soon as we could Sir," Alex says.

"The briefing's just started," Gunner says.

Raya walks over to Gunner, looking at the blade as she puts some gloves on. "Whoa, I haven't seen anythin' like this since my grandmother taught me to work with frosthur when I was in my teens."

Gunner looks at her with surprise. "You've worked with frosthur?" he asks, handing her the blade.

Raya looks at it with excitement. "Oh yeah, I worked with it for three years under my grandmother when she was trainin' me to work with metal. It's old knowledge that's been passed down from generation to generation in our family... she believed we were the last to know of frosthur and how to work with it."

"As time is passing it is getting more and more important that we learn how to work with this metal. Our mission is to mine as much of it as we can from the asteroid field, then bring it back here," Gunner says, taking the blade back.

"But wasn't most of it already gone?" Lance asks.

"If there's any left we need it. Even if there's hardly any," Gunner replies. He turns and his guards follow him. We go with him, curious to see where this next mission will lead us.

CHAPTER 18

GUNNER TAKES US to the hanger but stops us in front of a bigger ship this time. I notice that he doesn't have his crown on.

"Won't we be easier to notice with this one?" Lance asks.

"We may, but we need a bigger ship for the mining equipment and for cargo. We'll have to take our chances this time," Gunner says. And it looks like we will be. We get in, and I notice right away that this ship is much higher tech than what we had before. I put on my helmet to use the x-ray vision to check the ship's condition. I don't see anything being highlighted in red, and the information that's showing up on the visor tells me that the ship is ready to launch. Everything is good to go. Blair helps Raya bring some crates aboard the ship, then checks the supplies that are already there.

"We've got way more supplies than we need! Why so much?" Blair asks.

"You never know what might happen. It's best to be prepared," Alex says.

"That's right, we never know what we might need out there," Gunner says with a nod. "We need all the luck we can get," I hear him quietly say under his breath.

Alex and Gunner head to the control room. Fauve and I follow at a slower pace, taking our time to go through the main area. I look over and see that she is looking at her communicator and frowning.

"Is everything okay?" I ask.

"Yeah it's just, well…" she says, hesitating before going on. "It's my brother Radek. I haven't heard from him in a long time now. He always got back to me, but I'm worried something's happened to him, being in the army and all. I don't even know for sure what he does."

"I'm sure you'll hear from him soon, being in the army can make it difficult to respond to people sometimes."

"Thanks Franca," she says, smiling.

"Hey Fauve, you coming?" Alex calls.

"Yeah, coming!" she calls back. She looks at me, "Gotta go." With that she runs off. I continue walking until I get to some of the windows. We're traveling above the clouds, returning back to the stars. Radek… where have I heard that name before? It sounds familiar. I watch the clouds pass by, and after a moment it comes to me. That man at the meeting was talking about him being a part of the lost special force team… should I tell Fauve about that?

If she knows she will probably worry more, but it feels like she also has a right to know. I make my way to the control room. This one has three seats. Alex and Fauve are sitting on either side of Gunner and he's teaching them things about piloting. I guess I'll have to tell Fauve later.

None of them heard me come in so I quietly leave and let them be. As I make my way through the ship I realize that this one has some serious upgrades compared to what we had before. There's a full medbay, and each crew member has their own room. There's no prison on this ship.

There's a room where the mining equipment pulls ore into the ship. Right next to it is an empty room. Raya is standing in the middle of it reading a book. To the side of her are some crates filled with armor pieces and other things. She looks to be deeply focused on the book. I can't fully see her face because her pink hair is in the way. I've sometimes wondered what it would be like to be born with colored hair like that.

Raya looks up from her book and smiles at me. "Hey Franca, didn't see ya there."

"Yeah I just got here. Reading up on that metal Gunner was talking about?" I ask, surprised to see a book.

"This is an old book my grandmother gave me. Thought this would be a good time to refresh my memory on it."

I look over at the crates. "So you'll be setting up shop here?"

"Yeah, I'll be settin' everythin' up. I figure we might be on this ship longer than we expect, and would like to get some of my other work done."

The ship starts rocking, and I instinctively think there's something wrong with the ship. I put on my helmet and see that everything's fine. "Looks like we're running into more distortion," I say, taking off the helmet.

"Sometimes I think Alex doesn't pay enough attention to that," Raya says.

"Well, actually he has a hard time seeing it. You have to look for areas ahead of you that look blurred or stretched."

"Oh well if it's like that then no wonder we keep hittin' 'em. I wonder if the captain of that merchant ship would've been a help."

"Maybe he would've, but Bayu seems busy with his own life."

"Oh right that was his name. I forgot."

After a bit I head over to the generators. I'm relieved to find that good safety measures have been put in place. I spend the rest of the day in the control room. While I don't like flying ships myself I like to learn what I can in case I ever have to fly. The next day I go about the ship, seeing if anyone needs anything. The first room I make my way to is the cargo bay. When I get there I find that Blair is entering information into a computer system. "Checking inventory?" I ask.

"Yeah, everything looks to be in order for the next two years. I still think that's too much for a mission like this."

"It probably is, but you never know what might happen."

Blair nods. Seeing that my help isn't needed here I decide to make my way to the control room and see what's happening. On my way past the medbay I stop for a moment.

I can hear Fauve talking on her communicator. "I think I'm alright, but I'm not sure. For all I know they could still be out there looking for me." She looks at the floor, "oh who am I kidding? They're probably right on my tail. And I haven't told the others yet... I was hoping this issue would resolve itself..." Yep, she's still having trouble. That's going to bite us in the end. "Welp, I gotta go, I'll fill you in more later."

I leave before she ends the call. I need to stop listening in on conversations. I make my way to the control room. I find that everyone else is already there discussing what to do next now that we're in the asteroid field again. This ship is much faster than the other one.

"So, we're gonna start minin'?" Raya asks.

"Not yet. From what I'm seeing it's already been mined here," Gunner says.

"So the small amount that was left is gone?" Lance asks.

"Yes, someone knew it was there and got it," Gunner says.

"I thought we were the only ones who knew about it," Alex says.

"That's what we believed until I saw the damage last time. We might find traces of who was here mining it, so this may not be a total loss."

"I say we track them down and fight," Roxanne says.

"While fighting is sometimes necessary, it's not always the right option. We still need to figure out who it is so we know if they're on my brother's side or not." After that we spend time monitoring the radar system. If we see anything out of the ordinary we have to report it right away.

"What does frosthur look like?" Fauve asks, joining us.

"It has a bluish silver color to it," Gunner replies. I keep looking out. So far I don't see anything. Maylea is standing next to me but seems distracted looking at her communicator. I feel like this isn't the time to be doing that. I refocus my attention on the radar system, watching as the asteroids pass our ship.

In the midst of them a floating piece of metal on the radar catches my eye. "I see some metal to our left," I say.

Gunner immediately comes over to me. "Where is it?"

I point to the area, though it's harder to see the metal now because some asteroids have moved closer to it.

"Alex, turn to your left and get ready to pick up some metal."

"Got it," Alex responds. The ship turns, and as we pass the metal our ship's mining equipment activates, pulling it into the room the equipment is in. We all head through the airlocked door to the room and take a look at the piece of metal that's lying on the floor.

"This appears to be from some mining equipment," Gunner says.

I crouch and get a closer look at it. There's something written on it, but most of the words are covered in soot. I get out a rag and gently wipe the soot away. What's written there surprises me.

"Well, what does it say Franca?" Blair asks.

"It says 'The Burning Rift' on it," I say.

"That sounds familiar," Lance says.

Roxanne rolls her eyes. "Not again!"

"So you guys know who this belongs to?" Gunner asks.

"The Burning Rift is Bayu's ship," I say, standing up. "He's the merchant I mentioned earlier."

"That can't be good," Gunner says.

"Why not?" Maylea asks. "From what I saw he seemed peaceful enough."

"It's not the merchant I'm worried about, it's who he's selling to."

"He does have a point there," Lance says.

"Our next goal is to find this merchant. Bayu was his name you say?" Gunner asks, turning to me.

"Yeah, his name is Bayu. I'm not sure where he went though... he didn't say where he would be going next. Alex might still have his comm. link data saved."

"We might as well get on with it then," Gunner says. We head over to Alex and ask him to check his communicator.

"Looks like I can still get in contact with him," Alex says.

"Good, we'll need to meet up with him somewhere," Gunner says.

"I'll let you know when he responds to what I said."

A day passes before we hear anything from Bayu. While we were waiting we decided to stay near Durath, away from the asteroid field. Gunner doesn't want his brother to find out that we were there and doesn't want to draw any attention to us. From time to time Fauve checks the radar system and looks out of the windows to see if anyone's following us.

"Gotten anything from Bayu yet?" Lance asks.

"Nope, not yet... I wonder if he's ignoring us," Alex says.

"Well with our supplies we can sit out here for two years," Blair says jokingly.

"Two years? The supplies stored on the ship are only for a year," Gunner says.

"Blair knows his stuff with supplies. He can make two weeks' worth last a month," Alex says.

Gunner looks over at Blair. "Where did you learn to do that?"

"I had to work many times with limited resources, couldn't afford more and had to make do with what I had," Blair says.

Alex's communicator buzzes. He looks at the holographic screen. "Bayu just responded."

"What did he say?" Gunner asks.

"He said, 'I'm on the hunt for some treasure right now, unless it's worth my time I can't come to meet you.'" Alex pauses. "Should we ask him about the frosthur instead?"

"We can't talk about it that freely. We need to keep it as low-key as we can. I need to make sure he keeps quiet about it."

"What do you want me to say then?"

After a moment of silence Gunner speaks. "Tell him we have a business deal that will be more worthwhile than what he's currently doing."

Alex starts typing. Once he finishes we wait. It takes some time for Bayu to respond, but he finally does.

"What did he say this time?" Gunner asks.

"He says he's not convinced unless he knows more details."

"Tell him he'll be paid extra for his time."

Bayu responds right away. "He said 'I'll meet up with you, but it better be worthwhile, or you'll be paying for compensation. Where do you want to meet?'"

"Send him our current coordinates. We'll meet him right here."

Alex starts typing again. His communicator immediately buzzes. Alex looks up at us. "He says he's on the other side of the system and that we need to meet him halfway."

"Tell him it'll be worthwhile, and that this is important. I need us to not stray too far from Pike III if possible."

Alex types again and gets another response back. "He said, 'yeah right. Meet me between Rythor and Faratha IV or forget it.'"

"Alright, we'll meet him there. I don't have time to be arguing with a merchant." We spend the next day traveling to Faratha IV. This area of space doesn't have any distortion, so things go a lot smoother.

"Hey Franca, isn't that The Burning Rift?" Raya asks, looking at something on the radar system.

I move towards her to look, and a large ship can be seen on our scanners that's shaped exactly like The Burning Rift. "Yep, that's it," I say. I feel our ship starting to turn to go towards it. After fifteen minutes a carrier ship leaves The Burning Rift and comes over to our ship. Gunner, Alex, Raya, Lance, and I go there to meet it.

The door to our ship opens, and Bayu strides through. He takes one look at us and shakes his head. "The world must be doing bad if the king himself has decided to ride with you." He smirks. "I thought you were lying before. I just couldn't believe it."

I look over at Gunner to see his reaction. I guess Alex mentioned who Gunner was in an attempt to convince Bayu to come. Gunner looks annoyed. "I do as I please. Who I decide to travel with is no concern of yours," he says evenly.

"Am I the only one who sees this as a hazard?" Bayu mutters to himself.

"We get by just fine," Lance says sternly.

"Whatever makes you feel better I guess," Bayu says, not even looking over at Lance. We make our way to the main area to talk.

We all take a seat, and I notice that Fauve and Maylea don't come to join us. Roxanne comes but stays standing with her arms crossed, leaning against a nearby wall.

"So," Bayu says, taking a seat once everyone else has been seated. "No guards, no other ships?" he asks, gesturing with his hands as he talks. "That doesn't seem like a good idea for a king."

"I can defend myself far better than most realize," Gunner says shortly.

Bayu looks intensely at him like he's studying him. "And so can I, but I always have some of my crew nearby. Look, I've got other places to be, can we get on with this 'business deal' as you call it?" he asks, sounding like he's tired of this conversation.

"Fair enough," Gunner says.

"Finally," Bayu grumbles.

Gunner gets right to the point. "We're looking for a certain metal called frosthur. The asteroid field near Durath has been stripped of it, and we found a piece of metal with your ship's name on it. We're willing to buy it from you for a fair price."

Bayu leans back in his seat, crossing his legs. "Ah so you're following that craze. It's a high selling item right now... But I could part with it if your offer's good enough."

Gunner looks at him like he's sizing him up. "I'll give you a hundred and fifty thousand silver credits for it."

"I could easily get two hundred thousand for what I got on me from my current buyer," Bayu says indifferently.

"I'll give you a hundred and eighty thousand silver credits," Gunner says firmly.

"My price is two hundred thousand, no less. If you don't have it I'll be charging you for compensation for making me leave my current business for this empty meeting," Bayu says just as firmly. While he seems like he's being disagreeable he has a casual, at ease expression in his eyes. At moments it almost looks like there's laughter in them.

"Fine, if that's your price I'll pay it," Gunner says after a moment.

"It's a done deal. My crew will send it to the hangar bay immediately." He starts to get up but Gunner motions for him to stay seated.

"What is it now? I have a ship to run."

"I want to know who else is buying this."

Bayu leans back in his seat again, crossing his arms. "Information costs a bit too. But for the right price..."

"Why would you charge me for that?"

"Because you could try to compete with me in selling it."

"What do you want for it then?" Gunner asks in a challenging tone.

"Let's see... thirty thousand silver credits should do it."

"Alright, you have a deal," Gunner says. The slight relief in his tone tells me that he was expecting the price to be way higher.

Roxanne scoffs. "Merchants," she says disdainfully.

Bayu grins at her. "The man who's buying it is named Thatcher. Miners are currently mining the other asteroid field for it because he's paying such a high price for the stuff. Don't know why it's valued so highly by him."

"Can you buy it from the other merchants and miners?" Gunner asks.

"I could," Bayu says in a careful tone. "But it would cost me a high price to do that. I would have to outbid Thatcher."

"If you can get any I'll make it worth your while," Gunner says. "And I'll pay an extra twenty thousand silver credits per load if you keep it quiet that I'm the one buying from you."

Bayu narrows his eyes. "Why the secrecy? I don't want to be involved in drama. Me and my crew are here to sell things."

"I want to keep it quiet from the public," Gunner says casually.

"Fair enough," Bayu says sounding agreeable for the first time since he came aboard our ship. "Alright it's a deal," Bayu says, standing up.

Gunner, Lance, and I also stand up. Bayu shakes Gunner's hand, and then we all make our way back to the airlocked exit of our ship.

CHAPTER 19

BAYU STOPS AT the door of our ship. He turns and looks at Gunner. "My crew is already on its way with some of the frosthur."

"Some of it?" Lance questions.

"Yes some of it. The rest will be delivered on the second load. Our carrier ships are all down besides two and my mechanics are busy working on other projects," he says.

"I could fix them," I say.

Gunner looks at me in surprise. I shrug. If he's going to get more for us we don't want that to slow him down. It seems like it's pretty important to Gunner that we get it.

"You're still here working with this lot?" Bayu says, sounding surprised. Did he not notice me there before?

"Yeah I still work here, it's not that bad."

The expression in his blue eyes shifts from surprise to concern. "You'd still be much better off with us." He continues on. "If you want to look at the carriers you can but know that I'm not liable for anything."

"That's fine with me, I'll take a look at them." They can't be that bad.

"Oh, and I'm not sure if you actually have time to work on them, as me and my crew will be leaving right after we deliver this."

"I'll keep that in mind," I say. I've fixed things quickly in the past; I shouldn't have trouble with this.

"Alright, get on the carrier ship and we'll take you aboard," he says, turning to give orders to the crewmate that came with him.

"Make sure that you watch when it's time to go, we still need you here," Gunner says.

"I've been on his ship before. I should know when they're leaving," I say confidently.

"Alright then," Gunner says, heading back to the control room.

"You coming Franca? I don't have all day," Bayu calls from the carrier ship.

"Yeah, I'm coming," I say, quickening my pace. I get aboard the carrier ship and it starts to lift off the ground before the door is even shut. It didn't seem like Bayu was in a rush, but then again he's always focused on getting straight to business.

Right away Bayu's communicator starts making a sound. He taps his earpiece, picking up. "Hello? Yeah we'll be carrying out the deal in a few days' time." After a pause he rolls his eyes. "If anything I'm the one concerned if you'll pull through on your end of the bargain. Don't be worrying about us." With that he abruptly disconnects the call.

"What was that about?" his crewmate asks.

"Eh, it's just Lewis making sure I follow through on our deal."

"I forgot about that. When will that deal be finished? I hope we never make another one with him again," the crewmate says with a scowl.

"We'll be done with him soon enough. With everything going as it is I'll be richer than him in no time." The carrier ship lands in the hangar of The Burning Rift, and Bayu shows me the carriers in the adjacent hangar. "Now if anything goes wrong that's not my problem."

"I know that, I'll be fine," I say, getting tired of hearing him talk about not wanting to be held responsible for me.

"When you get done I'll pay you for whatever you fixed," Bayu says, pausing as if he's thinking of saying something else before abruptly turning and leaving.

I look around. There are about thirty carrier ships, and I'm the only one here. I put on my helmet so I can see what needs fixing. Every ship here has at least one part that is showing red, and many that are yellow.

It would take a couple weeks to fix everything, even if I worked fast. I won't be here long enough and will have to settle with fixing one or two. I browse the hangar looking for some easy ones to fix. I spot one that only needs a new control panel inside, so I decide to work with that one first.

I go over to the hangar's repair station. Most big ships have them. You can order a part and if a spare is already in storage it'll be teleported to you. I walk up to the computer system and a holographic screen pops up. I scroll through the parts in storage and find the one I need. I select it and wait. Soon it comes through a slot in the wall, falling onto a padded tray with a soft thud. I glance out the window, checking to see that our ship is still there. It is, so I resume my work.

I pick up the control panel and examine it. The part looks to be in perfect condition. When I first started to repair things I never paid attention to this, thinking I didn't need to since the part was new. I've learned since then that new parts have a chance of coming with defects. I go inside the carrier ship and walk to the control room. I test to see if the control panel works at all. The holographic screen won't come up, and the emergency controls don't respond.

I get out my bar turner and start turning the small metal bars that hold the repair hatch closed. It's a thin hatch that's about five inches wide. I wish it was bigger, but then the control panel would have to be thicker. Once I remove the hatch I get out my micro bot extractor and release some micro bots from my new mechanic gloves into the control panel. They go in, but come back right away. This panel is beyond repair, so I'll have to put in the new one. I take the bots back and start unscrewing the bars that hold the panel to the stand that it's on.

Once I get that off I set up the new one. Thorough examination reveals that it works fine. I step out of the carrier ship and make my way to the recycle chute. Parts that go there are melted down and made into new ones. As I'm heading there I glance out the window and stop. The crew's ship is gone... How did Bayu finish delivering the frosthur so fast? I thought it would take longer than that. I let out an aggravated sigh. Why do things like this always seem to go wrong?

Now I'm going to have to talk to Bayu... he probably did this on purpose so that I would stay and work here. I quickly go back to the hangar I arrived in. It looks like all the carrier ships are here. I leave the hangar and enter the large passageway, making my way to the front of the ship. This takes me more time than I wanted it to. I pass many rooms and areas before I come to a place I'm more familiar with. The medbay looks to be the same; few patients are in the room. It doesn't seem like the crew has many casualties.

I move on, now having better bearings. Many people pass me. Some of them turn their heads to look at me, but most of them don't seem to notice I'm here. I smile at them and keep going. I must be getting closer to the front end of the ship by now... I make it to an open room. At the opposite end there's a door with two guards. Both have guns and are staring neutrally out ahead. I walk up to them as confidently as I can. "Is this where Bayu is piloting the ship?"

The guard to my left eyes me suspiciously. "It depends on who is asking. Who are you?"

"My name is Franca, I was briefly hired to work on some of the carrier ships in the hangar. I need to talk to Bayu, as I was supposed to join up with my crew afterwards and there's been a mistake."

"Ha!" the guard says, spit flying out of his mouth. "A likely story. You're probably a spy from The Golden Terror here to gather intel. I'm not letting you by."

"I'm telling the truth, just ask him," I say, hoping that'll help. I can feel a lump in my throat as I'm starting to get frustrated with this. I take a deep breath to make sure I stay calm.

"He's not here," the guard says with a sneer. "And even if he was I wouldn't leave my post for this."

"Fine, I'll find him elsewhere." I say, turning to leave.

The guard grabs my arm. "Not so fast, we're going to have to detain you until we know who you are."

"What!?!" I say. Oh you've got to be kidding me. "Now wait a minute!" I say, struggling to get out of his grasp.

His grip tightens. "Oh no, you're not getting away from me!" He says, walking at a brisk pace and tugging me behind him. He briefly looks back at the other guard. "You got this Jones?"

"Sure do," he says confidently.

"Thanks," the guard says, pulling me away from the control room.

I struggle against the guard but give up after a few minutes. He's not letting go of me, and if I put up too much of a fight he may use handcuffs. I'd rather not deal with the pain of that. The prison ends up being at the other end of the ship. On our way there I pass some of the people that I saw before. Now they're looking at me.

As we're about to enter the doorway to the prison a woman with platinum blond hair walks up to us. "Franca?" Wynter says in a surprised tone once she comes closer.

"Wynter? It's been awhile," I say, glad to see her.

"Yes it has," she says, her smile fading as she begins to look concerned. "But what are you doing here?"

The guard's grip tightens on me. Kinda reminds me of how Roxanne is... "Wynter, I don't have time for this, I have to get the prisoner in the cell," he says, starting to pull me to the doorway.

"Hold up Zeph, you're not going anywhere with her just yet," Wynter says coldly. "What are you doing anyway? Shouldn't you be cleaning the forges?"

Zeph sneers. "I got promoted. I'm a guard now. You better behave Wynter," he says laughing. My hand is starting to lose circulation from how hard he's holding my arm.

"Anyway," Wynter says, turning back to me. "What are you doing here?"

"I didn't do anything wrong!" I say, trying not to focus on how my hand is falling asleep. "Bayu hired me to fix a few carrier ships, and my crew took off without me so I was trying to find him."

"Is that all? Zeph, release her now. She's a friend not a prisoner!"

"She's a spy Wynter, through and through. She's going in the cell," he says confidently, pulling me through the doorway.

"Zeph!" Wynter exclaims. "I can't believe this," she says, throwing up her arms in exasperation and walking away. He drags me down a passageway that has rows of cells off to the left. He goes all the way to the end of the passageway and takes me down the last row. Everything is dimly lit. I don't see many prisoners down this row. I'm okay with that... I don't feel like talking with anyone. The only problem is that I might be hard to find. He unlocks an old fashioned door made of metal bars, shoves me in, shutting the door with a click. I've never seen a prison with bars.

Zeph looks at the door with his arms crossed, then nods. "There, that should hold you," he says tugging on the bars to make sure.

And with that he leaves. I hope Wynter can get in touch with Bayu or someone who can help me. I pace in my cell. I wonder what Gunner plans on doing with all that frosthur?

I'm sure the rest of the crew knows by now. They're probably already on their way to Pike III figuring out their next steps. They would most likely figure I decided to stay... or went home like I'd always been mentioning. After some time of pacing I begin to grow tired. It's been a long day, and this pacing isn't doing me any good. I decide to go to sleep to kill some time.

I awaken to the sound of voices coming my way. "I'm telling you I'm not a prisoner!" a man yells in an agitated tone.

"Yeah, sure," Zeph scoffs.

"No really!"

Zeph opens the cell door across from mine and throws the man into it. The door slams shut with a clank. "Maybe now you'll understand that you can't escape from us," Zeph says triumphantly before walking away.

The man holds onto the bars of the door for a moment before sighing and letting go of them. He has short brown hair and brown eyes. His face is bleeding and his clothes are ripped. His left hand and arm are wrapped with cloth bandages, but they are torn as well, showing red underneath. He looks over at me mournfully. "So, he caught you too huh?"

"Yeah I guess you could say that." I say indifferently, bored by my circumstances.

"What'd that guy get you on?" the man asks, studying me.

"Oh he thought I was a spy for wanting to talk to the captain. And you?"

"Are you a spy though?" the man asks, ignoring my question.

"No," I reply.

The man looks up at the ceiling. "I guess you could say that I'm a wanderer now, going from place to place. I was escaping from some men who were after me." He looks at me and grins. "I got away, but had nothing to pay someone with to get a ride out of the settlement. Snuck on board this ship and that guard happened to check me for my registration code. Ended up here pretty quick. Now I have to figure out how to get out of here," the man says, checking to see if any of the bars are loose in the door. I wonder if the men that were after him were marauders, or if he's one? "How long have you been here?" he asks.

"From what my communicator says, eight hours. I don't feel like there's much use in keeping track of the time." It only adds to the stress of waiting in my opinion.

"How long do you think it'll be before we get out of here?"

"Soon I hope, I shouldn't be in here in the first place. My crew is long gone by now. You'll probably get out just fine, if you're not a marauder."

The man laughs hard. "The last thing I'll ever be is a marauder."

"Where would you go if you managed to get out?"

The man stays silent for a moment, hesitating. "I'm part of the army, so I need to report back." If what this man is saying is true, then we're on the same side. I can't tell for sure though. He checks his communicator and frowns. "I guess you can't transmit comm. link data in here?"

"Guess not," I say, checking mine again to see if anything had changed.

"Great. My sister's probably worried to death. I haven't had the time to get in touch with her." We stop talking after that. I sit in my cell and start to doze off. I wake up and walk to the door when I hear voices coming our way.

CHAPTER 20

"I TOLD ZEPH she wasn't a prisoner, but he wouldn't listen," I hear Wynter say.

"He'll be reprimanded for this. I didn't even know she was still here," Bayu says. I can hear his thick boots clomping down the row. "She wasn't in any of the other cells, so she has to be in this row. Why did he put her all the way back here?"

"Oh, he thought she was a spy or something," Wynter says in distaste.

"Franca? A spy?" Bayu bursts out laughing.

"I know right?" Wynter says, laughing with him.

"Zeph is going to be penalized for this one. I can't have him arresting guests or business partners." He stops in front of my cell. "Hang on a minute and I'll have you out of here," he says, getting out an old-fashioned key.

"Finally," I say, still feeling annoyed about the whole situation.

"Well, I didn't know you were here," he mutters as he moves the key around.

"Why's it not working?" Wynter asks.

"Bad lock. I'll have it here in a moment. There," he says as the door opens.

I step out of the cell, glad to be free. "Thought I'd never get out."

"Sorry Franca, Zeph doesn't know what he's doing," Wynter says.

Bayu hands me my rifle and things back. "Check that everything is there, I don't want to be responsible for anything that's missing."

I take my things back, and before I can say anything the man in the other cell clears his throat. "I was arrested by that same man. Can I be let out as well?"

Bayu looks over at him. "And your name is?"

"Radek. My name's Radek."

"You're Fauve's brother?" I ask, surprised. What's he doing here?

He looks at me, mirroring my surprise. "Yes, you know her?"

Bayu starts tapping his foot. I ignore him and walk up to the man's cell.

"Yeah I'm on the same crew with her. We've been tasked with finding your crew. She's been worried about you."

"Franca, I don't have time for this," Bayu says impatiently. He turns and looks at Radek. "You're being held for stowing away. I'll discuss your sentence after I get some things taken care of. Depending on what you were trying to do negotiations may be possible."

"But Bayu!" I say, wanting to explain.

"I'll deal with this later. First I need to figure out what to do with you."

"Here," Radek says, removing a chain from around his neck. "These are my tags. Please give them to her and tell her I'm alright." He holds the chain out to me and I take it.

"I will," I say, carefully putting it in my pocket.

With that Bayu and Wynter start to leave. I turn to follow them, wishing that Bayu had just let Radek go. I need to figure out how to get him out of the cell. He didn't tell me anything about the special force team, but he probably didn't want to in front of Bayu. We come to a stop once we get out of the prison. "Well, I better get goin'," Wynter says. "It was good to see you Franca!"

"Yeah, it was good seeing you too Wynter. Maybe we'll see each other again sometime," I say. You never know.

"Yeah, we just might!"

"Thanks Wynter," Bayu says as she leaves. We start walking. I assume we're going back to the control room. "If I didn't know better I'd say you stayed here on purpose," Bayu says.

"Oh? I thought you purposefully left with me still aboard," I say. I'm surprised he'd think I did this on purpose... why would I?

"I wouldn't do that. You know how I feel about non crew members hanging out on my ship. I don't have time to take responsibility for anyone who's not a part of my crew."

"No worries there, you won't be," I say with a little bit of frustration in my tone. It's my fault. I got lost in fixing that carrier ship and time passed me by. "So now what? I need to get back to my crew, and Radek is part of another crew that works for Gunner."

"You still want to go back there?" he shakes his head. "I'll never understand that." He ignores my comment about Radek. After a few moments of silence he speaks again. "Once we get to the control room we'll figure out when we can get you back to them, if that's what you want," he says evenly.

"Alright," I say. I guess Gunner will have to work on getting Radek back. We walk in silence all the way back to the control room. When we get there the guards let me through with no problem. I notice that Zeph isn't there. We go into the room and I'm surprised at how it looks. The room is filled with holographic maps. Some have moving dots on them. The control panel is long enough for six people to sit at it. Some crew members are diligently at work managing things.

One man is standing at the left side of the control panel, a woman is studying one of the maps, and another guy is looking at a holographic communication board that is off to the side of the control panel. Bayu takes a seat at the center of the panel. "Have a seat," he says, motioning to the seat next to him. I sit, looking at the control panel. I've never seen this model before. "Why are you looking at the control panel like that?" Bayu asks. "There's nothing wrong with it," he says sounding slightly annoyed.

"I was just trying to figure out what model it is."

"Model? My father built it."

The man sitting on the other side of him asks a question and he turns to answer. The woman studying the maps looks up at me and smiles. "He never likes it when people judge his ship."

"What'd you say?" Bayu asks.

"Nothing," the woman says quickly getting back to work. She goes back to looking at her map.

The man that's watching the communication board speaks up. "Uh, captain?"

"Yes?"

"Lewis is getting impatient. He says if you don't hold your end of the bargain he's coming for us."

"Tell him we'll be there by the end of the day."

"What about getting me back to my crew?" I ask.

"If I don't take care of this first we'll have him on our tail the whole way to Pike III," Bayu says, sounding like he's starting to lose his patience.

"Is this how all your dealings work?"

Bayu glances at me, looking like I almost offended him. He seems to shrug it off, answering casually. "Naw, this guy's just a mosquito. He goes after you day and night until he gets what he wants."

"Ya better watch out captain, or The Golden Terror will be coming after ya," the guy at the communication board jokingly says.

Bayu scoffs. "Isn't that a terrible name for a ship? Who would pick that."

"I guess it is," I say. I honestly feel indifferent about it. I don't think it matters.

"Considering it's one of the most important things, he could've picked a better one," Bayu says. "Anyway, we'll take care of this real quick and then I guess we'll have to head all the way back to Pike III."

"Maybe we can deliver a cargo shipment there," the woman studying the maps says.

"Yeah, maybe," he says. "Cole, where is he now?"

The guy at the communication board looks at one of the holographic maps that has some moving markers on it. "He's in Faratha IV's orbit now."

Bayu gets a compass out of his pocket. The metal is a silvery white color that radiates with a white light. He turns the ship to the northeast and puts the compass back in his pocket.

"I've never seen a compass like that," I say.

"It was my great grandfather's. My grandfather and father were both captains after him, and now I'm following in their footsteps," he says with pride.

"Why does it radiate with light like that?" I ask. I've never seen anything like it.

"It's a relic from the past. My great grandfather knew more about it but his journal was lost long ago. I've been searching for clues of its whereabouts for years but haven't had any luck so far."

"Do you think his journal is still out there?"

"Oh yeah it's out there, I just don't know where yet."

"Captain, Lewis says he wants us to be there sooner," Cole says.

"Well too bad. We get there when we get there," he says firmly. "If Lewis is gonna start a fight I'll let him have it." After a few hours Bayu orders for the ship to be stopped, and has his men deliver a cargo shipment to Rythor.

"Was that your deal with Lewis?" I ask, hoping that we can now start heading back to Pike III.

"No, that was a deal with someone else. We're heading to Faratha IV now. Then we'll see about heading back to Pike III," Bayu says firmly. I sigh. He's always about business first. Time passes slowly, and after six hours I can finally see Faratha IV on the radar system.

"Cole, let Lewis know we've arrived," Bayu says.

"Uh captain?" he asks nervously.

"What is it?" Bayu responds impatiently.

"He says he had other things he had to take care of on Faratha IV, you're going to have to land if you want to meet him here."

"Tell him I'll wait in orbit," Bayu says coolly.

"Sir, he says he won't be going back in orbit until he gets your shipment," Cole says, with a slight shake in his voice.

Bayu doesn't say anything.

"What are we going to do?" Cole asks.

"We'll meet him, but he'll be charged extra for the inconvenience."

It doesn't take us long to land in Faratha's hangar. Bayu arms himself with a handgun I don't recognize. He catches me looking at it. "What now?"

"Nothing, just never have seen that particular model."

"That's because it was hand forged. Do you have to know the models for everything? Now come on," he says in a frustrated tone.

"You don't expect me to go with you?" I ask. I don't see why I have to be a part of this errand.

"Of course I do. I can't leave you on the ship. If the crew of the Golden Terror attacked the ship I would be held liable for you. This way I can make sure that I'm not." Some tough men join Bayu and begin to leave the ship. I decide to humor him and go along. I don't know if I agree with this logic though. We get into Faratha's hangar, and don't see Lewis yet. Some cherry blossom trees are growing in planters in the hangar. The ceiling is transparent, letting in lots of light. Bayu types something into his communicator, then we wait.

After some time a man comes up to us. He's wearing black and gold armor. "My captain's waiting for you outside the hangar," the man says.

"He can come here if he wants his cargo," Bayu says without any hesitation.

The man laughs, but it sounds fake. "My captain will claim that you cheated him out then."

Bayu grins. "So be it then. He has fifteen minutes to get here if he wants his cargo."

The man runs back the way he came with a scowl. Bayu keeps checking the time on his communicator. After ten minutes a man comes with many people following him. They all are wearing black and gold except for him. His armor is gold and silver. He has a beard and long black hair, with striking green eyes. He walks up to us slowly, with his crew following. "So, you decided to waste my time with this nonsense," the man says to Bayu, sounding like he's close to being at the end of his rope.

"Actually it's you that's wasting my time," Bayu says casually. "The extra charge will be on your tab."

"I'm not paying that," the man says through his teeth.

I resist the urge to get my rifle out from the sling on my back.

"Lewis, you either take the deal or you don't get the cargo," Bayu says with a smirk. "Oh, and did I mention that any violence adds greatly to the charge?"

Lewis clenches his fists, then looks over at his crew. He nods the slightest and they all pull out their guns. "You'll finally regret all you and your father have done," he says pulling out a gun and opening fire.

Bayu dodges the gunfire and fires back, taking down one of the crew members. Bayu's men also spring into action. I get behind cover and get out my gun as I hear bullets whizzing past my ear. The people that were in the hangar scatter, and I hear a scream. At the back of Lewis's crew stands a sniper, aiming at Bayu. As I'm starting to take aim the sniper is brought to the ground by a guard. I lower my rifle, seeing that the fight has been broken up.

"Enough!" one of the guards from the hangar shouts. Lewis and Bayu are standing apart, glaring at each other.

"You'll pay for this," Lewis says, spitting at Bayu before walking away. His crew follows.

"Take this as a warning," another guard says to both of them. I stand up from my cover, activating the safety on the rifle.

"Are you alright?" Bayu asks. I can still see the fight in his blue eyes.

"I'm fine," I say confidently, not wanting to end up in the medbay again.

"Good," he says, turning to go back to the ship. I follow, glad that ordeal is over. We get back to the control room, and Bayu orders that we leave immediately.

"Sir, what about Lewis's cargo?" Cole asks.

"He hasn't paid me enough for it," Bayu says evenly. "If he wants it he'll have to pay triple now. He has three days before I sell it to someone else." I feel like asking about him sending me back to Pike III, but I know this isn't a good time. He's still angry from the fight. Bayu orders that we head to Yenath, to finish another deal before moving on to Pike III.

At the end of the day everyone meets at the mess hall. I take a seat at a random table, not able to find Wynter. Some of the people are singing battle songs and slamming their drinks on the tables. They're all riled up. I can tell they expect to fight Lewis and his crew again. Many of the people have armor now. I'd rather be back with the others but recognize that this is my reality for now. I finish my meal and head into the main passageway.

People are out here too, and there are craftsmen selling weapons, armor, and other gear at little vendors they've set up. Guards are everywhere. I look at the data of the ship that Bayu sent to my communicator. He marked where my room and the maintenance room is, suggesting that I put my things there. I do that and head to the room he assigned to me. The room I got is not nearly as fancy as the one at the palace, but it's not bad either. It's been a long day, and I'm glad to be getting some rest.

CHAPTER 21

WHEN I WAKE up I head back to the control room. The morning passes, and Bayu works in silence. A man bursts into the room. Bayu turns his seat around to see who it is. "What is it?" he asks, laying a hand on his gun.

"Sir, someone has landed in the old hangar. I don't know who it is, but they came undetected by our scanners."

"We'll never get anything done at this rate. Come on, let's go see who it is," he says begrudgingly, drawing his gun and getting out of his chair.

"You won't have to," Gunner says, moving past the man.

Bayu's eyes narrow. "What are you doing here?" he asks in a demanding tone.

"You failed to return Franca to us, so I've come to get her. We need her for our mission," he says calmly, not bothered at all by Bayu's stance. He comes over to me. "Are you ready to go?"

I nod. As much as I find The Burning Rift to be an interesting place, I was wanting to find out more about what Gunner's going to do with the frosthur.

"I didn't fail," Bayu says, taking a few strong steps towards Gunner. "I was going to return her after I took care of some important matters."

"It wouldn't have been that hard to have made sure she was with us before we left," Gunner says casually, not intimidated by Bayu in the least.

Bayu raises his voice. "I'm not liable for those who aren't a part of my crew. She should've been paying more attention."

"She was trying to help you. The least you could do was make sure she made it back."

Bayu looks like he wants to fight Gunner, but then his mood changes to something that's more dismissive. "Whatever. I don't have time for this, take her and go," Bayu says turning away from him.

"Alright let's go," Gunner says, turning to walk away.

"Wait," I say. I'd almost forgotten.

He stops in his tracks. "What?" he asks, turning to look back at me.

"I found Radek here, in the prison."

"What's he doing here?" Gunner asks Bayu in a demanding tone.

"We found him stowing away, and have yet to determine his sentence," Bayu says.

"He's one of my men, I'll take charge of him."

"This is my ship, I will run things," Bayu says, almost raising his voice to a shout.

Gunner stands his ground, seeming unbothered. "A legion of ships will come to my aid if need be."

Bayu stands taller. "Me and my father have fought many a legion. But fine, take your man. He means nothing to me."

Gunner turns and leaves the room and I follow. Once we're out of earshot he speaks. "We need to get back to the others quickly. We're running out of time..."

"Time for what?"

He opens his mouth to speak, but before he can the ship violently shakes, sending us both to the ground. I get up and run to the wall, looking out of the transparent part of it. A blur of gold pass by. "Crew! At the ready!" Bayu calls out over the intercom.

Everything breaks into chaos. People rush about, pushing us out of the way. I get shoved to the wall and Gunner ends up on the other side of the passageway. "We're under attack!" I shout to him, trying to be heard over the crowd. I can't tell if he heard me, but he looks frustrated.

Wynter walks past me fully clad in red and silver armor. "Man the missiles! We'll defeat The Golden Terror yet!" she cries out. The floor shakes as cheering resounds from the crew. Soon the ship's weaponry is firing. Wynter stands tall with a big grin on her face. She looks over at me and her smile fades a bit. "Franca what are you doin'? The ship needs repair girl!" she calls, bringing me out of my daze. I get moving.

The ship shakes again, and I fall to the ground. She cries out more orders. I get up and run in the direction of the damages. "Franca! Where are you going?" I hear Gunner call out amidst the yelling.

I don't turn back. The ship will need critical repairs if I don't hurry. I push and force my way against the people who are running away from the area of the last blast. Gunner calls after me again, but it's too loud for me to say anything he'd hear. If I turn around I'll lose all my progress I've made toward the area that needs repairing.

I get to the area that was hit and see that the wall is thinner there. This could be a bad weak spot if not fixed. We're lucky that missile didn't go all the way through. I run off to the maintenance room. I'll have to control a repair mechanism to restore the outside of the ship to its original state. Gunner watches me as I pass by. I would stop and explain what I'm doing, but there just isn't any time. I get to the area right before the control room I throw the door to the maintenance room open and go inside. The maintenance computers are displaying the condition of the ship. So far there are three areas that have been severely damaged.

The repairs will take at least twenty minutes and I have to decide which area the machines should repair first. I know that the one I went up to is the most critical. I select it and the repair machine makes its way along the ship to do the repair work. The ship shakes violently again, and once I get back up to my feet I find that the part of the ship where the medbay is has been damaged to the point of it being an emergency.

I've already sent the machinery to the other repair area... I cancel the repair and send it to the medbay. Then I realize the area that I had it repairing is actually more critical than I first thought... so many people are going through that passageway to get to the other parts of the ship. If I don't do something a hole could develop there and people might die... I send the backup machine out that way.

I double check that everything's doing what it's supposed to, then I go over to the side of the room where the space suits are. Those are there for anyone who wears a uniform, or doesn't have a place to connect a cable to their armor. I take a cable and put my helmet on before leaving the room. I'll have to help the backup machinery with some of the repairs because those tend to be slower. Mechanics don't always do as much maintenance on them or keep them up to date.

Before heading out I look behind me and see that Gunner is ordering some people around. We need all the help we can get in this situation. I put my helmet on and open a door that is only for the mechanics. Heading out I attach my cable to my armor and then to the side of the ship. I make my way to the area that needs repair and set up the personal shield I got with my armor and weapons. A purple force field surrounds me, and I get to work. I use my helmet add-ons to check if anything internal needs repair.

Nothing does, so I focus on the ship's frame. This ship has many thin layers of tough metal armor. This armor is made up of panels so that sections of it can easily be replaced. Some of the panels are bent. I get out my bar turner and start turning some bars, releasing the broken metal panels into space. They float away as the backup repair machine comes with some new ones. It starts to slowly put one on. I come up to the machine and enter a code into it so that it knows a mechanic is with it. Which makes me wonder, where are the other mechanics?

The machine pauses, then lets go of one of the panels so I can have it. I grab onto it and struggle to get it to its proper place. The panels are big and bulky, making them challenging to move on your own. It gets lighter and I look over and see that another mechanic is helping me. He gives me a thumbs up and starts using a bar turner to attach his end to the ship. I do the same and get the panel on. A missile flies by, almost hitting us. The guy doesn't seem to notice and keeps working. I don't know how he does that without having a shield like me. Though I have to wonder if mine is any good against missiles. I don't really know. Regardless I've got to keep going on the best I can.

We continue working in silence. I can't remember which channel Bayu's crew is on and things are too busy to try to figure that out right now. The silence is broken by a hissing sound. A flash of white light hides everything from view. For a few moments everything shakes. Once it stops shaking and the light dissipates I look to the left. The metal of the ship is steaming, and panels are distorted. Thankfully the crew mechanic was on the other side of me. I look over and see that he's working as if nothing happened. My force field flickers for a bit as it works to regenerate power. I guess it does work after all. I'm thankful I have it.

We finish working on our current area then go over to the new spot once it stops steaming. The backup machine follows us slowly. I'll have to work on that sometime. It looks like it's another thing that the mechanics have put off fixing. They also haven't done anything about the carrier ships... maybe they're overworked. Soon another mechanic joins us. With her comes the main repair machine. As we're working to quickly get the wall patched up another flash of white light blinds me. When I'm able to see again I find yet another damaged area towards the back of the ship. It looks like it hit where the prison is... I hope Radek is okay.

The other mechanics and the main machine go ahead of me. I stay with the slow one, wondering if there's a way I can help it along. As I'm thinking another flash of white light hits. Once I regain my vision I find that the panels between me and the other mechanics have been destroyed.

I stop the backup machine and get to work. As I'm moving to place the last panel down I realize the machine doesn't have any more. It'll have to go back inside to the machine's restocking area to retrieve more panels. I give it directions to get more, not knowing what else to do. We'll need a lot more if we want to get everything fixed. The other mechanics are still working at the end of the ship... some internal damage must've been done.

I look the other way to see how the backup machine is doing and to see if there are any other damages that way. A carrier ship leaves our hangar... who would be leaving right now? No one goes after it, and the battle rages on. The Golden Terror is too focused on taking The Burning Rift down. So this is what happens when two merchants have a disagreement.

I stay where I am, not sure what to do while I wait for the panels. I can't get to the other mechanics, and the repair I'm working on could turn into an emergency at any moment. I decide I can't wait for the machine to bring panels. I enter the ship, and put my helmet back in the maintenance room. When I get to the main passageway I find that it is just as busy as it was before.

As I'm going through it I begin to hear arguing over the rest of the commotion. "You have no right to order my crew around, and if I see you doing that again I'll kick you off the ship," Bayu shouts angrily.

"I have every right to be here and will do as I see fit. Some of your crew needed direction and asked me to help. I'm not going to turn them down if they need it," Gunner says.

"Regardless this is my crew and I'll take care of them!"

I press on, not caring to hear the rest of the fight. I finally make my way to the ship's part factory. Few ships have them these days, but people like Bayu who want to be self-sufficient usually have them on board. I make it there and find a wide array of parts. The ship keeps shaking as I make my way past rattling shelves. As I'm heading to the panels everything goes dark.

"I hope we find something here," Jalyn says wearily. I'm walking behind her and Greyson. Rays of sunlight reach through the pines. The ground is wet, and the smell of rain tells me there was a storm not long ago.

"Don't worry Jalyn. How can we know if we don't try?" Greyson says.

"What do you think Franca?" Jalyn asks, looking over her shoulder at me.

"I don't know, we might find it," I hear myself say. My best guess is we're somewhere on Yenath, but we could also be somewhere on Rythor. My foot slides in the mud, hitting a big root. I quickly put out my hand and grab onto one of the tree's branches, keeping myself from falling.

"You okay back there?" Greyson asks.

"Yeah I'm fine," I say, catching up to them.

Jalyn stops and pulls out a journal. "I think it's a little more to the west of us."

"That would be... this way," Greyson says, pointing deeper into the forest.

"Right," Jalyn says, carefully closing the old journal before walking in that direction. I notice Greyson keeps looking behind us. Something feels off, but I don't know what. I feel on edge, like we're being followed. I glance behind us too and see nothing. Looks like I've been assigned to guard the back of the group.

We travel for a long time in silence, listening to the sounds of the woods. It's a strange place in my opinion. The forest is eerily silent. I don't even hear birds chirping. I keep an eye on the forest behind us, but never see anything. Still, I can't shake the feeling that we're being followed.

We emerge into a decent sized clearing. A lone cabin stands quietly at the edge of it. Moss covers the roof. A spider's web glistens in the window when the sunlight catches a glimpse of it. A worn boat leans against the side of the cabin, and on the other is a garden bed that has long been forgotten in the shadows of the past. Time has almost washed away the dirt path that used to lead up to the cabin. Patches of it still show through the grass that has mostly overtaken it.

Jalyn makes it up the path, walking slowly as if to take it all in. Nothing can be seen through the cabin windows besides darkness. A loud creak sounds as she steps onto the deck, startling me. I'm reminded to keep a check on things behind us. She turns the doorknob, and the door slowly swings open with a creaking sound. Greyson follows her inside, taking out his weapon. I follow cautiously.

"Look, on the table!" Jalyn says.

She's found another map. "What's that one show?" I hear myself ask, barely hiding my excitement. I don't know why I feel excited, but I do.

"It shows some sort of a hill, or mountainside with a mark in the middle of some trees to the right of it."

Greyson's eyebrows furrow. "I don't believe there are any mountains in this area."

"There's a poem written to the side," Jalyn says, gently wiping some dirt off of the map.

"I didn't know he was a poet," I say.

"Oh yes, he wrote many poems throughout his explorations." She continues on, and I strain to hear her as things fade to white again.

CHAPTER 22

I **WAKE UP** to find that I'm lying on the floor. I groan... my head hurts. I put a hand to my forehead and feel something wet. I look at my hand. Blood. Just what I thought. A ship part is laying on the ground beside me. It must've fallen from one of the shelves and hit me. The ship shakes again. I've got to get back to work. If I can.

I stand up and continue onward to the section of panels with a mild headache. I pick one up, but it's cumbersome. I ponder the dream I had as I work. I've never explored Yenath's forests. I'd be curious to know how much my mind has made up, or if by chance the dreams have details to them that are accurate...

I exit the parts factory with three panels, leaning them against the wall to shut the door. All I can hear is shouting, clanging of metal, and gunshots. As I start to make it to the passageway I stop. There's a full on battle going on up ahead. We got boarded... I lean the panels against the wall. There's no way I can get through this to repair the ship.

"Franca!" Gunner calls, emerging through the crowd. A man grabs onto his armor and tries to cut through it with a carbon blade. Gunner punches him, forcing him to let go. He makes his way to me at a fast pace. "We've got to get Radek! Missiles are still hitting the back of the ship." I turn and follow him, having to run to keep up. He stops once we get inside the prison. "Show me which cell he's in," Gunner says.

I nod and make it to the last row of cells. I stop short when I get to Radek's cell.

"What is it?" Gunner asks.

"He's not here," I say. Where could he have gone? Bayu didn't sound like he was going to release him.

Gunner walks briskly over to the cell, looking inside. The cell wall at the back looks damaged, but there are no holes. "He didn't leave anything behind."

"You think he's in the battle out there?"

"No, if Radek was trying to escape he's either hiding here somewhere or has already left."

I'm reminded of the carrier ship leaving and mention it.

"It's possible that was him, but I'm not sure of it," he says, starting to walk out of the prison.

We get to the passageway and are immediately greeted by Wynter. "What are you guys doin'? We've still got work to do. Franca, the ship's being chewed to bits by those missiles." She turns to look at Gunner. "And we need you to command the fourth regiment. They've geared up and are preparing to head to battle!"

Gunner looks apprehensive. "I'll have to find you later Franca."

"Good!" Wynter says, rushing off with a smile.

"I guess we're going to have to stay till the battle's over. I'll meet you in the control room after the fight," he says.

I agree and go my separate way. I know there's another door for the mechanics to go through on the other side of the ship... I just have to get those panels and go. I pick them up and head to the maintenance room to get my helmet before moving to the other side of the ship. It doesn't take much to find the door. Going through the door I attach my cable and make my way to where I was repairing before. It takes me some time to get to that side of the ship. I wouldn't have to be doing this if my way hadn't been blocked by the battle inside. The going's slow because of the panels. A missile flies by, reminding me to activate my shield.

I make it over and find that the backup machine has been tirelessly working to replace panels. I don't see the mechanics or the other machine in sight. I start working alongside the backup machine, speeding up the process. I need to lay fifteen. I have to keep going back to the parts factory to get more panels. While I can't carry many I'm still faster than the machine would be.

Once the repairs are finished I set the machine to standby and tiredly make my way back on the ship. It'll get going again if more repairs need to be made. I need to check things on the computer in the maintenance room. Once inside the ship I'm greeted with the usual war cries and gunshots. I put the cable that I borrowed back in its place, and store my helmet in the room. The computers show one place that the machines are repairing. It looks like they're going to need more panels soon.

I head through the main passageway, trying to get back to the parts factory. Wynter passes by, charging towards the enemy yelling. I look ahead of me. I don't see how I can get through this without a fight. Even so it would take me forever. I decide to check on the medbay. Maybe someone there will know of a roundabout way to the factory.

I make my way there, and the lady who took care of me before rushes over. "Some of The Golden Terror's crew are heading this way! I need help setting up a barricade!" she looks at me with fear in her eyes.

"I'll do what I can," I say, looking around to see what I could use. I don't find anything. I ask her if there's another way to the parts factory. She tells me which way to go, and I head that way as quickly as I can. I'm glad that there was another way to it. I bring back a panel and set it up against the doorway. Getting out my tools I bolt it there. Just as I finish I hear bullets hitting it.

The woman looks relieved. "At least that'll hold for a bit," she says, walking over to one of the beds. I look and see that it's the mechanic I was working with earlier. By the looks of it he got hurt on the metal of one of the panels or something like that. All of the med beds are full. I'll have to get care for my head later. I ask the woman about the battle, wanting to know who's winning.

She shakes her head, unsure. The attackers can't seem to get through the panel, so there's nothing else for me to do but wait things out. I have no medical skills, so I can't help with tending to the wounded.

After what feels like a long time the battle cries finally come to a stop. The dead silence feels strange. It takes time before people come to check on us. Once people start calling through the panel I work to pull it away from the doorway. Looking at the other side of it I find that it's dented in many places. Some spots are worn enough that it wouldn't have taken much more to break through.

As I'm examining the panel Bayu rushes in. "Everything alright?" he asks gruffly, his voice sounding like he's been shouting a lot.

"Yes... just tending to the wounded," the woman says, glancing over at the beds.

Bayu looks relieved. "Everyone's staying at the mess hall right now, just so you know." He turns to leave, and I decide to follow him. I notice he has a slight limp.

"Sir, you're limping!" the woman says, calling out to him.

He turns to look at her. "I am, but it's fine. I'll have it looked at later." He looks at me for the first time. "You coming?"

"Yeah, I need to find Gunner."

"That man is insufferable," he grumbles under his breath. "He has a lot of nerve thinking he can order my people around," he states. By his expression I can tell he wishes Gunner was off the ship.

"Well he is the king."

"He's not the king to all of us."

"What do you mean by that?"

Bayu looks at me with a glimmer in his eyes. "There's more people here than just your people," he says in a serious tone.

With that we reach the mess hall, and he says nothing more, disappearing in the crowd. People are everywhere, tending to their wounds or each other's. They are joyfully talking about how they fended off Lewis and his crew. One man is bragging about the new scars he'll have. I can smell food cooking and decide to take a look at my communicator. I learn that it's around six thirty at night.

A woman walks up to me with some bandages. "Looks like you took a nasty hit. Let me take care of that for you," the woman says, holding up a wet rag.

I forgot about my head. "Oh thanks, but I'm not feeling any pain. I'm sure it's fine."

The woman frowns. "If we don't take care of that it'll be worse later. Might get infected."

"Really I'm fine." I say, looking apprehensively at the bundle of bandages that she's carrying.

She gives me a disdainful but determined look. "This lot is always so stubborn. I'm going to take care of this whether you like it or not." With that she presses the wet rag on my head, wiping away the dried blood. I wince, but don't say anything. Before I know it my forehead is covered with a lump of bandages. "That should do it," she says, taking a step back, proudly admiring her work.

"Thanks," I say as she walks away, feeling the bulk of the bandages. I look around and see Gunner is standing near one of the fireplaces in the room. I make my way over and see Bayu is also standing there. I head over to them. It would be nice to sit by the fire.

"Franca are you okay?," Gunner asks, coming over to me when he sees me. He looks at the wad of bandages on my head with concern.

"I'm fine, I didn't get hurt much," I say dismissively. I wish that woman hadn't put so many bandages on my head. She made it look worse than it is.

"There's not going to be enough room for you in the medbays tonight. I'll have to pay for the injuries you took." Bayu says, coming over to me. "Also let me know how much repair work you did, and I'll pay you accordingly. It'll be more than you'd get from that lot you go with," he says, looking like he's trying to purposefully insult Gunner.

"I wouldn't be too sure of that," Gunner says casually. "And why can't she have a bed in one of the medbays? I thought you didn't like being held liable for anything. And after all the trouble she's gone through to help you I'd think you'd do more than that."

"I'm doing what I can, but the health of my crew comes first," Bayu says, his eyes filled with a glint of stubbornness.

Gunner sighs in exasperation. They both seem too tired now to do much fighting. We move to sit around the fireplace, watching the flames dance. As I take in the heat of the fire, I begin listening to the music that is playing. A woman is singing in another language, but after a bit she starts singing words I can understand.

> "In good faith he saved us from the dark,
> Traveling long and far,
> In good faith he journeyed on,
> Going far over the mountains,
> Long against the wind,
> He found the treasure of men,

Raising it high and letting the light go forth,
He destroyed and overcame the darkness."

I find myself pulling out the piece of paper I've been carrying in my pocket from when I was in the underground settlement on Rythor. The picture is the same as I remembered it. A young man is standing on a hill, surrounded by shadows. A beam of light is shining from his fist, piercing through the darkness. I look at the unrecognizable symbols underneath the picture. Maybe they relate to this song?

"Where did you find that?" Gunner asks. I look and see that he's looking over at the picture.

"I found it in one of the abandoned houses below Rythor."

"What were you doing there?" Gunner asks in a curious tone.

"Oh, I just kinda ended up there," I say not feeling like going into much detail about it. No matter how you say it, jumping off of a building does not sound smart. Gunner doesn't press for more information. "What's the story behind it?" I ask, bringing my focus back to the picture.

"It's an old tale of a man named Rhorric. In a time of darkness he found an ancient relic of light that changed the path of man. It was so powerful that evil could not face him. He destroyed the darkness of the world," Gunner says confidently.

Bayu shakes his head and snickers. "You know very little of the tale." He looks at the fire for a moment before speaking. "It all happened on Pike III long ago, before you came and named it that. We will always call it Thauria. Rhorric, on a long journey to destroy the evil of the world traveled through many places there until he came upon a relic, The Artifact of Light. Not much is known about it now, or where it is. He hid it to prevent it from falling into the wrong hands. The people offered for him to be their ruler, but he refused, wanting to instead be a wandering defender of the land."

"Where did you hear of this?" Gunner asks.

"That legend has been passed down from the people of my great grandfather's time. It's a song the crew has sang from generation to generation to keep the story alive," Bayu says wistfully.

"This crew goes that far back?" I ask in surprise.

Bayu nods. "While some members are new many are descendants of the original crew. People have lived here way before any of you came along."

I look at Gunner and see he's staring into the fire, lost in thought. "What do the symbols mean under the picture?" I ask.

Gunner looks over at the picture again and studies it closely. "From what I know it says the same thing that the song does."

"Here let me look at that," Bayu says, impatiently holding out his hand. I give it to him carefully. The paper seems very old and fragile. He reads it quickly. "That is what it says. Though there is an addition at the end it says that The Artifact of Light is buried where only those who seek to fight darkness will find it."

"And where would that be?" Gunner asks.

Bayu narrows his eyes. "I don't know, and even if I did I wouldn't tell you. You're not worthy to wield it."

Gunner doesn't say anything to that. We go back to listening to the music. Bayu mentioned that there were people living here before us... I wonder if they only live as merchants now? I'm about to ask him more questions when he stands up. "I've got other business to attend to. When you're ready to turn in there's a couple of empty rooms at the back of the ship that you can stay in. We should be catching up to your ship tomorrow." Bayu says, giving me the picture back before walking off, not waiting for an answer.

Gunner goes back to watching the fire. I look at the picture. Rhorric sounds like he was a brave man. It's a curious story, I wonder if there's much truth to it. "It might be able to save us," Gunner mutters to himself.

I don't say anything. I don't know what kind of trouble we're in, but if it's that desperate we might need to try to find that artifact... if it truly exists. I doubt if Bayu would help us. The singing goes on, telling tales of old. Some of it I can understand, some of it is in the other language. I end up drifting off to an old lullaby of decades past.

I wake up to people talking cheerfully. Looking around I realize that I slept in my seat. I must've been more tired than I thought. I look and see that Gunner is chatting with a man about his armor. I rub my eyes. People are seated at the tables around us eating the morning meal. After I wake up I go and have my breakfast.

After the morning meal everyone moves to get to work. I wait for Gunner to finish his conversation before heading to the control room. We find Bayu is already there managing the ship. He looks at us with a look that makes me feel that he thinks we are incompetent. "What took you so long? Thought you'd be here sooner."

"It doesn't matter, we're here now," Gunner says.

"Well what is it? We have a lot of work ahead of us to get this ship back in order."

"I've come to let you know that we're leaving. I have urgent business to tend to and can't remain here any longer."

"Fine. I can't get you to Pike III right now anyway. Your ship should be in the hangar where you left it."

Gunner walks out of the room, and I follow him. When we get to the hangar he stops short.

"What is it?" I ask.

"My ship's gone," he says. "What did Bayu do with it?" He rushes back to the control room. He continues past the guards without question and opens the door.

Bayu turns around to see who came in. "You haven't left yet?"

"My ship is gone," Gunner says with his arms crossed.

"Well I didn't do anything with it. Of course the last of Lewis's crew did retreat in haste... maybe they took your ship when they were trying to escape."

"If they did that, then I need another ship," Gunner says, watching Bayu closely.

"All we got right now are carriers. The fighters all need repair," Bayu says.

We can't go back to Pike III in one of those... we'd be attacked instantly.

"Then I'll need you to take us back to Pike III."

"Back to Pike III? That's out of my route, now that I need to get some more ship repairs done."

"Well my ship was in your hangar, and you did let them make off with it. It was an expensive ship, but I'm sure you can pay to replace it."

"Alright. Fine. We'll take you there," Bayu says in aggravation. I can't say for sure how much that ship would cost, but I can tell that it would be a lot.

I look at one of the maps and see that in a few days we'll make it to Yenath. He'll probably drop off cargo there first. All we can do now is wait.

CHAPTER 23

ONCE WE GET to Yenath, Bayu has some cargo sent by two carrier ships to another cruiser. I never finished trying to repair those... I think I'll leave that to his mechanics this time. With the stops Bayu makes it takes us most of the day before Pike III comes into view. "Looks like I'll be dropping you off soon," Bayu says as he prepares the ship to enter orbit.

"Where's the crew? I thought we'd be meeting them in space," I say.

"They're back home," Gunner says.

Bayu gives him a quizzical look. "You mean home for you. It's not really home to them."

Gunner doesn't say anything. I mean it's true, I don't feel like the palace is my home. I'd be surprised if the others feel that way. We're all just wanderers who've been brought together from other places. "We're a people of wanderers from an oppressed land. We make our homes where we can find them," Gunner says with strength in his voice. A surprised look quickly crosses Bayu's face before he hides it. "What? You didn't think I knew how that feels?" Gunner asks.

Bayu doesn't respond to that. Soon we're in orbit making our way to the settlement's hangar. I get my helmet from the maintenance room, and go back to Bayu and Gunner before we land. "Finally," Bayu says as the ship makes it to the hangar. He sounds relieved that we will be gone. "Escort them to the hangar, then we'll be on our way," he says in a good-riddance tone. He gives Gunner and I payment as compensation for everything.

The guards escort us past the mess hall to the hangar. I can hear singing coming from there but can't make out the words. Once we set foot in Pike III's hangar they're gone. Guards approach Gunner immediately, and he orders a carrier to take us to the palace.

As we fly through the settlement I study the jungle. I watch as we pass floating houses and lanterns. If it weren't for the temperature being so hot here I wouldn't mind living in a place like this. I'd much rather be in a cold climate, since that's been my life.

The window I'm looking out of becomes covered in clouds as the carrier makes its way upward. Nothing can be seen for two minutes, then as we make it above the clouds beautiful reds and oranges can be seen as the sun is preparing to set. The ship skims along the clouds, once again reminding me of a ship sailing along the ocean. Ahead the palace stands firmly on the island, as if nothing could ever shake it.

It's windows are glowing with a golden light, matching the sunset. Mountain peaks can be seen poking through the clouds from the planet below. The carrier lands in the hangar, bringing our journey to an end. I step out and can't help but look at the hangar in awe all over again. It's so different from how Bayu had things set up. Guards come up to Gunner, but he waves them off. They stay at a distance instead.

We leave the hangar and begin to walk along the walkway. Moths gather around the lamp posts, and fireflies can be seen flickering among the pines. As the sunset starts to sink lower, the sunlight decides to hide behind the trees, peeking out through the branches.

The remaining light casts shadows on the land. The birds have grown quiet, settling down for the night. Gemstone lamps warmly glow orange. Each lamp holds a large gem that glows no matter the time of day. The walkway meanders it's way to the palace. I still think it's a bit long, but it does let you take everything in around you before you get there.

Once we get there the guards greet us and open the doors. We go through, and I feel a sense of relief now that things will be getting back on track. We go up the stairs and stop at the doors of the throne room. Gunner turns to me. "I've got some things I need to tend to, but the others should be in the same living area that you were in before. Do you remember the way?"

"Yeah I think so," I say. It shouldn't be too hard; I haven't been away from the palace for that long.

"You can get the guards to help you if you need it."

"Thanks," I say, starting to go my own way as the guards open the doors to the throne room. I pause to watch the light stream through the doors as they open. The windows of the dome catch the last glint of sunlight. The doors shut, and I turn to go before the guards can give me a wary glance. I try my best to remember the way, and only get turned around once. When I finally make it to the living area I find that it's empty except for Roxanne. She's pacing back and forth with a concerned look on her face.

"Hey Roxanne," I say, breaking the silence as I walk into the room.

She tenses and waits a split second before turning to face me. When she does her concerned expression is gone. "I see you finally escaped the clutches of that merchant."

"Yeah, it took me longer to get back than I anticipated. His ship got boarded, and I couldn't leave until the battle was over," I say with a laugh. I've decided to try and make the best of what happened. I'm glad I took those bandages off of my forehead, she would've never let me hear the end of it.

Roxanne rolls her eyes. "That's just like them."

"So, how have things been here? You looked like you were thinking about something when I first came in."

She glares at me. "Oh it's nothing. Fauve's just disappeared again. I was trying to decide if I need to go hunt her down or not."

"She's probably somewhere in the palace," I say, trying to be reassuring. Inside I know that might not be true. She could be off searching for treasure. I decide not to mention it to Roxanne. It won't help anything, and she'll just be critical.

"Yeah who knows," Roxanne responds. "If you're looking for the others some of them are training. Raya's at the forge. It's a workshop built to the left of the palace."

"Thanks," I say, leaving the living area. No matter how I talk to her it always feels like she wants to get rid of me. I might as well give up and just be on my way. I look to find a door that leaves the palace, but the only one I happen upon is the one Gunner used when we were on our way to the armory. Deciding to head out of it anyway I take a glance at the beach.

To my surprise Gunner is standing there at the edge again. The wind is blowing through his hair, and thunder roars from the clouds near the mountains. I turn my back and begin walking. He has a lot on his mind, and I don't want to disturb him.

As I turn the corner of the palace a small building emerges from the trees. As I walk up to the door I can hear the sound of machinery running.

"Come on, we've got to get more heat!" I hear Raya call out as I open the door. Against the wall to my left is a huge furnace, with a control panel off to the side of it. Some people are by the control panel, moving levers and pushing buttons. Raya's standing in front of the forge with sweat dripping down her face. A metal crusher is sitting to the right, straining to break large chunks of frosthur into smaller pieces. It doesn't take long for me to start wiping sweat from my brow.

"We're increasing the heat," a man calls to her.

The flames in the furnace burst in reaction, before calming down a little. The furnace is behind a temperature blocking glass wall. It was developed by scientists so that when extreme temperatures are used the heat from the furnace can't get to the rest of the room. A temperature reader can be seen on the wall next to it… it's currently reading six thousand degrees! "Let's see… seven thousand three hundred degrees should be hot enough to start… the furnace can handle seven thousand five hundred tops…" Raya mutters to herself, glancing up at the temperature of the furnace. She looks over at the people over by the control panel. "Not hot enough!"

They start pressing more buttons. Frosthur is unusual in that it's so cold that it takes extreme heat to melt it. A man bursts through the door, rushing up to Raya. "I found them," he says, trying to catch his breath as he hands her a set of tongs and a hammer that are bluish silver in color.

Raya looks relieved. "Thank ya for this. I thought I was goin' to have to try to work with tools that would be harder to use with this heat."

The man nods and turns, leaving the room.

Raya notices me and waves. "Can't stop to talk now Franca, but yer free to watch." She checks the temperature again. "Almost there!" she calls out, wiping the sweat from her forehead with her arm. A popping sound comes from the metal of the furnace as it begins to climb hotter in temperature. I don't know how much longer I'll be staying in here… the heat is uncomfortable. I didn't know frosthur needed to be heated at such a high temperature. I wonder what she's making?

Ten crates of frosthur are sitting to the side of the metal crusher. It's all raw material that hasn't been refined into anything yet. I wonder if she has enough to work with? I thought Bayu gave us more than that, since it took quite a few trips with a carrier ship to transport it all. I stop a man walking by to ask him about the frosthur. "Do you know why we have so little of it? I thought we had gotten more than that?"

"The captain had to make so many trips because of how heavy it is," Raya says, overhearing me.

The man continues on, and I have to wonder why this is all so important. Gunner acts as if it's our last hope. Once the furnace hits the needed temperature Raya gives the go ahead to start smelting. When things seem to be running fine she looks at the crates of frosthur and shakes her head. "There's not nearly enough," she says turning to me.

"What's Gunner wanting to do with it?"

"He didn't say, other than that we would need to start making armor and weapons. I don't know of any other metal that's stronger than frosthur."

"It seems like other people are working to get their hands on it as quickly as they can."

"The last thing we need is for marauders to get it," she says as she watches the furnace. I stay with her for a little longer before calling it a day. I'll check in again once she's done smelting to see what she's going to make first. I step out of the workshop, relieved as a cool breeze sweeps over me.

The stars are shining brightly above in a clear night sky. Moonlight casts its light on the land, wrapping the island in its gentle light. The clouds have calmed down and are setting peacefully around the shore. To my surprise I find that Gunner is still standing there, watching the sky. He turns and heads back to the palace, shaking his head. I find myself following him, curious of what's going on.

I wish he would be more transparent with us, so we would know what's happening. Maybe that's wishing for too much. I enter through the doorway a few moments after him and see that he is making his way to the throne room. He starts to turn around and I immediately hide in a nearby hallway. After he pauses for a moment he continues onward. I know I shouldn't be following him, but I have so many unanswered questions.

He walks up to the doors of the throne room and opens them himself as there are no guards there. He forgets to close the door and walks slowly to his throne. Moonlight shines through the palace windows. Picking up a sword handle that's leaning against the throne he presses a button, and the blade comes out, letting moonlight reflect on it. The blade is a familiar bluish silver. He's silent for a moment, then shakes his head. "Father how can I do this without you? If only I had a fraction of your wisdom..." He says, looking at the blade.

I stand frozen in place at the door. If I move right now he will hear me. He puts the blade away, turning. He sees me before I can get out of sight. Again I feel embarrassed. Why do I always get caught? "I'm guessing there's not enough frosthur?" I expected him to say something about my listening in. I walk into the room, passing the large wooden doors.

"Raya said it's not nearly enough," I say, trying to hide my embarrassment.

He sighs. "I thought so. We're going to have to head out and get more immediately."

"Why do we need it so badly?" If we're on the verge of war I want to know.

"Because my brother's not playing games anymore. Things are getting worse by the day, and if I don't figure out what to do soon more lives will be at stake." Gunner looks out the window, "I wish I knew what my father would do, because no one else seems to know. If I confront my brother it will most likely lead to war, but if I let him be he will destroy everything with the path that he's taken." He looks back at me. "Getting frosthur may be the last defense we have for the people. At this point it is our last hope."

"Maybe we can get more from Bayu?"

For a moment a defensive look crosses his face. "Bayu can't be trusted. He's only out for his own gains. I'll only go to him again if absolutely necessary." I knew Gunner didn't like Bayu, but I thought he would be more willing to put up with him again if we needed to.

"Isn't there a deal that you could work out with your brother?" I ask, trying to find another solution.

"No, I've already tried that. He wants me gone, and now that our father has passed away he doesn't feel like he has to keep the formalities anymore. I would rather not fight, and have been holding off for a long time, wishing to mend things with him. But when it costs the lives of others? Then I can't stand aside any longer." Gunner says with a trace of sadness in his voice.

"And your mother?" I ask, immediately regretting the question.

He hesitates. "When we were escaping from The Sarthrian Empire one of the enemy soldiers shot her ship down... she didn't make it."

"I'm sorry to hear that," I say, not knowing what else to add to that. I kind of remember some talk of that happening, but it feels like it's been a long time since I've heard that story and had forgotten.

"It's okay, not everyone remembers what happened," Gunner looks at his communicator. "It's getting late. We'll have another long day ahead of us and it's best to turn in."

I agree with him and make my way out of the throne room. Now that I'm starting to get the layout of the palace I'm having less trouble getting back to our quarters.

I get there and find that Roxanne is talking on her communicator. "If I don't get a hold of her soon I'm going to have to notify Alex about this... where did you last see her?" she asks as she paces the room. She makes eye contact with me and turns away so I can't see her face. Fauve's still missing? I hope she's okay. I walk over to one of the seats and sit down. I want to know if I should be out searching for her. "What?" Roxanne asks me as she ends the call.

Before I can say anything Fauve bursts through the door, out of breath. "You called?" she asks, trying to slow her breathing.

Roxanne crosses her arms. "Where have you been? Maylea and I have been searching for you."

"Oh, I was just exploring around the palace," Fauve says, shifting one foot to the other.

"For two days?" Roxanne asks, clearly not believing a word of it.

"I also looked around the island. There are some good spots for camping around here!" she says cheerfully.

Roxanne clenches her fist. "This isn't time for fun and games Fauve. We need you here and can't keep stopping things to look for you."

"I just get restless is all. I said I would be back," Fauve says casually, as if none of this is a big deal.

Roxanne doesn't back down. "We don't have time for that. Things are getting serious now. You have a duty here Fauve, and you're expected to do it."

"Sorry," Fauve mutters, looking like she knows there's no way out of this one.

"It's getting late. From what I see on our communicator we have another mission in the morning. We better get ready for it." With that Roxanne heads to her room, almost slamming the door.

"You okay Fauve?" I ask. I hope she's not in danger.

She forces a smile, trying to sound confident but failing. "I'm fine. They've lost my trail now... so we shouldn't have to worry about that anymore."

"That's good to hear," I say, not feeling assured at all. Soon the others return, cheerfully greeting Fauve. Most of them are concerned, but glad she's back. After talking for a bit we all turn in and prepare for the next day. I find myself quickly drifting off to sleep.

CHAPTER 24

I WAKE UP in the morning and head over to the standing mirror to make sure that I'm ready for the day. Now that my armor is new I don't look so rough. I notice the weariness in my grey eyes. I must be more tired than I realize. I leave my room and am greeted by the others bustling around. "Got everythin'?" Raya asks me, shouldering her heavy pack.

"Yep, I've got all my gear," I say, glancing at my armor.

"Maybe you could help me carry some of mine?" she asks. Roxanne glances at her and shakes her head, shouldering her pack with ease.

"Sure," I say, moving to pick up her other pack with my free hand. I carry my helmet in the other. The sound her pack makes tells me that it's full of metal pieces and tools. Raya leads me to our ship and shows me where she's setting her gear. Alex and Gunner are already planning the route for today.

"So we're checking the asteroid field near Rythor this time?" Alex asks.

"Yes, I suspect that's where the merchants are currently getting frosthur from. There's nothing left in the field near Durath," Gunner says. The trip to Rythor is long, but uneventful. I'm starting to see how boring ship travel can be. Despite Fauve telling me that she's not being hunted down anymore I still catch her looking out the windows and checking the radar system. If she's in that much trouble, then aren't we as well? Surely those people that are after her wouldn't just attack her and not the rest of us. Days pass before we make it to the asteroid field. To our surprise we find that it's silent here.

"Hey Franca?" Fauve asks, motioning for me to come over.

"What is it?" I ask, walking up to her.

She looks around to make sure that the others are occupied before speaking. "You do see that ship over there, right?"

I look out the window and at first I don't see anything. As I look closer though I can just barely see the outline of a black ship off in the distance. While it's far away it seems to be keeping up with us. "Yeah I see it. It's not even trying to follow us from behind," I say, watching it closely.

"I thought I had lost them but no, they've been with me this whole time," Fauve says in disappointment.

"Do you think they'll attack us Fauve?" I ask in a serious tone.

"Well…"

"We have to know; we may be in danger. And if they're this determined to keep following you things aren't right."

She hesitates before speaking. I'm about to break the silence when she finally does. "They're looking for an opportunity to catch me alone. I think it's unlikely that they'd attack us outright."

"We should let Gunner know about this… it's been unresolved for a long time."

She looks at me for the first time in a while and I'm surprised to see the weariness in her eyes. "This is my life Franca. It's always been this way and will be as long as I work to uncover artifacts. I'm almost always being followed by someone or other."

"Well why does it have to be that way?" I ask. If it were me I'd be trying to change my circumstances.

"Not everyone who looks for these artifacts are focused on preserving history. Many of them want to sell them and are not careful when excavating. I hate to see broken artifacts... I'm trying to save them. If they weren't worth so much maybe it'd be different... it'd be easier for me to get to them first." Before I can respond the ship shakes, throwing me off of my feet.

"We're being attacked! Everyone at their stations," Gunner orders. Roxanne bursts into the main area and takes control of one of the turrets. Lance takes the one on my side. Fauve rushes to the control room and I put on my helmet. Raya comes to my side to help with the repairs. From what I see so far the shot didn't do much damage. It's strange that it made it past the ship's shields. I hear another missile fire, but we dodge it. Alex never does that... maybe Gunner's piloting the ship?

I make my way to the control room to look at the radar system. It's detecting a large ship. I look out the window and see that it is dark grey in color. The black one has disappeared. Soon other ships appear alongside it, all grey. Then many ships that look just like ours surround us.

"Look at that," Alex says in amazement. "Where did they all come from?" he asks in wonder.

"They've been here all along. Invisibility cloaking comes in handy at times," Gunner says. The enemy ships start firing at us. Gunner's warships jump to our defense, staying around us. I count at least fifteen. Ships on both sides crash and burn. Through it all our ship isn't touched. Roxanne fires her turret whenever she gets a clear shot. Soon all that's left is the ship that attacked us first.

It takes off, heading towards Rythor. "After it!" Gunner calls out to Alex. Our ship speeds up in response. The ship makes a sharp turn back into the asteroid field. We follow, turning and twisting to follow the ship's path as it weaves through the asteroids. "Hold back so he thinks we've lost him," Gunner commands.

Alex slows down the ship, and we follow at a slower pace. We watch it from a distance, and after an hour a mining ship approaches it. Carrier ships go to it and return, then the mining ship leaves. The ship we've been following takes off, and we once again go along at a distance. As it gets closer to Rythor's orbit it abruptly turns and lands on the planet's moon. Gunner has us land a small distance away so that we can see what's going on. The moons near Hayventh are covered in ice, but this one is more like a miniature planet with grass and trees.

We get our gear on and step off of the ship. Roxanne gets out her advanced scanner device.

"Roxanne, what do you see?" Gunner asks.

"There are men loading crates of frosthur onto a carrier ship."

"That's what I thought. How many crates are there?"

"There are at least thirty," she responds.

"Thirty? We were only able to get ten!" Lance exclaims.

"We can't let that shipment go through," Gunner says.

"Want me to take them out?" Roxanne asks, putting away the advanced scanner device and getting out her rifle.

"Not yet."

"Do you think they're merchants?" Blair asks.

"Those ships that attacked us looked like they belonged to marauders," Alex says.

"We'll have to do a surprise attack then," Blair says. We all sneak closer to the marauders except for Roxanne. Raya was hesitant to come into battle with us but didn't want to be left alone on the ship either. She decided to go with us, but at the back of the group. Gunner gives Roxanne the signal, and she fires a shot, immediately killing one of the men.

Before the men can react Blair and Lance start firing, sending everything into chaos. I look at their armor, and see that it's all dark grey, but has a symbol of a Tiger on it with "The Corruption" written under it. "More marauders," I say.

"They're not marauders. I don't have time right now to explain," Gunner says, his attention turning towards something to the right of us.

I look to see a man standing to the side of the battle, watching Gunner. His armor is a deep black, different from the other men. The sword he carries has a blade that is of the same material. When I look closer I see that it is jagged, dripping with blood. Lance sees the man and fires a shot at him. The bullet hits his armor, and ricochets off of it. The man doesn't even flinch.

He walks in our direction, ignoring the gunshots. Most of the men are laying on the ground, with the remaining ones retreating. He stops at a safe distance from us. "What are you doing, attacking my men?" the man asks angrily. "I have a shipment to deliver."

"I know what you're doing," Gunner says, standing tall. He puts his gun away, as there is no use in using it. The man is wearing a helmet that bullets would not be able to go through.

The man glares at Gunner. "Sure you do. But let me say this. You won't be king much longer once Ty finishes his plans. You might as well give up now."

"You're to turn over this shipment," Gunner says calmly, not backing down.

The man smiles and laughs. "I'll be rewarded for bringing the dead king's body to my master."

Gunner draws his blade. It is a silvery blue in color with white light shining around the edges. The handle is like his crown, glowing brightly with what looks like white gemstones. I can't tell what they are, but they're not gemstones. The man yells, raising his sword and striking at Gunner. Their blades meet, and Gunner's lets out a flash of light with each strike. I can feel vibrations in the ground as the blades clash together. Gunner's blade hits the ground as he misses the man, and the force creates a depression in the ground. The ground trembles, almost causing me to lose my footing.

They swing strike after strike, neither one willing to give in. The man starts to look tired, but keeps going. Gunner is breathing hard, but keeps pushing his attack. Their fight carries on for a little longer before the man steps back, wiping sweat from his brow. He signals to the last of his men, and they fire off a weapon that releases a smokey thick mist into the air.

The smell of smoke fills the air as my vision is blinded. I try to get out of it, but it seems to be everywhere. Ship engines power up, then are gone. We're left in silence as the smokey mist hangs in the air.

"Is everyone okay?" Gunner asks as it fades away. We all say that we are.

"We've got a problem," Roxanne says.

"And what's that?" Lance asks.

"They made off with our ship. We're stranded."

"Great. What're we going to do now?" Blair asks.

"I will get in touch with my army, they should be nearby and will come back for us," Gunner says.

"Maybe we can find an abandoned ship or somethin'," Raya says. I notice that Fauve's been unusually quiet. I wonder why?

"It's getting late, we should start setting up camp," Maylea says.

"Right," Lance says. I have a portable tent in my gear, but I don't know what the others have. Everyone decides that we need to camp somewhere hidden. As we're looking for a place Gunner glances at the sky every now and then. We lost all that frosthur...

"Uh Gunner?" Blair asks, catching up to him.

"Yes?" Gunner responds, stopping and turning to him.

"Why isn't your army here yet? When you called them before they came right away."

"They reported that there were more ships tailing us... from a different group. My men didn't know who they were and decided to lead them away from us," Gunner replies before continuing on. Blair nods. We continue on, and eventually come to a place that looks good for building our camp.

"Alright, we're setting up camp here," Gunner says. Raya and Lance go deeper into the forest to get firewood for a campfire. I'm about to go help them when Fauve motions for me to come over to her. She's standing to the side, away from everyone. I go over to her while Maylea eyes me suspiciously.

Once I get closer she motions for me to follow. We go off deeper into the forest, away from the others. Once we're out of earshot she speaks. "I haven't said anything to the others, because I'm not sure I should," she says after glancing around. "On one hand it might help us, but on the other it will reveal to everyone the life I've been living."

"We won't know how they'll react until you tell them," I say. In my opinion we could use all the help we can get.

"Well, I have a ship I can call over with my communicator... it only holds two people, and it's full of artifacts right now..." Fauve says, biting her lip.

I pause. This could help us, but I don't know how the others will feel knowing that she's been doing other things besides helping us this whole time. "Well it would help, though it's possible Gunner's army may come and get us."

"And what if they don't?"

"Then other than finding an abandoned ship yours is our only hope."

"I think I could leave and get help, then come back. Do you think it would be okay to wait a little before saying anything?"

I'm not sure what to say on that one. Gunner acts like we're racing against time. This would cause Fauve some trouble though... "Why don't we ask Gunner? He won't feel the same way about this as the crew does," I suggest. He knows more than I do about what's going on anyway.

"I guess I could... okay, I'll do that," Fauve says, agreeing quicker than I thought she would.

"We better get back to camp." We make our way back and find that almost everyone has a tent set up. Fauve starts helping Blair with the remainder of the tasks. I walk over to Raya, who doesn't seem to have a tent. "It doesn't look like you've set anything up yet," I say.

"I left all my supplies on the ship, so everythin' I had is gone." She waves her hand dismissively. "Eh I'll be fine. I'll just sleep under the stars." I can tell that she's trying to not let on how much it bothers her that her stuff is gone.

"You can have my tent," I say, handing a folded tent to her. "I'm used to sleeping out in the open without one and don't mind."

She shakes her head, "I can't do that to ya."

"No really, I don't mind," I say, starting to set it up for her. I look over to see where Fauve is. She's adding wood to the fire. Gunner goes deeper into the forest, and she doesn't follow him. Maybe I should've offered to talk to him for her? As it gets dark everyone gets closer to the campfire.

It feels like winter is just starting here. Everyone has a day's worth of rations on them, so I don't have to start hunting yet. I'm prepared to if needed. The stars are shining brightly on us, and one falls.

Gunner returns to camp and lets us know that his army is still fighting with that other group that was tailing us. I wonder if those were the ones who were after Fauve? Everyone turns in for the night, and I lay on the ground by the fire. I drift off, listening to the crackling of the flames.

I squint as the light of the sun shines on my face. Wayford's gates stand tall before me, with guards on either side. Pine trees are standing just outside of the log walls, and watchtowers are positioned near the gates. I look to my left and see that I have some pelts slung over my shoulder. Gotta bring those in. The guards nod at me as I pass, and I merge with the rest of the hunters on the other side.

I make my way towards the hunter's district. The familiar smell of cooking meat reaches me as people drift from stall to stall. The smell of pine wafts through the air over a breeze that feels refreshing under the warm sun. I come up to the leather craft stall and put my hides on the counter.

"Got more hides for me ay?" Kade says.

"Yep, got some wolves out south," I hear myself say. I look over as a woman with auburn hair comes and stands next to me.

"What can I do for you?" Kade asks, turning to her.

"I'm looking for some blankets," the woman says, glancing over at me. I've never seen amber eyes like hers. I wonder where she's from? We get some travelers, but most prefer warmer climates. Her clothes are ragged and light... definitely not something you would want to wear out here. It is the summer season, so some people think the cold weather's not a danger anymore. And of course, for all I know she may be just passing through.

Kade smiles at her through his thick red beard. "Sure thing, I'll get some for you to look at." He moves away from the counter. "Oh and Franca, I've been meaning to tell ya..." He says, looking over at me as he sorts through some blankets on the table. I feel the woman's attention shift to me. I try my best to ignore it. I never like being watched like that.

"Yeah, what's up?" I ask. I bet it's another hovercraft or ship to repair.

"My wife says something's funky with her hovercraft again. Something about a rattling sound?"

Called it. "It'll take me two hours to fix it. I'll see if I have the parts for it when I get home."

"Sounds good, you'll get store credit, as usual," Kade says appreciatively.

"You fix things?" the woman asks curiously.

Uh oh. "Yeah, I can repair things," I say hesitantly.

"Do you think you'd be interested in a job as a mechanic on a ship?" the woman asks, her eyes glinting with adventure.

"Well, I'm not sure..." I begin to say.

"Why not Franca? You're always telling me you'd like a change in scenery. I bet you'd come back with all sorts of stories," Kade says.

"How long would I be gone?" I ask the woman.

"I can't tell you that, but..." Her voice fades out and I can't hear the rest of what she's saying. I nod in response, and Kade starts talking. Everything gradually fades to white.

CHAPTER 25

I WAKE UP to Fauve shaking my shoulder. "Franca wake up," she whispers quickly in a hushed tone.

"What is it?" I ask in a low voice, starting to get up.

"Shh! I've got to talk to you," she says, looking around at the others to make sure they are still asleep.

"Again?" I whisper back, looking over at Lance. He's standing a small distance from our makeshift camp, carrying his gun in both hands. While he is facing away from us right now, he won't be for long.

"Yes come on," she says, grabbing my arm and pulling me up.

I sigh. What could it be now? I had hoped she had gone to Gunner and spoken with him on the matter. I think about my dream as we head deeper into the forest and walk among the shadows of the night. I find it curious that I didn't recognize Jalyn in that one... I wonder if I dreamed of Wayford because I'm homesick? I don't feel that way...

Once Fauve's sure that we're out of earshot she speaks, still keeping her voice low. "Franca I've got to go. One of my rivals is getting close to discovering an artifact I've been trying to trace for a long time..."

"Go? You can't leave us here like this! Didn't you talk to Gunner?" I ask, shocked that she's even thinking of leaving us right now.

"Shh! Keep it down! I'm going to send back help before I head to the ruins," she says, looking off in the direction of camp.

"How can you be sure that will work? Our plan before was to use your ship to get help, then have you return in case we still needed it."

"Of course it'll work. The others are tough and don't need much assistance. And besides, the help I send back will get there before they notice anything," Fauve says, sounding confident about this.

"Why are you even telling me this then? You could've left and gotten a head start." Usually that's what she does anyway.

"Well actually, I'd like for you to come with me on this one."

"Come with you? Why would you need me with you?" I ask, feeling intrigued. This was not how I expected things to go. I can't see why she'd think that I'd be of any help.

"Because. I need a ship mechanic on hand... in case anything were to go wrong. I can't take any chances on my ship getting in the way of making it to the artifact before my rival. And it has been making this sound..." We both pause at a rustling noise. We resume our conversation once we realize it was just the wind.

"Fauve I can't leave the others. They might need me to hunt or repair something here. And also, how stable is your ship? It sounds like you might need a different one for this."

"I don't have time for that. The others have a day's worth of rations on them, and we'll be back by then," she says, starting to sound desperate. "Look, you don't really have to go with me the whole way. If the people we find to help us have a cruiser you can get a ride back with them. By that time we'll know if my ship will make the journey alright."

"I don't know about this..." I say, hesitating. I can tell by the look in her eyes she will leave whether I go with her or not. If she were to get stranded or distracted she might not send help back, or even return to us. Gunner still hasn't heard anything from his troops... I don't know what happened to them. If we got back by tomorrow Fauve's plan would probably work out. I'm not sure if anyone would notice that we'd gone. They might think I was out hunting, and Fauve... well they're no strangers to her disappearing. "If we can make it back before we'd be missed I'll go. Otherwise I can't." I say, having a sense that I might regret this.

Fauve pauses for a moment, then responds. "Okay, I'll get us back here as soon as possible," she says, walking along a nearby creek. I follow, already questioning my decision. I don't want her to get stranded or something, but I feel like we're also knocking on trouble's door by doing this. We make it to a small clearing, and sure enough her ship is stationed there. It's a scouting ship with two seats and some storage in the back. An older model for sure, but not ancient. At least not by my standards. "Here it is!" she says, walking confidently up to it. "Hold on while I clear some space for you," she says as she opens the air locked door.

I start looking closer at the ship as she moves things to the storage behind the seats. The ship seems to be in fine shape, maybe the engine is sounding a bit rough from age? Before I can put my helmet on to check the condition of the ship Fauve grabs my hand and pulls me towards the door. "I just checked my sources on where my rival is and we don't have much time," she says, rushing to the pilot's seat.

I quickly get in and shut the door as she powers the ship up. I hope she doesn't forget about the others... I can tell already that her focus is shifting to other things. The engine makes a sound, and then stops. The engine groans as it starts running. "It's a little slow," she says smiling at me.

"Yeah," I say, with a sinking feeling in my stomach. The ship becomes surprisingly quiet as it warms up. Soon we're in the sky, floating above our troubles. I look at the moon below as we begin to leave it behind. I wonder what kind of wildlife lives there? As we pass it I turn my focus to our first mission; getting help.

I know that Gunner's troops might be nearby, and it would be good to keep an eye out for them. Hopefully we can find them. If we don't we will have to resort to sending out a distress signal. I start looking at the ship's control panel for the radar system, and make the discovery that there isn't one.

"Fauve, where is your radar system?" I ask, feeling unsettled. We shouldn't be flying in space without that.

"I don't have one. Most of the time I just use this ship for storage on Rythor. The carrier ships on our old cruiser were more convenient, and covered up my tracks better," she confesses.

"I wish I had known about that before agreeing to this," I say.

Fauve makes a face as the engine starts making a sound. It's getting louder and louder. She kicks the area in front of her feet, and the sound stops. Something falls in the back of the ship. Who knows what that was. There's a pile of junk by my feet... I wonder when the last time was that she had this ship cleaned? "Aren't the stars beautiful today?" she asks, trying to divert my attention away from the ship.

"Nice try."

"Yeah I know... it doesn't sound too good does it?"

"No, it doesn't." I will admit however that the ship does have a good speed to it. It takes us all day to get near Durath. Neither of us have seen Gunner's troops so far. We've been keeping an eye out for any cruisers that we could contact, but have found none so far.

Fauve squints and looks ahead as the ship starts rocking from the distortion.

"Can you help me look for the distortion Franca?"

"Yeah, sure," I say, feeling annoyed. This is exactly why we needed a radar system, along with the fact that it's harder to navigate around other ships. Why did I agree to this?

By early morning Durath comes into view. As soon as we come closer to its orbit, Fauve's communicator starts buzzing. "Hello?" she asks casually.

"Fauve what are you doing? Aric is almost on site, and you're nowhere to be seen," a man's voice says in a frustrated tone. He's speaking so loud that I can hear him through her earpiece.

"Sorry about that, closing in now," she says, somehow getting the ship to go faster.

"I swear Fauve sometimes I wonder what you're doing in your free time that makes you so late to things. Can't whatever you're doing wait?" She hasn't told him that she's part of the military?

"Well I'm almost there, so it's nothing to worry about," Fauve says in a carefree tone.

The man on the other end starts to sound agitated. "Aric expects you to be on time. The stakes are high on this one, and the Wayfarer is ahead of us."

"Already?" Fauve asks, sounding a little alarmed. "Whatever, we'll still end up ahead in the end."

"You better hope so," the man says in a threatening tone. "Now get down here!" he yells, abruptly ending the call.

Fauve looks over at me. "He never gets off my back."

"What about sending help to the others?" I ask. I have a feeling things are not heading in the direction I had hoped.

"We'll get to that, it'll just have to be after this."

I don't like where this is going. We can't just drop everything like this.

"Look, this is important too. And it's a little more time sensitive. This won't take long, we'll be back with the others before you know it," she says as we enter Durath's atmosphere.

I hope she's right, and that this isn't going to become a tangent. We fly over the settlement, and head north, beyond the sandy cliffs. Durath has a semi-arid climate, supporting dry grasslands with some wildlife here and there. Some areas are just sand and cactus for as far as the eye can see. We seem to be heading towards an area that is more like that. The engine starts making sounds and Fauve kicks the ship again, silencing it. Looking out in the distance I can see some sandstone ruins, with ships stationed near it. She lands the ship among them, and I discover that all the others look to be in similar shape to hers. The first light of the sunrise greets me as I exit the ship. I leave my helmet in the ship, not wanting to carry it with me. Fauve runs up to a man, leaving me behind.

He shakes his head in aggravation as I catch up. "You're late… if you hurry you might catch up to Aric. He won't be in a good mood though." I immediately recognize his voice from earlier. He barks orders to some other people, who are getting ready to search the ancient tower nearby. Someone calls out to him, needing assistance with something. As he leaves us I turn to say something to Fauve, only to discover that she's running towards the ruins. I sigh and start running after her. The sandstone structure lies sprawled out ahead of us. Time seems to have eaten away at some of the walls, but otherwise everything seems to still be intact. Three watchtowers rise above the walls… I wonder how stable those are?

I expect Fauve to pause at the steps, but she doesn't. Soon I'm running up them, trying to catch up. I can feel the sun beating on me as I reach the top of the steps. Old columns reach into the sky, missing whatever they use to support. The columns lead up to the entrance of the ruins. Fauve heads to the entrance, checking over her shoulder to see if I've been following her before heading inside.

Torches that are placed along the walls are already lit, and in the center of the small room is a set of stairs heading down. I can see the warm glow of torchlight coming from below. "Looks like I'm really late this time," Fauve mutters to herself as she descends to the lower level.

I follow, curious to see what's below. Ruins have been discovered on all of our planets... unfortunately marauders have been drawn to them, causing exploration to be limited. I get to the bottom of the steps and see we're in another room that's a little larger than the other. At one side of it a man is standing at a closed doorway, looking at the symbols that run along the door frame.

His hooded tan cloak seems like something you wouldn't want to wear in the heat of the desert. "What took you so long this time Fauve? We can't afford to lose this artifact," the man says without turning around. I pause. His voice sounds familiar, but I can't place him.

"I got here as soon as I could. Have you spotted the Wayfarer yet?" she asks.

He steadily continues on with his work, not looking up from it. "No, but when I do she's not going to get away from me this time."

Fauve walks up to the doorway and begins to examine the symbols. I follow, curious if I can make sense of them. To my disappointment they aren't legible to me. Some of them remind me of the ones under the picture I have. I think they're in the same language.

"Who is she?" the man asks, taking a moment to glance at me before turning back to the symbols. He's making note of something in his communicator.

"Oh that's Franca. She's a friend of mine."

"As long as she stays out of my way she can be here."

"This is Aric," Fauve says to me. "He's an expert in capturing looters, and is one of the best trackers out there. If anyone's going to catch the Wayfarer, it'll be him."

Aric doesn't say anything and keeps busy. Next to the doorway are three levers. Two of them are up and one is down. Aric turns to them, and pulls down the one on the right, and flips the one on the left up. Fauve steps back, and I follow suit. I've heard the ruins are filled with traps and other dangers. The sound of gears can be heard as the thick sandstone door moves upward into the ceiling. Aric continues on at a hurried pace down the narrow hallway. I wish I could go at a slower pace, having never been to any of the ruins before.

Aric lights torches as he goes, then abruptly stops. Fauve almost runs into him, and I almost run into her. "What is it?" Fauve asks. I look around her to see that he's looking at the ground.

"She's been here," he says, examining a track in the dirt. He starts walking at a pace that's almost running.

"Aric wait, what if she has others with her?" Fauve asks.

"I don't care about that. I can't let her get away," he says, his voice laced with anger and pent-up frustration. Why is Fauve working with this man? Aric's footsteps get heavier as he starts to run. Fauve and I can barely keep up. We make it to an empty room.

There's an archway on the other three walls. Aric runs towards the archway on our left and jumps as an arrow shoots at his feet. Fauve follows him, sidestepping something. I do the same, not knowing where the trap is. I would prefer to not get hurt, if possible.

We come to another room. This one has a flat walkway that bridges a gap, leading to another archway. Aric and Fauve go ahead without any hesitation. I can't help but look at the pitch black below us on either side. Tired of running I have to slow to a walk. My breath echoes in the silence. I try my best not to think about the void below me. It'd all be over if I fell. Once I make it to the other side I enter another room.

Aric and Fauve are there, examining some symbols on one of the walls. "So there's a chest containing the artifact somewhere in this room," Fauve says.

"Yes... it has to be in the ground," Aric says. This room feels familiar to me, but I don't know why. All that's in the room are some supporting columns, nothing else. I feel a draw to the columns and walk up to one of them. There are some symbols on it, but I don't know what they mean. Fauve and Aric keep talking, ignoring me. They probably see me as useless here. If only I had more knowledge about the ruins...

The column consists of rounded bricks, and I notice one that's ever so slightly depressed into it. Before I can think through what I'm doing I press the brick in and start to hear a rumbling sound.

"What did you do?" Aric demands, turning and walking up to me briskly. We feel a slight shaking in the ground as a sandstone panel moves to the side and a chest raises up out of the ground.

"How did you know about that?" Fauve asks in awe, looking at the column.

"I don't know," I reply. It just seemed familiar to me.

Aric is already at the chest, removing a broken lock from it. Fauve and I make it to the chest as we hear a click. The chest opens, and Aric throws the lock to the side in frustration. There's nothing there.

"Maybe there was nothing there in the first place?" Fauve asks.

"No, she has it. She had to have taken it," he stands, and starts walking back the way we came at a fast pace. Fauve and I follow best we can. "There's still a chance I can catch her!" he says, starting to run.

When we get to the room with the bridge I slow down to cross, warily watching the darkness below. Aric doesn't seem to notice it and continues on. We make it to the outside of the ruins, standing at the top of the steps. "Where could she have gone?" he mutters, catching his breath.

"Maybe she's still inside?" Fauve asks.

"And if she isn't? Then we'd be wasting our time here," he says, spitting on the ground. "She always does this. Takes artifacts and runs off," he grumbles, taking out a scope and looking off into the distance.

The sun is higher in the sky, and what I thought had been intense heat before was nothing like what I'm feeling now. I look over at the ships of the other treasure hunters. Maybe now we can continue on our mission and leave this all behind. "I guess we're free to go now?" I ask.

Aric freezes, then turns around. "I don't know who you are, but you can't interrupt us on this. You have no idea of the importance of our mission." With that he looks out towards the land again. "There," he says, pointing off in the distance. "Those tracks could be hers." He starts walking off towards them. Fauve reluctantly follows.

"Sorry Franca," she says over her shoulder. Now what? If I take her ship I'll leave her stranded, and she's too far away from the settlement. Everyone else here could leave without her, and who knows where they would take her if she asked for a ride.

I go down the steps, following them. I can't help but glance up at the towers, wondering what they were used for. These ruins seem to be out in the middle of nowhere. I look ahead and see we're heading for some hills. Sand is covered with yellow grass that looks like it's long dead. A gentle breeze is blowing through Fauve's light blond hair. Besides the wind and our footsteps there are no other sounds. As we near the hills I look at the sun, watching the time go by. The others will think we've gotten lost. And in a way we have.

CHAPTER 26

ONCE WE ARRIVE at the foot of the hills, Aric kneels and studies the ground. "She went this way, and not long ago," he says to himself. He continues up the hill, not looking back. I wonder if he cares if we follow him? What would happen if we just left? I don't think he could stop us anyway... we all come to a standstill as we hear voices up ahead.

Aric starts moving much quieter and continues to the top of the hill. When I reach the top I see some people up ahead. Their clothes are rugged and tattered, and they're all carrying packs.

"Look, they have some things from the ruins," Fauve whispers.

"I don't see the Wayfarer among them..." Aric says quietly, taking out his scope. "Those are marauders!" he quickly puts the scope away. Before we can react he gets out a gun and charges down the hill yelling and firing it off. Fauve gets out a handgun and heads into the fray, while I stay on the hill with my rifle.

There are five of them, so we're not that outnumbered. I raise my rifle and look down the scope. While Fauve is shooting one of them another is coming up behind her with a blade. I aim and fire, taking him out. Fauve continues on, oblivious to the danger she was in. My rifle is jerked out of my hands, and a cloth is put in my mouth.

Two marauders come into my field of view. "That's a good one," one of them says, admiring my rifle.

"Come on man, we don't have time for that. The others are in trouble, and they got our buddy," the second guy says. The first man ignores him and heads back down the hill with my rifle. I feel someone tying my hands behind my back with rope. There were more people with this group than Aric anticipated... I wish he hadn't charged at them like that. Down below Aric cries out in pain.

"We've got you now," one of the marauders says. Aric takes a few steps back from them. "Men, tie him up," the marauder commands. Aric runs away, heading back in the direction of the ships. A few of the others follow, while I'm brought down to stand next to Fauve, who is also tied up. After a few moments the marauders return empty handed. Hopefully Aric sends someone back to get us. The marauders hurriedly continue onward, taking us further into the hill country.

They seem to know where they are going, and gloat about the loot they got from the ruins. I wonder if they got the relic that Aric was looking for, or if the Wayfarer got it first? Either way it sounds like it has fallen into the wrong hands. Throughout the day they stop, and we are given water. I'm not sure why they care, but I'm grateful as I haven't had water since I got here.

The day goes on, and I can't help but think about the others. Did they get off of Rythor's moon? Or are they still there, waiting for us? My guess would be that they think we're still on the moon somewhere. From what I can tell Fauve said nothing of her ship.

Before I know it dusk hits, and the sun begins to make its descent. I'm surprised to find myself beginning to shiver. The wind has picked up, and it has a bite to it. The man leading the group raises his hand, and everyone stops. "We're going to have to set up camp here. Check to see if the prisoners will be warm enough. Give them a cloak if needed."

The others instantly obey, getting gear out of their packs and making camp. A woman comes up to me with a cloak. "It's going to be okay. They might let you go before they leave Durath," she says with a whisper. Her hazel eyes have a soulful expression, and I can't help but wonder why she's with these people.

She shakes her head, understanding me in some way. "No, I have to stay. Maybe someday I too will be free," she whispers, going behind me to untie me, checking over my armor to see if it's warm enough. It has temperature regulation features, so I don't think I'll need a cloak. I feel relieved to be untied. The woman moves back in front of me. "With that type of armor I think you will be warm enough for the night," she says. A marauder that happens to be walking by nods at her as he passes. Her brownish red hair glows in the last light of the sun.

She goes behind me to bind my wrists back together again. I brace myself a little, expecting her to tie the rope tight like it was before. To my surprise she leaves it a little loose. Not enough for me to get out of it, but enough that I could possibly work my way free...

She gets in front of me again. "How's that?" she asks, her hazel eyes looking into mine inquisitively. I nod, unable to speak still because of the gag. "If you do get free, head north," she whispers, smiling at me.

With that she leaves me, not looking back. I watch as someone else ties Fauve's hands back together. A campfire has been started, and there's a pot set over the fire. They sit us next to it, and then leave us alone. Their leader is laughing and joking around.

"Why are you so happy? They took down two of us!" a man says angrily.

Their leader grins "Oh they're going to pay for it. We're taking them to the master... he'll know what to do with them." The others cheer and laugh, except for the woman who helped me earlier. She has been keeping an eye on us from a distance, when no one's watching her. I don't like the sound of what their leader is saying.

To my knowledge the marauders have no master... but what if we've all been wrong this whole time, and that this has been an organization that leads their attacks? That would explain the tattoo some of them have. Gunner did comment on them not being marauders.

Food is passed around, and our gags are removed so we can be spoon fed. I hate that. It's best to take the food anyway though. It's some sort of soup and seems to be hearty. I look off at the landscape beyond and notice a silhouetted figure standing off at a distance, watching us.

The person disappears into the darkness. The marauders stay up late into the night. At times I think I see someone in the distance but wonder if it's my imagination. The wind has picked up a little, but my armor has kept me warm. Eventually the marauders get out blankets and sleep on the ground around the fire. Fauve and I are set apart from everyone else and are left leaning against a cold rock. One of them stands guard on a nearby hill.

The person I saw earlier is standing behind the guard. I can't make out anything about them because they are wearing a hooded cloak. Everything seems to come to a standstill for a moment before the person takes down the guard, gagging and tying him. Then the person makes their way towards us.

They say nothing as they untie us and take the gags off. It's too dark for me to see their face. "Go, and don't turn back!" a woman whispers. I stand up, and turn to say something to her, but she's gone. I motion for Fauve to follow me and make my way towards the hills. If we can get over some of them without being noticed we can start planning our route back to the crew. I check to make sure she's following me.

The moon shines brightly on us as we travel across the sandy terrain. I feel grateful for my armor as the biting wind presses against us. "When do you think we can start heading back to the crew?" Fauve asks.

"We need to get out of the marauder's reach as soon as we can. We should head east a ways, then turn north," I say, shivering as I hear shouting in the distance.

"They've already caught on to us."

I just nod and start running. Now that we've gotten over some hills I can see cliffs in the distance, and some mountains to the east. We decide to go ahead towards the mountains. Maybe there's somewhere that we can hide there. The shouting continues behind us, and I quicken my pace. We climb hill after hill, and still they press on after us. We come to a stop at the mouth of a canyon. "Maybe we can hide here," I say.

"You can, if you know where they'll look," a woman says. I turn to see the woman who had helped me earlier.

"How did you get here before us?" I ask.

"I saw that someone was waiting in the shadows to free you and figured you would come in this direction to escape. Now come on, we don't have a lot of time." She heads into the canyon at a brisk pace.

"Do you know who set us free?" I ask.

"I can't say for sure. Legend has it that the Wayfarer will help those in need if she is around," the woman says.

"I hope it wasn't the Wayfarer," Fauve comments.

As we head down it gets cooler. I can hear shouts of confusion behind us. The woman looks over her shoulder before turning to her left, going into a cave. I follow without hesitation, though I worry that this could be a trap. She could easily turn us in.

"I don't know about this," Fauve says to me quietly.

The woman has us stop once we're in the cave. "They shouldn't find us here."

"I hope they don't… you aren't going to turn us in are you?" Fauve asks.

"No, I've rescued more than a few this way."

"Why are you with them then?" I ask.

"It's… complicated. I ran away from my family and ended up with some of them. Later our group was captured by the marauders, who threatened to kill us all if any of us left them. The others seem to have adjusted to this life, but I want to be free."

"But you're afraid you'll get the others killed by leaving," I say.

She nods. "Exactly."

"Aren't you risking that by doing this?" Fauve asks.

"They always think that I've been kidnapped by the prisoners each time," she responds with a laugh.

"They don't sound so smart to me," I say.

"The people from my group used to be, and some still are. They're just caught up in all of this." She tells us to keep quiet as we hear the marauders coming closer.

"The master's not going to like this," one says.

"That's why we must find them, at all costs. Especially the one with the dark hair. Our master has been looking for her," the leader says. After a few minutes the voices begin to grow distant, and then fade all together.

"Why do they want me?" I ask. And who is their master?

"I don't know," the woman says. "You do seem to draw a lot of attention to yourself."

"I'm still trying to figure out who freed us. Was it one of your friends?" Fauve asks.

"No, I have no idea who that was, but she seemed to want you free. She wasn't a part of our lot."

"We may never know. Anyway, we best get going. We're way off track," I say.

"I'll show you the way out and point you in the right direction," the woman says, leaving the cave. We follow, and walk in silence, listening to the sound of the wind. The moon is high in the sky, outshining the stars. We get out of the canyon, and she takes us north for a ways.

She stops at the top of a hill. "If you keep going that way you'll find your ship," she says, pointing straight ahead of us.

"What's your name?" Fauve asks.

She smiles. "My name's Niyah."

"Why don't you come with us?" Fauve asks. I give her a curious look. The ship only holds two.

"You could ride in the back," Fauve says to me, smiling. I don't think she knows how much stuff she has.

Niyah grins appreciatively. "No, I must stay. Maybe someday I will find a way to free the others and myself. Until we meet again." With that she turns, heading back down the hill.

We watch her leave, then go our own way. It takes time to pass the ruins. The ships that belong to the other treasure hunters are gone. I wonder if they're searching other ruins on Durath, or if they've moved on to one of the other planets? It doesn't take long to find Fauve's ship glinting in the moonlight. "Alright, back on course!" Fauve says cheerfully. I open the air locked door, noting how cold the metal of the ship is. Fauve tries over and over to get the engine to power up, but to no avail. "Sometimes it won't start if it's too cold."

"Guess we'll have to wait until the sun comes out," I say with a sigh. I don't know why I'm surprised; I should've guessed that this would happen. We get out of the ship, and I sit, leaning against it. Might as well get some shut eye since I don't have anything else to do.

"Franca, we can't sleep now! We should be exploring the ruins!" Fauve says, pointing at them.

I shake my head and yawn. "No Fauve I need some rest. You go ahead if you want to. I should be fine here."

"Alright, if you say so," Fauve says, turning from me and walking off into the distance. I should be fine. Those marauders don't know where I am, and the sun will be up in a few hours. Soon I find myself in a deep sleep.

I wake up as a light breeze blows my hair across my face. The desert looks the same as usual. Taking a stand I look at the horizon and see that the sun is just peeking through. No sign of Fauve. I bet she's still in the ruins.

I wait longer, but still no Fauve. I could wait here or see if she can be found. Her ship could use some work, and she isn't here. why not work on it? I open the air locked doors of the ship and get my tools and helmet out of the ship and put it on. Looking through the helmet I can see the engine has many parts that are worn; some to the point that they should've been replaced long ago.

Opening the air locked door again and looking through some of the junk in the back quickly shows me that Fauve doesn't carry any spare parts with her. Not much can be done without that since I don't have any supplies with me. Crawling under the ship gives me some relief from the sun as it begins to warm up the land.

Getting out my bar turner I find that half of the bars weren't even tightened in the first place. The bottom panel of the ship could've fallen off at any moment. I remove it and begin tightening loose parts, trying to repair what I can on the worn out ones. The wind starts picking up, but I ignore it, focusing on the work I'm doing.

"Franca! Get out from under there!" Fauve says in a stressed tone.

"Not now Fauve," I say, stabilizing the last worn out part.

"Franca, we're about to be overtaken by a sandstorm!" I put the bottom panel on as quickly as I can and we get in the ship. I can't see the ruins because of the sand. The ship engine powers up right away, and Fauve puts it in full throttle. The ship shakes in the wind, and rocks can be heard hitting against the sides. Fauve keeps us just ahead of the storm and pulls up when she can.

As we leave Durath's atmosphere Fauve relaxes her grip on the ship's controls. "That was close," she says. "We might have to go to Pike III to get help."

"I think we should head back to the moon first," I say. "They may have already figured out a way off or got some help."

"Good point," Fauve says, nodding. "We'll head there." The ride to the moon is uneventful. Fauve doesn't have to kick the ship, which is a relief to me. Maybe the work I did was enough to stabilize things for the time being. We have to work together to avoid the distortion, and successfully go around most of it. We get to the moon, and Fauve lands in the clearing that she did before, hidden among the trees. She still doesn't want them to know about the ship. Which is funny, considering that they've probably figured out that she has one and went missing.

We get out and notice that everything is silent. "Now let's see, I think our camp is this way," Fauve says, pointing in a direction that seems wrong to me.

"If I'm remembering correctly it was that way," I say, pointing to the right of us.

She shrugs. "Yeah, maybe it was. I guess it doesn't matter which way we go since we'll find it eventually." She may be right, but I would prefer to find the crew quickly if we can. Gunner acted like we were short on time and may have moved on without us. I hope that we can find them in time. The wind blows hard as rain pours down. That's odd, the sky was clear a second ago. I get a bad feeling in my gut. We go to the right, and begin to push our way through the forest, coming to the clearing that was once our camp.

CHAPTER 27

WE ALMOST DIDN'T recognize our camp when we saw it. Through the wind and rain I can make out the remains of the campfire. "What now?" Fauve calls over the storm. The thunder is crashing and roaring so loud I can barely hear her.

"If we can, we should see if there's anyone still here, but it's unlikely," I call out. I continue on, but I'm not sure if Fauve heard me or not. She follows me anyway. I lead the way to the campfire. Once we get there we don't see anything there either. I see multiple lightning bolts striking not far ahead of us. It doesn't take long to see that the lightning is coming closer to us at a quick pace. I turn around to see that Fauve is already running.

The rain makes it hard to see, and the ground is becoming muddy. I catch up to her just as she stumbles, and I reach out in time to catch her. Thunder booms over us as she regains her footing. We continue onward. She seems to be remembering where the ship is. I'm too afraid to look back. It looked like a wall of lightning was coming at us. I trip on a tree root and quickly put out my hand and grab onto one of the tree's branches, keeping myself from falling.

Fauve doesn't hear me call out and continues on through the trees. The loud thunder startles me into regaining my footing, and I start running again, trying my best to keep up with her. We get to the ship and I barely shut the air locked door before Fauve powers it up. It lifts into the sky and we take off. I hope we didn't miss anyone. It didn't seem like any of the crew were there. Looking down at the moon I see that there's a fire spreading among the trees. We fly in silence for a bit, recovering from the storm. I wish I'd stop shivering.

"So," Fauve says, breaking the silence. "I guess we're heading to Pike III now?"

"Yeah, I don't know where else to look." If they're not there then we're too late. We might be able to get Faine to tell us where Gunner went, but that's unlikely. Another day passes, leading us back to where we were. Once we pass Durath, Fauve stops talking altogether, having to focus since the distortion has gotten worse here. I wonder what's causing that? It seems to be spreading.

She misses some of it at least. When she does hit the spots I hear the ship rattle. Maybe the whole thing is loose. I feel a sense of relief wash over me the next day as we enter Pike III's orbit. That relief fades as we get to the atmosphere, and the realization comes to me that our missing radar system will be a problem. Ships are flying towards us on their way off of the planet. Fauve swerves and dodges one that emerges out of the clouds. That one seemed to appear out of nowhere.

"How are we going to get through this without a radar system?" I ask.

"I'm just going to have to watch closely for the other ships!" Fauve exclaims, leaning closer to the glass and squinting, dodging more ships.

"Why didn't you get a radar system for it?"

"I don't know! I bought it years ago for a discount. I only planned to fly it around Rythor on errands." We swerve out of the way of a ship just in time. I find myself grabbing onto the edge of my seat as she tilts the ship on its side to fly between two ships.

"I don't like this," I say. I didn't mean to say that out loud.

"Neither do I," Fauve says, speeding the ship up. When will this flight be over? I think we're going way too fast... eventually we stop swerving around and slow to a stop. We've come to the line of ships that leads to the hangar. I let out a breath I didn't know I was holding. I notice that Fauve's hands are shaking.

"Shouldn't we be going up to the island?" I ask.

"Oh, right," Fauve says, swerving out of the line and tilting the ship upward. We emerge above the clouds, and I'm more glad to see the island than I thought I would be. The clouds are rolling up to the shore like always. As we get closer to the island I tell Fauve to head to the visitor's hangar. The one that connects to the palace only opens up for ships it recognizes, and I doubt Fauve's ship is on that list. As we're landing I can see the guards coming into the hangar.

We get out, and they recognize us immediately. "The king would like to see you," one of them says, turning to lead us to the palace. He didn't give any room for objection, not that we would. I wonder how much trouble we're in? We're lead along the familiar path, but at an urgent pace. The guards stop a man who's running down the path. "The search has been canceled, we found them," one of the guards says.

"I'll tell the others immediately," the man says, turning and running back up the pathway. The guards barely open the palace doors for him in time. In a few moments we arrive at the doors, and the guards open them for us.

"What happened? Where have you been?" Gunner asks as soon as we get inside. I didn't expect him to be here right away.

"It's a long story..." I say, not wanting to talk about it. I should've known better than to go with Fauve on her wild goose chase.

"I'll get the details from you later. You both are just in time for the meeting," he says coldly, turning and walking quickly towards the throne room. We follow, and I can't help but wonder if something's wrong other than what Fauve and I did. The guards step out of Gunner's way, and nod at him as he passes. He barely looks at them and quickens his pace. We make it to the throne room, and I see that his advisors aren't there. Gunner doesn't stop but continues through a door to the side of the room. I almost come to a stop when I get through the doorway.

A long dark oak table lined with gold is in the center of the room. Gold columns support the room and have gems in them. A rectangular stained glass window lines the room towards the top of the wall. The chairs at the table are also made of dark oak and are lined with gold. A seat is left open at the head of the table, and the advisors are seated on either side of it. The crew is taking up the rest of the seats.

"Where were you guys?" Blair asks, sounding surprised.

"Yeah, we thought you were gone for good," Lance says.

"It's a long story," I say again, sensing that there are more important things that need to be discussed.

"I'm just glad you're back," Alex says. Raya nods in agreement. Fauve sits with her, and I take a seat next to Alex.

Gunner sits in his seat and takes a moment to make sure we're all here. Then he begins to speak with care. "It's time we discuss the danger that our star system is in. Things have been more critical than I've let on. As some of you know, my brother and I are not on the best of terms. When my father passed away, he left me his journal. And in it he revealed a discovery."

"Sir should we be telling them this?" Faine interrupts.

"They're going to find out anyway," Gunner says dismissively. "While my father was still ruling he sent people to explore the other side of Pike III. They found a mountain range that you can't see from here, and once they got out of the tree line they saw a dwarf planet not far from us. He sent the explorers to the planet, curious about it. It's a rocky planet with no atmosphere.

"It had a lot of caves, and in one of these caves the explorers found something strange. Tiny stars had formed there and seem to keep forming. These stars are small enough to be set in armor, or weapons, if the metal can contain the heat."

"So that's why you've needed the frosthur!" Raya exclaims.

"When it is used with the stars, the extreme cold of the metal is balanced out, making it easy to handle. It is the only metal that can withstand that heat," Gunner says. "The explorers returned, and my father's attention was on other things. He did nothing with the stars. Later after his passing I sent people to mine some frosthur, and with tools made from it was able to gather some of those stars. A new sword and crown were made for me with this metal, and some of the stars were added to them. From what we've seen anything made with frosthur is bullet proof."

"If a weapon is made with those stars in it does the weapon harness its power somehow?" Alex asks.

"Yes, it does. Nobody knows the full power of these weapons yet."

"How did that man get a hold of that weapon?" Roxanne asks.

"My brother happened to be spying on us when we were forging my weapon. He went and somehow made his own. That man was working with him, and I suspect he is buying all the frosthur he can."

"So he has more frosthur than us," Lance says.

"We barely have enough to make another weapon, while they may be able to make eight or nine at this point."

"Maybe we could get more from Bayu?" Raya asks.

Gunner shakes his head. "From what I've seen there isn't any more being sold by the merchants. However, I was reading the section of my father's journal on frosthur, and he mentions something about a different metal. I can't find any accounts about it in our database, but my father believed it could withstand more heat than the frosthur."

"The only database that has more information than ours would be the one on Faratha IV," Arlan says.

"Right," Gunner says. "I think it's worth it to go and see if there is anything there of value to us. Since I'm the king I have access to resources the public doesn't."

"Even with this, your brother will still have the upper hand, and he's planning on attacking soon," Faine says.

Gunner pauses for a moment before speaking. "There's nothing that I can do to save the people but try."

"So we're heading out then?" Blair asks.

"Yes we're heading out," Gunner says.

"Alright, let's get started then," Lance says.

"Franca I need you to stay here," Gunner says. His advisors stay seated.

Alex gets up from his chair but hesitates. "Can I stay too? I'd also like to hear what happened." The longer this meeting is going on the more I'm wishing I hadn't gone along with Fauve on her plan.

"You may," Gunner says, nodding his head. "Franca, I'd like to know what happened to you and Fauve. I wanted to ask you because I'm not sure that Fauve would be honest," he says calmly, turning his focus to me.

"Well," I say, not knowing quite how to begin. "Fauve let me know that she had a ship... it could only fit two and she said we'd send help back. She said we'd be back before daylight, but had an errand she needed to do..."

"And what was this errand?" Gunner asks.

Alex shakes his head. "I can't believe she wouldn't tell us this."

"She's part of a group that searches for ancient artifacts in ruins. They're trying to save them from marauders," I say, feeling guilty. This was Fauve's secret, not mine. If I don't tell Gunner he'll just become suspicious of us both. It won't be good if either of us are thought of as spies or traitors. This was something that she needed to do.

"What? When did she start doing this?" Alex asks, with anger briefly flashing in his eyes. "We've needed her here countless times. We learned we couldn't depend on her, even when we needed her, and this was what she was doing?"

"I don't know how long she's been doing this, but the group has no idea she's part of the military. I assumed that us leaving would be a quick thing."

"I recognize that Fauve may have made it sound like there was no trouble, but before you go along with her again do consider that the crew needs you," Gunner says.

"I'll be more careful next time." Or I'll try to be. I do like adventure, and in some ways liked exploring the ruins. But Gunner's right, I'm the ship mechanic and it's important that I stay with the crew.

"Alright, we've got to head out. I'll be with you in an hour," Gunner says to Alex. Alex and I get up from our seats and leave. We don't speak until we're out of the throne room.

"I just can't understand why Fauve wouldn't tell us this," Alex says.

"She didn't mean it in a hurtful way," I say, trying to help smooth things over. From what I can tell, it was the only way Fauve could do it. Maybe I shouldn't have said anything in front of Alex, but I was put on the spot.

"Well, I guess she has her reasons. Someone will have to talk to her though. We need her, especially now. Things are getting critical, and while I like Gunner, working for him is dangerous," he says.

"Maybe Gunner will speak with her. If not, I guess I could," I say, hoping I won't have to do that. We make it to the ship and find that things are almost all ready.

Roxanne glares at me as I pass her. I wonder what she's angry about now? She grabs my arm and pulls me to the side. "How could you abandon us like that?" she whispers harshly.

"We were going to get help. Fauve got sidetracked." I say, surprised that Roxanne would care if I stayed with the crew or not.

"Look, everyone's survival depends on us all sticking together. Maybe you don't have much fighting experience, but the enemy is always eager to pick off the ones who separate or fall behind."

I'm taken aback by her earnest tone. It almost sounds like she's been worried about me? "I'll try to keep it from happening again. I didn't know that we would be gone for as long as we were."

"Alright, the sooner you start paying attention the better," she says, returning to her old self. Before I can say anything more she walks over to the others. Gunner arrives, and we all get on the ship.

"Have you been to Faratha IV, Franca?" Blair asks me.

"I've been to the hangar there, but no further," I say, looking out the window at the clouds as we leave the island.

"I got to go there once, back when the settlement tours were still being done," Blair says, taking a seat next to me.

"Oh yeah I remember those. I decided not to go on them because I already knew I wanted to be on another arctic planet, so Hayventh was the perfect choice for me."

"You actually like the cold?" Blair asks in disbelief.

I laugh. "Yeah, I do. I don't mind the cold, but I guess that's because I grew up with it."

"I grew up in the southern region of the Sarthrian Empire," Blair says.

"Wasn't that area mostly desert planets?"

"Yeah there were a lot of planets that were just desert and rock as far as you could see. I grew up on one of those, which is why I felt the most comfortable with living on Durath."

"Do you have any family there?"

"The planet we lived on was dangerous. I spent most of my time trying to protect my family. When Nareth asked for people to go with him it looked like a new life for me. I tried to convince my family to come, but they didn't want to leave."

"Maybe they'll find a way here later," I say, trying to be encouraging. It's unlikely that any of us will ever want to risk going back to The Sarthrian Empire, and even more unlikely that anyone else will escape from there and make it here.

"Yeah, I've thought of going back for them, but I know that would be dangerous," Blair says. "What about your family?"

"My parents live on Hayventh, but the rest of my family stayed behind," I say, feeling that I have something in common with him. We talked for awhile, talking about the past and how oppressive The Sarthrian Empire was. Three days go by before we get close to Faratha IV. As it comes into view I make my way to the control room. Gunner and Alex are in a deep conversation about the different ships you can fly in the army. Fauve is studying the radar system.

I wonder if she's still being chased? I try to get a closer look at the radar.

She turns around and startles when she sees me. "Franca you scared me! What are you doing here?"

"I finished talking with Blair and wanted to be in the control room when we land. I want to see what Faratha IV looks like."

"Well it won't be long before we're there!" she says as she leaves the room.

I glance at the radar system, and see a few ships move out of its range.

CHAPTER 28

I WATCH OUT of the front glass of the ship as we get closer to our destination. I see that we're in Faratha IV's atmosphere, coming close to landing. The cherry blossom trees are vibrant, coming in pinks, reds, whites, yellows, and golds. It seems familiar in a way but isn't. Off to the west is an evergreen forest. I wonder what the hunting is like here? Never looked into that.

"There it is, Rosevale," Blair says. I'm amazed at how big it is. The settlement is carved into a mountain. Crystal blue waterfalls flow out of the mountain, and the settlement is wrapped in cherry blossom trees. The buildings are made of pure white stone and stained glass windows. We get ready to land, heading to a different hangar than the main one. It's located at the back of a tall building with a tower that's in the center of the city.

"I didn't know Faratha IV had more than one hangar," Maylea says.

"My father loved knowledge and wisdom, so he had a private one built here," Gunner says. We step out of the ship and see that the hangar is made of marble. Gunner walks ahead of us to meet the guards. He says something to them, and they nod. They open the hangar door, leading us along a private walkway. Green grass grows between the walkway and the railing, adding a splash of color. The walkway is made of white stone, and is lined with lamp posts.

I look at the building ahead of us. The windows are all made of electric blue colored glass. Our walkway leads to it, guiding us to a private entrance that's guarded. The guards that are with us talk to the other watchmen, and they open the doors for us right away. We enter, and I'm amazed at how large the database is. Shelves and shelves of holobooks fill the room, with plenty of seating areas to go to. The holobooks look like cards. You scan them with your communicator to read them. An assistant greets us as we come in. "Welcome to the database my king, what would you be interested in today?" she asks.

"First I'd like to check to see if my father left anything for me here," Gunner says confidently.

The assistant smiles. "Of course. Right this way," she says, gesturing for us to follow her. She gets into a teleporter that takes us to a higher floor. "The headmaster of this database, Ben, has something that might be of interest to you," she says as we come to a large office area. She opens the door, and we all follow. A middle aged man is sitting in a seat behind a huge wooden desk.

"My king, I wondered when you'd visit again," he says smiling.

"Ben," Gunner says with a nod. "Business kept me from coming sooner."

"Your father told me to hold onto something for you, but to only give it to you when you asked for it," Ben says.

"Do you know why he decided to do that?"

"I do not know. I can only assume he wanted you to have this when the time was right," he says, pulling out a worn leatherbound journal from his desk.

Gunner opens it quickly, and frowns. "All of the text is in a language I don't recognize."

"Is it? Let me see if I can recognize it," Ben says. Gunner hands him the journal, and after a few moments Ben speaks. "It has been many years since I have seen text in this language. Only one person left in the star system knows how to translate it."

"And who would that be?"

"That would be Queen Aaricia. Her people live on the edge of our star system, just beyond Hayventh. I can add their location to your communicator's map."

"Then that is where we'll be going next. Thank you for your time Ben."

Ben smiles. "It was a pleasure." We follow Gunner out of the database and back to the hangar. I take in the scenery of the trees and settlement before we go. If I could stay here longer I would.

"I didn't know that there's a Queen in our star system," Fauve says.

"She's always been there," Gunner says. "Her civilization lives on one planet. Most people don't know of her because she wants nothing to do with us."

"Will she even speak with us then?" Alex asks.

"She may, if she's curious enough," Gunner says.

"Why would your father put the journal in another language?" Maylea asks.

"I don't know. Maybe it was to keep my brother from reading it."

We go through the air locked door of our ship and take off. "There were so many holobooks on working with metal. If only I had time to borrow some..." Raya says, looking out the window at the database as we leave.

"You'll get another chance I'm sure," Blair says. The ship turns, leaving Faratha IV behind, embarking on another journey. It takes us three days to get to Hayventh. It's funny to think that when I was first captured we were going in the opposite direction. So much has happened since then. A part of me wishes that I could stop and stay a while at Hayventh. I head to the control room.

"I don't remember seeing any planets beyond Hayventh," Alex says.

"It's closer to the neighboring star system than ours. The planet that she rules from is a good distance from Hayventh," Gunner says.

"Looks like some ships are following us," Alex says pointing to something on the radar system. I look over his shoulder, and see three ships are following us.

"I don't know who they are. If they stay with us after we've passed Hayventh we'll know that they're following us," Gunner says.

I go over to Fauve. "Those are the same ships again, aren't they?" I ask.

"I wish they'd stop following me. I don't even know if I have what they're after," she says.

"Either you tell the others about them now, or I will. This should've been done a long time ago," I say. I should've done that from the start. I thought she would do it, but I was wrong.

"I wonder if there's a way to scare them off," Fauve says, ignoring my comment.

"Scare what off?" Roxanne asks. She pushes past me to look out the window.

"Fauve, what are those?" Roxanne asks in an exasperated tone. "Don't tell me these are some of your friends that you've brought along."

"I don't know, they've been with us since Pike III..." she says, leaving out the part that they are after her.

"I better make sure that our radar system is working properly. Gunner should already know about this." Roxanne turns and walks over to the control room. She mentions the ships.

"We're aware of them. I can call my troops if needed," Gunner says.

Time passes by, and the ships continue to follow us. Roxanne keeps a close eye on them, ready to take control of one of the turrets if she needs to. "This will tell us if they are following us," Roxanne says, watching the ships as we pass Hayventh. It feels strange, I don't think I've ever seen anyone fly past it.

The three ships continue with us, even after two more days pass. Roxanne reports back to the control room for orders and stays to watch the radar system. Eventually we see a planet far off in the distance. The closer we get the more our ship starts rocking. I head to the control room to see what's going on. "Looks like we've found more distortion," Alex says.

"There's a lot more of it up ahead," Gunner says. As we get closer we can see that the planet has a misty atmosphere, causing it to appear all white.

"Do you think this planet is the cause of the distortion?" Alex asks as the ship rocks more.

Gunner shakes his head. "No, I don't think so. There's something else that's causing it." Things get unstable right up until we get to the atmosphere. We're blinded as our ship goes into the mist, forcing us to rely on the ship's radar system and auto pilot to get us through. As we emerge from the mist we see a mountainous landscape covered in golden light.

"I've never seen a planet like this," Alex says.

"Neither have I," Gunner says.

"You've never been here?" I ask.

"No, my father came here once when we were charting out the star system. The Queen wanted us to leave her and her people alone, so we did." I can't stop looking at the landscape below. All of the trees are a golden orange or yellow, and the streams that run through the land reflect the trees and sky. Gunner has us land on a landing pad that's in the forest, right outside the city.

We step out of the ship, taking in the scenery. Leaves are gently falling from the trees, and the grass has an orange-red glow to it when the sunlight hits it. Deer can be seen among the trees in the distance if you look hard enough to see them. The forest is in a peaceful silence, reminding me of how much I miss being out in the wilderness.

My gaze turns towards the city, which is overshadowing everything around it with its high towers and walls. The towers look to be made of marble with many windows. As we get closer to the city I see that the posts of the gate are made of marble inlaid with gemstones. The gate itself is made up of golden rods. As we reach the city gates two guards come out. Their armor is made of white chain mail that has gemstones embedded in them. "State your business," one of them says in a hard tone.

"I'm Gunner, king of Ohniran, and I wish to speak to the Queen."

The guard narrows her eyes. "And what proof do you have of this? If you wish to enter the city I will let you, but only if you give us your weapons." Raya groans, hesitating before putting her weapon in the pile with the rest. The gates open, and the guards walk before us, calling some others to take the rear.

Ships fly above us, going to and from the many towers dotting the city. We seem to be in a marketplace. People go to and from the stalls, and I notice that all of their clothes are embedded with expensive gems. Some of them stop what they're doing to stare at us, watching with caution.

The guards take us through the center of the city towards the palace. The closer we get to it the more it seems to tower over us. The walls are all made of white marble, and thousands of gemstones can be seen embedded in the walls. The doors are made of pure gold, and open automatically for us when we reach them. We go through, and the inside is just as embellished as the outside was.

We're taken directly to the throne room, and while everything looks to be far more expensive than what Gunner has. Unlike Gunner's palace, the one here doesn't have many windows. Sitting on the throne is a tall middle aged woman with long flowing blond hair. The gemstones in her dress glimmer in the light that's coming from the nearby gemstone lamps.

She looks cunningly at us, like someone who already has plans for you before you even speak. "Well, I never thought I would see you nomads again. Gunner isn't it? It's been so long since your father told me about you that I'm not even sure I know your name anymore," she says in an icy tone.

Everyone seems astonished by her. Aaricia's smile only makes me feel worse, not better. But it's not her tone or smile that shocks me the most. It's that besides her clothing and age, she looks exactly like Fauve.

Gunner looks back and forth between Fauve and her. "You both look the same," he says in surprise.

She looks over at Fauve. "Why yes, she does look like me. As an heir to the throne should."

"What?" Fauve asks in surprise.

"You didn't know?" Aaricia says laughingly. "Why did you think you were being followed for so long? It was only my people trying to tell you the truth, so you could live here with me."

"But," Fauve stammers. "I grew up in The Sarthrian Empire with my family," she says, turning a little pale.

Aaricia's expression darkens. "You were taken away from us when you were too young to remember. Long has your uncle searched for you, but to no avail. He swore that whoever took you away would pay the price for what they did."

Fauve shakes her head. "I-I don't understand."

Aaricia smiles. "Don't worry, with time you will." Gunner clears his throat. Aaricia turns her attention to Gunner, her smile fading. "Oh, is the prince growing impatient? I obviously have more important matters to attend to. You should be glad I'm giving you my time at all," she says coolly with a glint of anger in her eyes.

"I'm the king now—" Gunner says.

Aaricia looks at him with raised brows. "You? Why are you the king, and not your brother?"

"Because that's what my father wanted, and I am capable of ruling," Gunner responds.

"So your father has passed, this is useful news."

Gunner's hand turns into a fist for a moment, but he makes his hand relax and doesn't comment on what she said. "I have something my father wrote to me in another language that I need help translating."

Aaricia looks at him smugly. "And what will I get in return for doing this?"

"I'll pay you a high price for the work."

Aaricia laughs. "Your currency means nothing to me. It will have to be something else. Let's say, your people working as slaves for mine for a few decades?"

Anger flashes in Gunners eyes, but he keeps his calm. "This is a business deal is a matter between you and me, and has nothing to do with my people."

"Oh is it? It's a negotiation, and if you aren't willing to offer something that I want I'll take it from you."

My throat is getting dry. Fauve is wiping sweat from her brow. The others look nervous as well. Things are quickly going downhill.

"That's not how negotiations work," Gunner says, barely keeping the edge out of his tone.

"For all I know it is your people who took my daughter from me. Or in the least have been keeping her from me. Why is it that she is here now instead of with The Sarthrian Empire? I won't do business with the likes of you," she says harshly.

"I have nothing to do with why she's here, I didn't know any of this before coming," he says, unable to keep the tension out of his voice.

"Of course you don't, that's what anyone would say."

"You do understand that my father rescued his people from The Sarthrian Empire, therefore rescuing her as well."

Aaricia pauses, looking at him. "If that's true, then I'll be merciful and let you go. Except for my daughter," she says. The guards step forward, grabbing us and forcing us out of the throne room.

"No, you can't do this!" Gunner says as the guards put his hands behind his back.

"Wait, they're my friends!" Fauve exclaims.

"Now, now. Don't worry about them. You don't have to concern yourself with the likes of them anymore," Aaricia says. The throne room doors close with a thud, and we're escorted through the city, back to the gates. Our weapons are returned, and we're forced to go to our ship. Gunner powers the ship up, and we head back into space. Many ships surround us, and don't turn back until we're near our own planets.

"What do we do now? We can't just leave Fauve there!" Alex exclaims.

"I'm trying to think of something. While the Queen only has one planet, she has a large army, and we don't know the strength of her allies. I will figure something out," Gunner says.

"You better, Fauve is important to us." Alex says.

"For now we need to head back to Pike III. Queen Aaricia will be watching us closely and will make sure we stay away. I want to see if my advisors know of any other way to translate my father's journal, and they may have some ideas on how to get Fauve back."

"Then that's what we'll do," Alex says in a disappointed tone. I feel like this is all my fault. Had I mentioned the ships sooner we might have had a chance to prevent this from happening. I'm determined to do whatever I can to help get her free. I owe it to her. Days pass, and when we get to the palace we find that everything is in disarray. People are everywhere, rushing around with weapons and armor.

Gunner catches Faine by the arm. "What's going on here?" he demands.

"It's terrible. The people on Rythor are dying from all kinds of calamities. Earthquakes, thunderstorms, fires. There's even been flaming tornadoes striking the planet. Instead of using the small stars that we found Ty has been shrinking stars around Rythor to power his weapons with. The absence of the stars is causing all these weather problems and throwing everything into chaos. He's grown so powerful no one knows what to do." Faine pauses and then looks Gunner directly in the eyes. "You are the only one who can stop him."

Gunner looks around at all the people. "I know. It's time." He lifts his head and squares his shoulders. "Faine, get my strongest set of armor."

"Yeah!" Faine shouts, smiling. "Now that's what I'm talking about. A real king defends his people."

Gunner smiles sadly, and heads to the armory. We all follow. "I'm afraid that my weapon is the only one with this power... you all will have to make do with the weapons you have," he says, sounding like he wishes he could give us something better.

"We can do that," Lance says.

"We're ready to fight!" Roxanne says. Maylea just sighs.

Gunner smiles at us. "I'm glad to have you all by my side. Alright team, let's see what we can do to stop this." We all gather our gear and prepare to head to Rythor.

CHAPTER 29

WE GET INTO one of Gunner's battle ships. Soon the hangar fades away, leaving us as we skim over the vast ocean of clouds. Stars are just beginning to shine in the sky, and the clouds around the island refect the warm glow of the sunset. Everything here is surrounded by a sense of peace, as if the problems of the world don't exist. It almost feels like this place is calling out for me to stay, and leave everything else behind.

I think of the people who are suffering on Rythor. I must make this stand with Gunner. I hope to return to the island when I can. The wages of battle are uncertain; I know I can take care of myself, but there's never a guarantee that I'll leave it with my life. The sky darkens to a deep black as we leave Pike III's atmosphere. Alex sits at the controls, maneuvering the ship with ease. We go to meet an army of ships waiting for us.

"Now this is what a real battle feels like!" Roxanne says, surveying the army as we slowly pass them to take the lead. The adrenaline and energy for the battle ahead flows around her. I can't help but feel inspired by that energy as it surges around me.

"Alright men, power your force fields!" Gunner commands through his communicator.

"Yes sir!" They shout so loud that I can hear them through Gunner's earpiece. The radar system shows them following us as we leave Pike III behind. Our ship travels smoothly along. For a moment I forget that the distortion is out there. All that training Alex did with Gunner has made a difference. The hardest thing about this journey is the time it takes to get there. The waiting feels longer than it usually does.

"Stop here," Gunner says when we are near Durath.

"What's wrong?" Alex asks.

"Ty is there, on Durath. I've been tracking him with my communicator. He left Rythor when we were leaving Pike III."

"Why would he be there?"

"We know each other well. He's been preparing for my arrival. We both knew this would come."

We descend through Durath's atmosphere, and fly over the landscape. The semi-arid climate is in its rainy season, leaving everything green here. Some areas of the planet are a sandy desert. Gunner lands his ship near a canyon, and his army lands around us. There are so many that some have to land farther away.

"This is where your brother is?" Lance asks.

"That's what my tracker says. This is his hideout."

"Can't we meet him somewhere else?" Blair asks, warily looking at the canyon.

"Ty knows that I'm coming to confront him. No matter where we go he will choose a location that's in his favor," Gunner says, heading towards the mouth of the canyon. We follow, with the army right behind us. No river or stream can be seen passing through the canyon. Our path slants downward as the canyon descends into the ground. The sunlight that was guiding us grows dim as we lose sight of the sky.

I follow close behind Gunner, waiting for my eyes to adjust to the lighting. Once they do I find that the ground ahead is littered with rocks and boulders. Ledges set higher up, and at the end of the canyon is the large opening of a cave.

The sound of shifting rocks causes Roxanne to pause. She raises her rifle, looking through the scope. She fires, and a man falls off of a ledge ahead of us.

"Take cover!" Gunner shouts, hiding behind a boulder. I barely press myself against the wall of the canyon in time as a bullet flies past me. Ducking, I crouch behind a small boulder and take my rifle off of my back. The army jumps into action, charging at the marauders who have shown themselves and begin forming a front line. My hands shake from the adrenaline that's coursing through my system. I do my best to still them and turn my focus to what's going on around me.

Gunner shouts something to me, but his words are drowned out from the battle cries and gunshots. Maylea darts to a fallen woman, trying to take cover as she tends to her wounds. I carefully look around the edge of my boulder, and fire a shot, taking down a marauder who was aiming at Maylea. Once the woman regains consciousness Maylea works to get her out of firing range. I take out a few others that were firing at Alex.

Roxanne lets out a war cry, catching a marauder scout off guard as she tackles him to the ground. He was just getting past the front line. We press forward, pushing the marauders towards the cave. Roxanne and I both move to take cover behind the same boulder. She has blood on her hair near her ear, and has some blood running down her neck. It doesn't look like she's done anything to take care of the wound.

"You're bleeding. I can cover you while you take care of that," I say.

She scoffs. "I'm fine. Worry about taking care of yourself." She aims her scope and takes out another marauder.

I focus back on the battle, not saying anything. More marauders flow from the cave at the end of the canyon, seeming endless. I look behind me. We've lost about fifty men. Something has to change if we're to turn the tide of this battle. That's when I see Raya bringing some sort of machine on wheels to the backline. She turns a few bars with a bar turner before some of Gunner's soldiers take the machine closer to us. They pull back a part of it, and pull a lever.

It fires a long missile-like bullet, and when it hits the ceiling above the marauders it lets out a sonic boom, disorienting them. Rocks fall down upon them, and in the confusion many are taken down before the others scatter. We move forward, guns at the ready. We're coming closer to the cave. A few marauders are running away from us, glancing over their shoulders.

"This way!" Gunner calls, rushing after them, taking the lead. Roxanne and I run to catch up to him as he passes the front lines. We enter the cave and stop short. Ahead of us it takes a sharp turn so that you can't see what's ahead. To our right is a large chasm in the ground. Small ships are flying through it. Gunner sends a scout into the cave in front of us to see what's beyond the sharp turn.

"Well? Gunner asks when he returns.

"Another army is standing in a large cavern on the other side, ready to fight. Some ships are coming out of an opening in the wall that seems to be from a chasm, heading up to a ledge that looks down on the cavern."

"Those ships are delivering supplies to my brother. He's overseeing the battle," Gunner says. "Men, I want you to charge after the army. The three of us are going to meet my brother."

They charge ahead, shaking the ground with their shouts.

"How are we going to do that?" I ask, hoping that he's not planning on doing what I think he is.

He nods at the ships passing in the chasm. "Those ships are only five feet below us. It won't be hard to land on one and ride it up to the ledge."

"This'll be fun," Roxanne says with a grin.

I look at them hesitantly. The last time I tried that it didn't go well. "Isn't there another way?" I ask.

"While my soldiers fight better than the marauders that make up Ty's army, they won't be able to fight forever. The sooner I confront my brother, the more lives that will be saved." He walks to the edge of the chasm. I take a stand next to him but further back, and Roxanne stands at a short distance from me, watching for us to go first.

Gunner watches the ships pass, and then jumps and grabs onto a wing. It's my turn. I look at the ships, thinking about the jump. I know I can do this. I step towards the ledge, and get ready to make the jump.

"No!" Roxanne says, tackling me before I can make the leap. We skid along the ground.

"What's wrong with you?" I ask, feeling frustrated. Why did she do that?

"You either put everything into that jump, or you follow the army," she says harshly. I notice something different in her eyes. Is that fear, or passion for the battle? She immediately lets me get back up and watches me. If I'm honest with myself she's right; I was about to make a half hearted jump.

I close my eyes for a moment, calming my breathing. I know I can do this. I'm sure I'll make it this time. I have to. I open my eyes, and see two ships coming. I jump, putting everything into it. Time seems to slow down as I stretch out my arms, reaching for my target.

The ship's wing dips from the impact before returning to a level state. Both of my hands grip tightly along the edge of the wing.

I look over my shoulder and see that Roxanne is on the ship behind me. Turning my focus ahead I find that the chasm is not clear of boulders, and is not nearly as deep as it had looked from above. I quickly raise my legs to miss one. I try to pull myself up to be on top of the ship like Roxanne, but the way mine is swaying makes it too hard.

The ship moves to one side of the chasm to avoid a boulder, scraping me against the rock wall. My gun catches on one of the jagged edges, and before I can do anything the strap that kept it on my back tears. It falls away into the dark, leaving me to regret the loss. I do have a blade that I took from the armory, but I don't have as much training with that type of fighting as I'd like.

The chasm opens up to the cavern that scout was talking about earlier. Our ships are flying near to the ground, but should be ascending to the ledge soon. It looks like it has a short metal wall that's been built around it. I can just see Gunner in the distance hanging onto a ship ahead. As the ship makes it over the ledge he lets go, falling out of sight. I look over my shoulder at Roxanne, and watch as her ship tilts on its side. She loses her grip, dropping to the ground below. Some of Gunner's troops rush in her direction as she gets up.

I turn my focus back to the ledge as my ship rises in the air. I know Roxanne wouldn't want me to let go. My arms are growing tired... I know I won't be able to hold on for much longer. I ignore my shaking arms as I watch the ledge coming closer. If I don't time this right the ship will turn around, going through another cave to get more supplies. When I see the ledge below me I wait until I'm past the short wall. I let go, feeling the wind against my face. I land and roll just as a large crate of supplies crashes to the ground next to me.

I lay there for a moment, trying to catch my breath. I have to get up before anyone sees me. I make it to a stand, trying to get my bearings. Gunner is laying ten feet away from me, unconscious. "Gunner!" I say, going over to him. Kneeling beside him I take his pulse. Still alive.

"So, you've finally come."

I look and see a man standing a short distance away, watching me. He walks towards me with an air of darkness. He has short black hair and a light shadow of a beard. Two scars run over his left eye, reaching to his jawline. His armor is pure black and radiates of darkness. Something seems oddly familiar about him, but I don't know why.

He stops in front of me, not paying any attention to Gunner. The air around him is a chilling cold. Black ice crystals hang from parts of his armor. "I knew I would find you again, with time," he says. His eyes have no expression.

"Who are you?" I ask. I'm guessing that this is Ty, or someone who works closely with him.

"I'm not going to play that game with you Franca. It's time that you recognize that my side is the winning side, or die," the man says, not answering my question.

"I don't know you," I say, straightening my shoulders. I will hold my ground. I have to.

"You really don't know? Maybe Evan was telling the truth."

"What does Evan have to do with this?" I ask. I glance at Gunner and see that he's still unconscious.

"He was supposed to rescue you from my evil brother's clutches," the man says with a trace of anger in his tone. He steps closer to me. Chills go down my spine as I feel the darkness that surrounds him. I shiver as the temperature drops. So this is Ty. I try to ignore the fearful feeling that comes over me. This feeling seems to be coming from the darkness.

"He tried to kill me," I say, refusing to believe that Evan was trying to rescue me.

"Evan failed, you've fallen to the deception of my brother," Ty says, glancing at Gunner with a hateful glare. He looks out at the battle taking place in the cavern before focusing on me again. "Come with me Franca. With the information you have and the power I've gained this war will quickly end."

"Information? I don't know what you mean," I say.

His eyes reveal the rage he'd been hiding. "Don't be a fool, if you don't tell me you'll die. I'm not afraid to kill you; your life means nothing to me. The information you have is a generous trade for sparing your life."

"We came here to put a stop to this. Don't you know what's happening to the people on Rythor?" I ask accusingly, changing the subject. I have no idea what he's talking about. Maybe this will buy me enough time to prepare to defend myself. I can feel the sweat on my brow. I'm going to have to fight for my life.

"Of course I know what's happening to them," Ty says, glaring at me. "It's Gunner's fault that they're suffering. If he had shared the power from those stars with me this wouldn't be happening. I don't care for them anyway. They belong to my brother. And like him, they also deserve to die." He looks at Gunner again, who is still unconscious. "My struggles against him will be over soon. Killing him will be easier than I thought."

I put my hand on the handle of my blade. I wasn't planning on fighting Ty alone, but I'll have to. I can't let him kill Gunner.

Ty looks at my hand sharply. "Franca, don't make me kill you." He warns. "All I need is for you to tell me what you know and turn away from my brother."

He waits for a fraction of a second for me to respond. I lift up my arm just in time to block his strike. His blade has shadows moving along it. The vibration from the strike causes my blade to recoil. His strikes convey the darkness of his soul more than any words could express. Every swing is filled with rage and a desire for the death of others. My sword gets a dent in it with each hit. It won't last for much longer... it's being torn to shreds.

Gunner groans, but doesn't move. If I don't do something he won't have long before Ty kills him. My blade is almost useless now. I take a few steps back from Ty, throwing it at him. I take Gunner's blade from its sheath and quickly block another attack. The blade shines with light around its edges. It's heavier than a regular blade, but is still manageable. I know you're supposed to spend a lot of time training to use this, but I have no other options. The shadows that run along Ty's armor fade whenever the light shines from Gunner's blade.

Ty strikes again at full force. I raise the blade and block the hit. The recoil is less, but still there. I have to put extra strength into balancing that out. He strikes again and again, taking different angles. I'm starting to tire... fighting with this blade is draining my energy. Ty has forced me to step back enough that we're fighting right next to Gunner. It wouldn't take much for Ty to turn his blade and kill him.

I need to get him away from Gunner. There's a a tunnel to the side of us. I make a run for it. I feel the movement in the air as Ty's blade almost clips my shoulder. His footsteps are pounding after me. I enter the tunnel, going as fast as I can. It opens up to another room. I continue running, turning down another passageway.

Hopefully I'm buying Gunner some time. The thud of Ty's footsteps follow me, not giving up the chase. My path leads to a cave with no other exit. Great. A dead end. Ty slows to a walk, catching his breath. If he was a foot taller his head would touch the low ceiling.

"This'll be easy," he says, watching my dismay with joy. I'm trying my best to fight him off, but I don't know if I will make it. He looks over his shoulder. "What took you so long?" he asks someone behind him. A man with a bluish grey helmet and armor rushes into the room.

"I got held up in battle," the man says, removing the helmet.

"Evan?" I ask, feeling a sense of dread.

He smiles. "It's too bad you didn't join me when you had the opportunity, you could have avoided all this."

"Evan. Give me the axe," Ty says coldly, not taking his eyes off of me.

My blood runs cold, but I stand my ground. The axe that Evan is holding has a jagged blade on one side, and a spike on the other. Blood drips from the blade, and pieces of torn metal hang off of it. One hit from that and it'd be all over. Evan takes Ty's sword, and gives the axe to him. Shadows run along it. Ty takes the long handle in both hands, walking slowly towards me as I back away. I raise Gunner's blade, wondering if I'll be able to block the axe with it. I feel my back touch the cold wall of the cave. "This one's for the Wayfarer," he says, raising the axe above his head.

"Stop! What coward would refuse to face me in a proper fight?" Gunner asks.

Ty is distracted enough for me to dart to the side, missing his strike. The axe hits the rock wall, causing everything to shake. I stumble, but keep my footing. There's a crack in the wall and ground where I had been. "This is my business, not yours!" Ty yells, his full anger showing as he faces his brother. While we were distracted Gunner got Ty's blade away from Evan.

"You've gone too far this time brother," he says.

"You're about to breathe your last breath," Ty returns without any hesitation, charging forward, striking at him. Gunner stands his ground, striking back in return. Ty takes each swing in stride, as if he's been training with this power for a long time. Both brothers seem to be equal in strength, but it's clear that Ty has the advantage. With the axe he can reach Gunner from a further distance. Evan stays near the only exit of the cave, unable to do anything. Gunner gradually makes his way over to where I am, and asks for his blade. I give it to him and move over, trying to avoid getting hit and end up standing next to where the crack in the wall and ground is.

Gunner starts pushing Ty back, using both blades to make a series of quick strikes. I notice that a necklace has slipped out from under Ty's armor. It has a blue gemstone on it that's glowing. I feel that it's important, but I don't know why. Gunner's blade hits Ty in the thigh, but I'm unable to see if it did any damage because of the shadows that move along his armor. Ty groans, but continues to fight as if nothing happened.

In desperation he brings his axe down over Gunner's head. Gunner darts to the side, barely missing the blow. I wish I could help fight, but there isn't much I can do at this point. Gunner strikes the low ceiling with his sword, and a beam of light and energy causes rocks to fall around Ty. He successfully dodges the rocks, continuing his attack. Evan turns and runs, fleeing from the battle. Soon Gunner is next to me again.

Ty looks at the crack in the ground. He swings his axe down upon it with all his strength. The ground crumbles beneath Gunner and I. All I see below me is darkness. I watch as I begin to fall, and then I jerk to a stop. I look into Ty's eyes as he holds my wrist with one hand. "What will it be Franca? Live or die?" he thunders, hurting my wrist with his grip. "Will it be me? Or my brother?"

I don't want to die today. I know that going with Ty would be the easy way out. Sorrow fills me as I realize that Gunner's probably dead, or dying. For a moment I think of what it would be if I was to be spared. To see my family and friends again... Even so, I know that I have to stand for the light, I cannot join the darkness even if it means death. It's what I stood for as a lead hunter on Hayventh. Doing the right thing is the reason why I went the whole way on this journey. I start to tremble, knowing my life is coming to an end.

"Well? Make your choice or I'll throw you down!" Ty says in a rage. He looks at me darkly. I know it's time for him to let me go. His gemstone necklace catches my eye. One of the links looks like it's about to snap. A loud cracking sound comes from the ceiling above us. The only way to save everyone may be to take him down with me... I just have to distract him a little longer. I feel a bit of comfort knowing that others will be saved from Ty, even if I can't save myself.

I shake my head. "I'll never join you!" I say as I grip my hand around his wrist. Pulling myself up just a little I grab onto the gemstone with my free hand as he's starting to let go of me. The necklace snaps. Ty barely reaches in time to grab my wrist with his other hand.

"Give me that! Now!" he says, trying to pry the gemstone from my fingers. But it's too late. A rock breaks loose from the ceiling, crashing down. It smashes into the ground next to him, which was already weakened. My stomach drops as we fall together, into a void of darkness.

CHAPTER 30

THE WIND IS knocked out of me as I land on my back. Once again I realize that if I hadn't been wearing armor I would have died. The darkness that surrounds me is pitch black. If it weren't for me struggling to breathe and the pain I'm in, I would have already believed that I was dead. I start to open my hand, but quickly close it. I don't want Ty to see the glow from the gemstone. If he's still alive.

The sound of someone stirring next to me is telling enough. Ty groans, and brings himself to a stand, picking up his blade. I feel a glimmer of hope. Both blades fell with Gunner, he might be somewhere nearby. And if I survived the fall there's a good chance that he did too. I try to get up, but a sharp pain in my chest keeps me down. Maybe Ty will leave me alone if I pretend to be dead? His communicator glows dimly, sparking as it lays on the ground where he had fallen.

In the corner of my eye I see a shadow move. Gunner tackles Ty, bringing him to the ground. They struggle against each other before getting up with their blades. Gunner's blade shines in the dark as light glows around it's edges. They start fighting as if they'd never stopped. Ty strikes again and again, never letting up. I can see what he's doing. Gunner is slowly backing towards a dark pit. It looks like a fissure.

"Gunner look out!" I shout.

Ty glances in my direction, losing the rhythm of his strikes. Gunner advances forward, gaining the upper hand. In desperation Ty strikes quicker and quicker, until Gunner's heals are at the edge of the fissure. As Ty is stepping forward to give a final push Gunner moves to the side. Ty goes past him, unable to stop his momentum. He yells as he falls into the fissure. Gunner spends a few moments looking over the edge. "No..." he says, lowering his sword. All is silent except for his heavy breathing that has grown shaky. Once he regains his composure he turns his back to the fissure, stepping away from it.

"Franca? Where are you?"

"I'm over here," I say, opening my hand so that he can see the gemstone.

"Are you alright?" he asks, kneeling beside me.

"I'm not sure. I have at least two broken ribs," I say, wincing as I try to move.

"I need to find a way to get you out of here," he says. "Will you be alright if I go and see if there's a way out?"

"I'd rather go with you," I say. My adrenaline is wearing off, and I'm feeling leftover fear from the battle. Every breath hurts.

"Alright, lets go," Gunner says, gently helping me to a stand. I can't help but groan from the pain. I use the gemstone to light our way. We slowly explore the area, and finally find a narrow tunnel. The going is slow and painful.

At the end of the tunnel we find a network of caves. It's hard to know which one will lead somewhere, so we have to just try our best. We wander through the caves for what feels like hours before finding one that has an incline. Many times I have to rest due to the pain I'm in.

I wonder how the battle went? With Ty gone it should've lead to a victory. I'm guessing that Evan is leading the marauders now... I imagine that we'll have to deal with him later. Just as I'm losing hope that we'll ever get out of this cave network we see a faint light ahead.

I'll be so glad to get out of the dark. Our mood lightens the closer we are to getting out of the cave. We finally find the opening and have to wait for our eyes to adjust. We leave the cave as soon as we can, feeling greatly relieved to be alive. I never thought I would be so happy to see the desert. I immediately look at the sky to see what time it is.

The sun has almost finished setting, and the stars are shining in the sky. I realize how tired I am for the first time. I look around. The canyon is nowhere in sight. It's just rolling hills of desert.

"Where do we go now?" I ask, breaking the silence.

"If my communicator was working I'd get in contact with my army to get us out of here. Mine broke in the fall like yours did. The chances of locating that canyon are low. We need to find water."

"If I've kept track of things right, the canyon should be that way," I say, facing the direction I think it is in. I remember where the sun was when we first came to that canyon, so it should roughly be in that direction... might as well see if we can spot it while we search for water.

"Lets go a little ways, then see what we think," Gunner says. "We may need to stay at the cave entrance for the night."

We begin to travel in that direction. The going is slow as I still have to stop and rest at times. It hurts just to breathe, let alone walk. Movement in the distance catches my eye. A woman on horseback is riding across the land. She stops her horse at the top of a hill and looks around. She's wearing a flowing red and white dress, and her brown hair blows gently in the breeze. She looks our way and moves the horse towards us in a gallop. "Someone's coming," I say to Gunner.

He watches her cautiously as she comes. Two other people ride to catch up with her and follow along. The woman stops her horse in front of us. "Hail travelers! You seem lost," she calls to us. Now that she's closer I can see that her dress is embroidered with golden thread and diamonds. The sleeves are white with golden cuffs.

Upon her head sets a crown of desert flowers and gemstones that accent her jade colored eyes. All of her jewelry has diamonds, and her necklace has symbols on it I don't understand. Her horse is a beautiful brown and white appaloosa with a flowing white mane and tail. The two people with her stop nearby, watching us warily.

I look around at the landscape. It's true that we don't know where we are. This part of Durath looks unfamiliar to me. "You could say we've lost our way," Gunner says.

"It's common for adventurers like you to get lost out here. Come with me and stay at my kingdom. You can rest there," she says before he can finish what he was saying.

"There's a kingdom here?" Gunner asks with surprise.

"Oh you must hail from a very distant land then. I'm Elira, Queen of the kingdom of Athrene. Come, there's a much better place for talking," she says.

"How will we go with you? We don't have a hovercraft," I say.

"Hovercraft?" she scoffs, "Who cares about those things? Horses are much better!" She makes a loud high pitched whistle. After a few moments two white horses come galloping over the nearby hills. She smiles, noticing my surprise. "I don't like to go anywhere without a few friends," she says cheerfully.

How am I supposed to ride a horse in this condition? Not only do my ribs hurt, but I've never ridden in my life. I could risk puncturing a lung doing this.

"My friend here is injured. I'm not sure how many broken ribs she has, but I doubt she can make the journey this way," Gunner says, noticing my discomfort.

"I could call for the one hovercraft we have. It hasn't been used in a long time, but it should be able to travel this distance," she says, nodding at one of the people who came with her. The woman nods back at Elira, and rides off in the direction of the kingdom. Elira looks at the two horses that came to her. They have halters, but no saddles. She whistles at them, and one joyfully approaches Gunner. He grabs hold of the halter, and we wait for the woman to return with the hovercraft.

"What are you doing away from your kingdom at this hour?" Gunner asks.

"I was out for an evening ride. It's not uncommon for me to find folks who have lost their way, so it's always good to check the land for the night," Elira says.

The woman that Elira sent away returns, driving the hovercraft instead of riding a horse. I painfully get in, thankful that I will be having a smoother ride. We begin our journey, travelling over the rolling hills of the land, passing towering rock formations.

The grass in this area is a vibrant green. Even the bushes seem much greener than what I would expect. To our left is a field of golden flowers. Horses are grazing, and their ears perk up as we pass. Some decide to gallop alongside us. Herders beckon to them, wanting to put them up for the night.

Far off is a large cliff with a few waterfalls flowing down it. They channel to streams that run through the fields. As we get closer I can see an elaborate wooden palace sitting on top of the cliff. Warm light comes from its windows and people can be seen on the balconies.

A large pathway leads up to the palace, and I notice that there's another structure next to it. Fire flickers from iron lanterns that are set on intricately carved wooden posts. Some people are riding along the pathway on horseback. Elira nods to them before they pass us, and they nod in return.

We make it to the palace, and I see that it's much bigger than I initially thought. Elira gets off her horse and a woman comes to take it over to the other structure. I watch Gunner get off of his horse. It takes me a bit to get out of the hovercraft. The main doors of the palace are already open, and lots of people are inside sitting at tables.

"We need to get you to the medbay," Elira says as my breathing gets rougher.

I nod in agreement, feeling the pain more than I was before. We head through the rectangular room to a large door at the back. A guard opens the door for Elira, and we go through to a medbay. There are fourteen beds here, which don't seem to be nearly enough for a palace. Maybe there's another medbay somewhere else? A nurse makes her way over to us.

"What happened?" She asks, looking at me with concern in her eyes.

"This traveler has broken ribs and needs rest," Elira answers.

"How long would I need to be in a medbed?" I ask. We can't stay long, we need to get back to the others.

"It will depend on how bad the breaks are," the nurse replies.

"It's getting late, you both need rest," Elira says.

Soon I find myself in a medbed, and drift off as the lid closes. I awaken to see the morning sun coming into the room. The nurse that I saw from before enters something in her communicator, and the glass lid opens. I sit up, and find that Gunner is there.

"How long have I been asleep?" I ask. I feel no pain in my ribs at all.

"It's been a week," Gunner says.

"A week? We've got to get back to the others!" I say, rising to a stand.

"No, we're not leaving yet."

"Why not?"

"Franca, Ty didn't die that day like we had thought. He's now ruling over Ohniran, from the palace on Pike III."

"What? How did he survive?" I ask.

"His armor must have saved him. It was more powerful that I realized. That and the fissure may not have been as deep as I had thought," Gunner says. He starts walking out of the room and I follow, thanking the nurse before we leave. We stop on a balcony at the front of the palace, and I find that we're well into the morning. The view is of the expanse of land beyond the palace. With Ty ruling he will surely turn the people against us, and things will be harder. He'll probably be a lot stronger when we face him again.

"We're going to have to come up with a plan," I say, looking at the land ahead.

"Yes, I'm going to have to come up with a strategy. I can hide out here for a time... Ty would never think to look for me here. He will be expecting me to challenge him eventually, and will send people out looking for me."

I listen to the waterfalls, taking in how the water moves around rocks. Its pathway twists and turns, but it always manages to get back on track. Gunner's path will be difficult. But we have to do what's right; Ty will destroy everything if he is left to his ways. "You know Gunner," I say. He turns to look at me. "As long as we keep trying and don't give up, we'll find a way. This road won't be an easy one, but we've made it so far already. I know we can do this."

Gunner smiles. "Thanks Franca," he says, continuing to look out on the land.

I ponder everything I've been through on this journey. Our ship losing power, my fall into Rythor's underground city, the palace at Pike III and the shore with the clouds. It was all an adventure that I will never forget. Who would have known that a snowstorm would lead me here, on a mission to defeat the darkness that threatens our world.

I think about all the people I've met. Each person has helped me to grow in one way or another. The crew taught me how to work with others. Roxanne and Maylea pushed me to develop internal strength. Fauve showed me the joys and consequences of a spontaneous life style. Gunner brought to my attention how important it is to protect the light of the world. And Jalyn, real or not, was an example to me of not giving up even when things seem hopeless.

I put my hand in my pocket to get the gemstone out. Instead my fingers brush against a metal chain. I pull it out and see that I still have Radek's tags. I should've given them to Fauve sooner. That is my one regret. I gently put them back in my pocket. I have to save Fauve, there must be a way. Maybe we can get the others together, and then rescue her. I know we'll see the crew again, we just have to find them. I reach in my other pocket, and pull out that picture I've been carrying around.

I think about the dreams I've had, finally able to give them my attention. It's odd, but they seem to fit together somehow. Meeting Jalyn at Wayford, leaving Hayventh, then working for her as a mechanic while she searches for something. And through it all, it seems I gained a friend, before parting ways.

I watch the horses grazing in a distant field. I don't really know what those dreams meant, or why I had them. If Jalyn is real somehow, I hope that she finds what she was searching for. And who knows? Maybe those dreams were of the future and I'll meet her someday. I listen as crickets chirp nearby. I feel deep inside that the adventure has only begun, and that there's so much ahead of me. I have decided that I won't give up. I will continue to fight the darkness, and see where this path leads.

www.ingramcontent.com/pod-product-compliance
Lightning Source LLC
Chambersburg PA
CBHW030650260626
47157CB00007B/2582